I0522507

desert world
ALLEGIANCES

LYN GALA

DSP PUBLICATIONS

Published by

DSP PUBLICATIONS

5032 Capital Circle SW, Suite 2, PMB# 279, Tallahassee, FL 32305-7886 USA
http://www.dsppublications.com/

This is a work of fiction. Names, characters, places, and incidents either are the product of author imagination or are used fictitiously, and any resemblance to actual persons, living or dead, business establishments, events, or locales is entirely coincidental.

Desert World Allegiances
© 2015 Lyn Gala.

Cover Art
© 2011 Justin James.
dare.empire@gmail.com
© 2011 Cover Design
Mara McKennen
Cover content is for illustrative purposes only and any person depicted on the cover is a model.

All rights reserved. This book is licensed to the original purchaser only. Duplication or distribution via any means is illegal and a violation of international copyright law, subject to criminal prosecution and upon conviction, fines, and/or imprisonment. Any eBook format cannot be legally loaned or given to others. No part of this book may be reproduced or transmitted in any form or by any means, electronic or mechanical, including photocopying, recording, or by any information storage and retrieval system, without the written permission of the Publisher, except where permitted by law. To request permission and all other inquiries, contact DSP Publications, 5032 Capital Circle SW, Suite 2, PMB# 279, Tallahassee, FL 32305-7886, USA, or http://www.dsppublications.com/.

ISBN: 978-1-63216-345-5
Digital ISBN: 978-1-63216-346-2
Library of Congress Control Number: 2014949322
Second Edition March 2015
First Edition published by Dreamspinner Press, September 2011

Printed in the United States of America

This paper meets the requirements of
ANSI/NISO Z39.48-1992 (Permanence of Paper).

Thank you to Donna, Kelly, Stella,
and everyone else in my beta group
who helped me with both this book
and the logic of this whole universe.

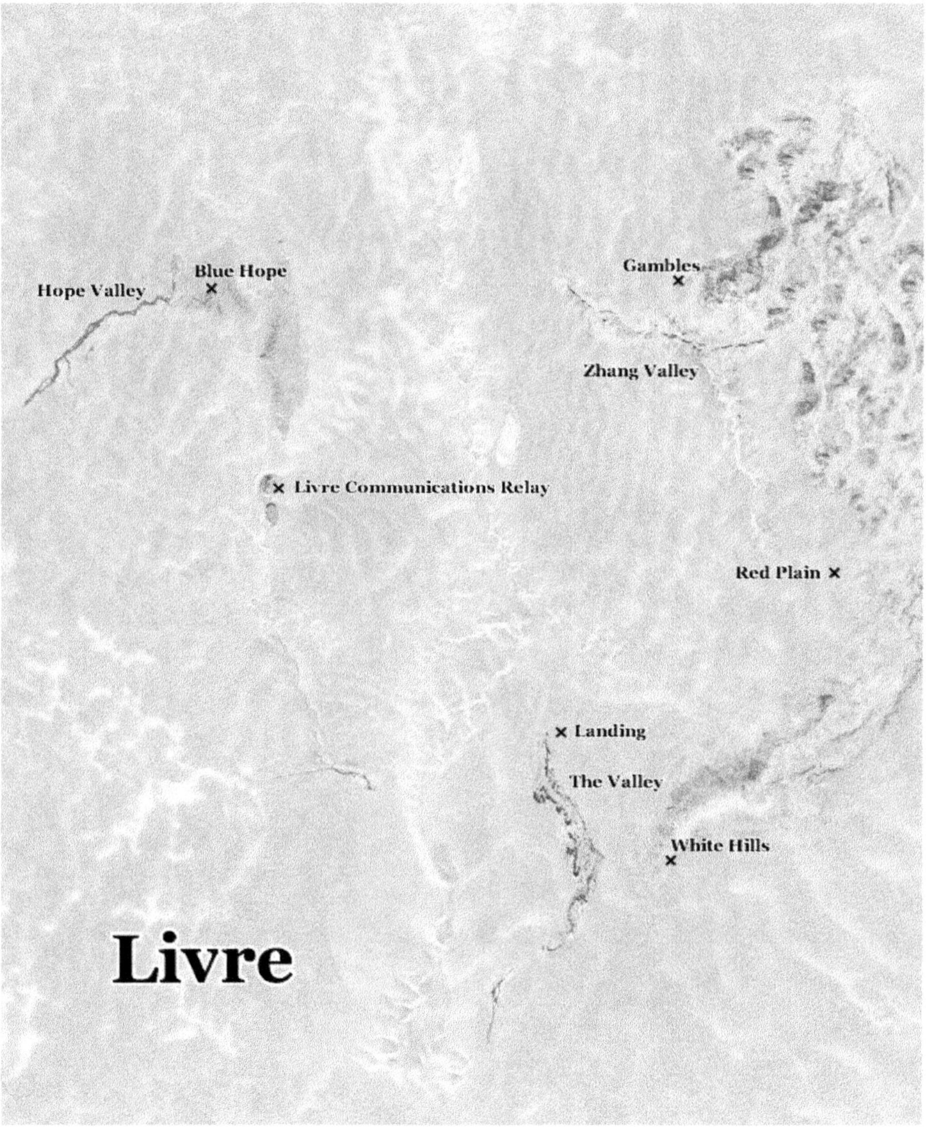

Hope Valley
Blue Hope
Gambles
Zhang Valley
Livre Communications Relay
Red Plain
Landing
The Valley
White Hills
Livre

chapter
o n e

"MAYBE WE shouldn't be doing this," Temar suggested again. If nothing else, they should not be doing this when both moons threw pale light over the fields. Both he and Cyla were fair and blond, and Temar felt like a white flag raised in the middle of a fire-blackened field. The field wasn't black, and the tiny green plants stood out in line against the dry ground, but he still felt exposed.

"Maybe George Young shouldn't steal water from us," Cyla answered sharply. She stopped, and Temar flattened himself to the ground and wished his sister would listen to him, just this once. "He'll be sorry when we get proof." The bitterness in Cyla's voice made Temar's heart ache. Since their father's death, she had grown harder. It scared him.

"We have proof. Sort of. We just need to wait for the council meeting at season-end."

"I'm not waiting. Not anymore." Cyla's voice was fierce, and Temar was caught between wanting to go home and wanting to keep his sister from doing anything unforgivably stupid. Maybe she saw his indecision because she leaned closer, resting her hand on his arm. "He will be sorry."

"Or we'll be sorry when we're caught," Temar warned. He wished he had the right words to convince her that they were making a mistake.

"Then we don't get caught." Cyla looked over her shoulder at him and smiled. He hated it when she got that expression, the one that never failed to get them in trouble. She winked, and then she was dashing across the field. For the length of several breaths, Temar lay on the warm ground, eye level with long rows of tiny plants that swayed gently in the breeze. Their verdant leaves unfurled from stems firm with water. Even before their father died, their own farm had turned into a ragged collection of pipe trap weeds and chokeweed. If Cyla was right and George Young had their water quota, that would explain why his fields produced so much more than their own. If Cyla was wrong…. Temar cringed at the thought of working restitution days on Young's farm.

"Wait," Temar hissed, and then he ran after Cyla. They were close to the Young farmhouse now. Like all farms on Livre, the buildings were tall and narrow, pushed into the rock cliff wall to avoid taking up any more land than required. Most of the planet was a desert, ruled by shifting dunes and sandrats, and every inch of the sheltered valleys was needed to create life.

"See anything?" Temar asked. He flattened himself on the dusty path, next to Cyla.

"Nothing." Her eyes swept the buildings where Young and his workers lived. "We find the evidence and then we go to the council."

"Or we go to the council, show them my water readings, and ask them to investigate and find real evidence for themselves." Temar's stomach ached. He was no terraformer or soldier who could live on adrenaline. No, give him a glassblowing shop, or at this point, even a farm with a clear water allotment, and he'd happily live his life being remarkably, blissfully boring.

"They already refused, and this is not the place for a debate."

"No, Naite Polli didn't refuse. He only said we had to wait until season-end, for the regular session." Temar bit his tongue before he started shouting in frustration. Even though they hadn't damaged anything, a landowner could demand at least one labor day from any trespasser, so he really didn't want to get caught. He doubted Cyla had considered that, however. Sometimes she was a little less than logical in how she approached life, and it drove him insane. Maybe if she were younger or less stubborn it wouldn't have annoyed him so much, but she had these ideas, and then he couldn't get her to see reason. She'd tell him he was too young to understand that adults had to do whatever it took to get the job done, but since she was only three years older than he was, the argument didn't seem exactly fair. Twenty-one was old enough to know they were both going to be in serious trouble if they were caught on George Young's land. And twenty-four was too old for her to sneak around someone else's property.

It was like her request for a special council meeting. If Cyla had listened to him before she stormed off to talk to Naite Polli, Temar would have told her she was making a mistake. Naite represented the unskilled workers of Livre, and he was a hard man who had very little patience for bending the rules. Of course Naite refused to hear them during season, but not all the council members were that inflexible.

Temar would have gone to Dee'eta Sun. The woman represented the artisans, and Temar had watched her work glass with a skill and patience that he envied, catching the molten sands on the end of her pole and then twirling them into incredible shapes. Dee'eta would understand that sometimes circumstances required you to move faster than you expected. After all, with glass, one second too fast or too slow and the entire piece could warp hopelessly out of shape or shatter into a million pieces. Cyla had thought Naite Polli would side with them because he worked the land, but Temar would have sought out Dee'eta Sun and explained how one more season without water, without hope, and without credit to hire workers, and their land would be as gone as a piece of glass that shattered when the blower moved it to the punty rod.

Cyla studied him, the light of the blood moon making her hair look pink. "We need evidence so significant that they can't wait for season-end." With that, she took off running. The water tanks squatted on tall stilts, the angle of their tilt making them look like giant, white beasts, leaning down to touch the ground. Maybe they were leaning down to eat Cyla. He knew it was a silly child's nightmare, but the tanks still waited to swallow her up as she threw herself to the ground under the closest one. That one was positioned a good six feet lower than the second one, so the valves and meters should be easier to read.

"Luck of the stars," Temar whispered before he went running after her. She was an idiot, but she was his only family. If she was going to be stupid and get sentenced to work days for George Young, at least he could go down with her.

"So, let's do the test." Excitement colored her voice while she screwed a drip meter onto the bottom of the release valve.

"We're going to be sentenced to a week of workdays if the council hears we tampered with someone's equipment," Temar muttered, but he took out his flashlight and put it in his mouth while he adjusted the tiny gears used to measure the water. If they pulled a cup of water, and the measure on Young's tank didn't match their draw, that should be enough to prove to the council that he was stealing water from the common line that ran between their farms.

"Young is going to be sentenced to slavery for a decade when we have our proof."

Temar tightened the connector nut and pulled the flashlight out of his mouth. "No one gets sentenced to that much slavery," he pointed out.

"Yeah, but no one has ever stolen this much water before. Twenty years of water theft should mean at least a decade. I'll have him out digging up pipe traps in the midday sun."

Temar looked at Cyla with some concern. There were days that anger settled under her skin, making her seem ugly. If Young was stealing water, and Temar agreed with his sister on that one, then the man deserved slavery, but Cyla's joy at the thought made him a little uneasy. Instead of watching her start the test, he wandered back toward the second tank. He'd expected a second set of pipes, leading to the ground watering system, but instead the taller tank led into the first one.

"Cyla, these are run in series," Temar said.

She made an incoherent noise in response.

"Cyla," Temar said, a little louder.

"Shhhh."

"Then listen. These are set up different than Dad's."

This time she stopped and looked at him. "Dad's tanks were set up back when ships were still landing. Literally. I'd be surprised if Young didn't upgrade. After all, with all the water he stole from us, he can afford the best." She gestured toward the tall house with the dark windows. Unlike their own house, it wasn't lopsided from age and gravity. "I need to get a one-cup measure, and we can go home."

"Then get it." Temar looked around nervously. Under the bright moonlight, the white tanks looked pink, the newly sprouted wheat took on a purplish hue, and the dusty ground between the rows was striped with shadows from the leaves. A breeze pushed all the seedlings to the west, their leaves dipping down to touch the ground. Cyla was taking her time, and the sour fear in Temar's stomach was solidifying into something hard that made his gut ache. He knelt next to her on the hard-packed dirt.

"What's wrong?" he whispered.

"The valve is stuck." Cyla grunted as her fingers slipped off the tank, and her knuckles hit one of the struts with a dull thud that reverberated softly through the entire tank.

"Unlucky stars," she hissed before sticking her knuckle into her mouth.

"Let me." Temar got his fingers around the valve and tried to turn it. Even if it was stuck, years of pulling weeds had given his fingers an advantage. He twisted the piece, feeling the metal groan under his fingers as it slowly yielded. Then the unthinkable happened. Something snapped with a crack that echoed through the tank, and water gushed over his hands. Warm water, in quantities he'd never seen, poured over his skin, like a smooth fabric sliding over him.

For a second, Temar was too shocked to react. He knelt as water—actual running water—spilled over the ground and tumbled over him in unfamiliar patterns. Even when he finally got his hands moving again, he couldn't find any way to reverse the direction of the valve. Something had snapped, and now the nut spun loosely around the end of the pipe. "It's broken!" The water pushed against Temar's fingers as he felt for any mechanical cutoff or valve or emergency switch, but there was only the tank and the pipe and water pouring over him in horrifying quantities.

"Shut off. Where's the shut off?" Cyla shouted in her desperation, and a siren ripped through the air with its high-pitched wail. She ran to the other side, her feet actually kicking up water that had dirt suspended in it. *Mud.* The unfamiliar word floated to the top of his memory from school. They had it on Earth, where water ran over the face of the planet, but on Livre, where nearly every molecule of water had been harvested from the larger of the two moons, melted, purified, and then carried to the planet, mud didn't exist. Or it *hadn't*. Temar found his knees slowly sinking into the softening field.

Footsteps pounded the ground, followed by the sound of men and women slipping and cursing and the strange slap of hands and bodies against water. "Where's the cutoff?" Cyla's scream carried above the siren, above the chaos of the night. Now Temar had his hand flat against the pipe, the water spraying out like the tail of a peacock from a child's book.

Hands caught his arm, pulled him, and Temar slid in the wet earth, falling on his face into mud that pressed itself to his mouth and nose until he pushed back, choking on it. More hands caught him, pulled him, and Temar didn't fight.

chapter
two

SHAN LOOKED out the thick glass at the twisted trunks of the wind trees and at the barchan dunes. The sand inched south in the wind, and when the afternoon came and the winds changed, the same sand would move back to its original position. More or less. The trunks of the trees were scarred white from the constant attack of weather and wind and sand, but right now, Shan's attention was focused on the three men and two women behind him. He suspected he was about to lose the argument, and maybe it was the masochist in him, but he refused to give up. Slavery was evil. He would not participate in enslaving others.

The eldest member of the council leaned forward, her fingers steepled in front of her face as she stared at them with great concentration. "This is more than a petty crime." Lilian Freeland's voice was soft, but full of the authority that came with wealth, or what passed for wealth on such a poor planet as Livre. Her sheep and her crops provided for half the valley, and in such difficult times, that was wealth enough. "This is not a child's prank, calling for a simple fine."

"I doubt either intended so much damage." Shan didn't turn around when he addressed the group. Instead, he watched their ghost images in the reflections of the glass. Naite rolled his eyes, but Shan didn't expect anything else. They were brothers, and some tie in the blood meant that, whatever side Shan took, Naite took his own position opposite.

Bari Ruiz spoke, his voice slow and careful. "They are both very young. The young make mistakes."

"Young people break dishes, not water tanks." Naite leaned forward, his large hands braced on the polished table. "Look at the water they wasted, the crops they ruined! Do you know how long it will take to repair the tanks? Our supplies of welding materials and metals are limited, and these two idiots risked permanent damage to get revenge for some imagined insult George Young offered their dead father." His voice rose until it boomed in the small room.

George Young's name put a sour look on even Bari's face, and there was not a more generous and forgiving soul on the planet. Bari had been voted in to represent those who focused on raising children, and his patience was endless... until someone brought up George Young. Clearly, Landholder Young could annoy even the most patient man on the planet.

For a moment, Bari followed the grain of the wood in the table with his finger. "They grieve their father."

"Their grief should not cost the community entire fields," Naite quickly answered.

Shan hesitated, not sure how to convince the older members of the council to show a little more forgiveness. Before he could organize his thoughts, Kevin Starwalker cleared his throat. Lilian tilted her head to the side and rested her cheek on her hand as she considered him.

Kevin stood, his eyes carefully avoiding all their gazes and his heavily calloused fingers playing with a small carving. Tiny white scars stood out on his dark knuckles, the mark of a carpenter. Shan knew he would look for a practical solution. Right now, he was pressing his lips together so tightly that they were nearly as white as his hair. "I dislike ordering young people into slavery, but if we don't, what will happen to these two?" Kevin finally looked at each of them, his dark eyes obviously looking for any other solution—any way to protect the community without condemning two young souls.

Shan finally turned and stepped forward. "I can take them into the church until they decide where to take employment. Their father's land can go to Landholder Young, to repay him for the damage." Shan fervently prayed for them to listen to his words, even if he was the youngest on the council. As the representative of the church, his opinion should carry some weight. Hopefully, it would carry enough weight to keep these two young fools out of slavery. Of course, they would still suffer the loss of their father's land, but that wouldn't hurt as much as loss of their freedom.

"Their father's land wasn't worth two tanks of water." Lilian dismissed the idea with a wave of her hand. Like Kevin, her hair had turned white, but she was pale, with washed-out blue eyes that made her look almost fairy like, as though she had slipped out of some Earth novel and landed on Livre. But he doubted a fairy would choose their poor world—a world so poor that they could not afford to leave able-bodied workers living in cells and eating the food provided by those who fought Livre's dunes to carve out fields.

However, Shan wasn't ready to give up. "We could enter a judgment and order them to devote half their wages to repaying Landholder Young."

Naite's face left no doubt about his opinion. "They aren't trained. The work they'll get will be little more than they need to feed themselves." Naite crossed his arms, daring Shan to disagree with that. Lilian held up her hand to stop any more debate.

"They aren't children," she said firmly. "They may have only meant to damage the irrigation system, but even that would have killed the seedlings, and as the children of a farmer, they knew it. They are too old to claim the ignorance of youth and too young to offer anything in compensation."

"Lilian." Shan stepped forward, begging her with his gaze not to condemn these young people by taking a position against them. "Slavery is not a system that reflects well on us as a community. Every time we pass judgment on someone, ordering them into bondage for some length of time, we damage ourselves—our own souls."

Shan prayed she would listen to him. He couldn't sit still and allow slavery to take more lives. True, both of them were of legal age, but Temar sometimes came to the church, watching from the shadows. He was such a lost soul, such a young soul. Shan remembered feeling that lost. Someone else had reached out to help him, and now his heart ached with a need to help this young man who had stood in the back of his church and who had obviously never found what he was searching for. Maybe if Shan were a better priest, he would have found a way to connect with Temar before he had done something so idiotic.

"This is an old song," Naite said, his voice heavy with disapproval. "Are you going to sing it every time the issue comes up?"

"If I have to." Shan worked hard to keep his voice and face free from the annoyance he felt.

"I'll sing it for you." Sarcasm dripped from Naite's words. "Slavery is unfair and evil and not godly. But there is a problem, little brother." Naite stood and walked the length of the table before coming around the end to face Shan. "Cyla and Temar are not being unfairly targeted. They have no good judgment of their own, or they wouldn't have tried such a dangerous stunt. A few years of being treated like the children they are—of having to work and live where they are told and facing the consequences of their actions—that's the best thing for them. I don't think it's unfair to give these two time in a structured environment in order to grow up."

"It's unfair for anyone to lose his freedom."

Naite laughed. "When I was sold for three years, I didn't see you coming to save me, and it's a good thing you didn't. Three years with Landholder Sulli taught me discipline and honesty I never would have learned from our father. Cyla and Temar could use a few of the lessons I learned when I had to work to regain my freedom."

"Yes, Landholder Sulli is a good man," Shan agreed. He held up his hand to prevent his brother from getting them all off track. Naite defended Tom Sulli the way most men defended their parents or their lovers, but Shan didn't think his brother had ever been in Tom's bed, during or after his time working for the man. "You were lucky, and I thank God for that every morning, but not all people are as good as Tom Sulli. What happened in Blue Hope—"

"Blue Hope is not here!" Naite threw up his hands and walked away, his back stiff with anger. "That sandrat in Blue Hope paid for what he did, and I would never put up with hatefulness like that in our community." Naite dropped into his chair on the other side of the table. "Just because one sick pervert in Blue Hope abused a slave does not mean the system is corrupt."

"And just because Tom Sulli helped you turn your life around does not mean the system works." Shan felt his carefully hidden frustration rising in his chest.

"The system has worked for fifty years. It works better than expecting the laborers to raise crops and feed people who are jailed. Trust me, if criminal convictions led to jail time, half my workers would be out stealing water in order to get condemned to a little rest and free food." Naite laughed like he had made a huge joke, but then Naite's sense of humor had never been his best trait.

"The fact that the jail system failed does not mean the system of slavery is our only alternative."

"No, it's just the best one."

"It is evil." Shan pronounced each word carefully as he fought a need to scream.

"There's slavery in the Bible." Naite smiled, a smug expression that clearly suggested he'd planned that little attack.

"So are incest and infidelity and hate. God is not endorsing any of these acts. God did not wake up on the eighth day of creation and say, 'Let there be slavery.'"

"He didn't say, 'Let there be sanctimonious priests,' either, but look what we have, anyway." Naite had a smug look on his face, and Shan wanted to tackle his brother to the ground and start pounding on him.

"Naite Polli." Kevin Starwalker spoke the name, and even though he didn't have any inflection in his voice, he still managed to make his disapproval clear. Naite leaned back, his dark face pinking slightly.

"Perhaps you should look up the root word in sanctimonious," Shan said, not even feeling guilty about getting the last word only because Kevin had stepped in.

"Perhaps both of you should look up the meaning of manners," Bari said, his voice a whisper that might not have been heard, only the room had gone silent, save for the wind whistling against the metal joints of the square building. However, when Shan glanced over, Bari didn't offer an apology. "We must think of what is best for Cyla and Temar. If we take their wages, they will not have any sort of life. A term of slavery would allow them to finish their punishment and move on."

Kevin spoke up. "They could learn from some hard labor. Their father may have blamed George Young for his troubles, but his crops died because he never took care of them. Disliking Young is one thing, but blaming him for theft is unacceptable. He's honest, even if his values leave something to be desired. If Cyla and Temar work the fields, they'll learn what their father should have taught them."

Clearly Bari and Kevin were both leaning toward condemning two young people to slavery. Shan didn't even bother looking at Naite. He looked to his last hope—Lilian. She had withheld her judgment until now, which meant she was unsure. When the woman felt passionately about an issue, she had no qualms about manipulating and cajoling the rest of the council to do whatever she wanted.

Lilian was staring out the window. The sand in the air reflected the sun, so that the landscape shimmered in shades of gold and red. The flickers of light shone against the thick glass and spawned prisms and rainbows that scattered across the dull, gray walls of the room. She fingered the wooden talisman that hung from a cord around her neck. "Slavery is not to be taken lightly. What happened in Blue Hope is a reminder of the seriousness of such a judgment."

"Absolute power corrupts absolutely," Shan agreed, hope chipping away at the sinking feeling of defeat in his guts. Dee'eta Sun made a small clicking sound that might have suggested she agreed with him, but she remained silent.

"This is a difficult situation, and some of us are going to leave here unhappy." She stopped, and the room fell silent.

While on paper the council might be a meeting of equals, some were more equal than others. Lilian's years, wisdom, and her friendships with half the town gave her voice a weight that the rest of them lacked. "If these young idiots had skills, they could work off this debt. The fault for that is their father's, but it doesn't change the fact that any restitution would cripple them for their entire lives. While I don't vote for slavery easily, I think this time, it is the only choice. The debt will be paid, these two will have some time to grow up, and maybe they can learn some skills which will improve their futures."

Shan had to smother a very unpriestlike desire to slap the smug look off his brother's face. Naite was the poster child for slavery—the perfect example of what the system was supposed to do. As much as Shan did thank God that Tom Sulli had treated his brother so well and helped him heal from their father's abuse, sometimes Shan wished his brother's papers had been purchased by George Young. Maybe then Naite would have been as passionate about abolishing slavery as he was about defending the system. Maybe. Naite was so stubborn, he still might argue for slavery, simply to annoy Shan.

And now Shan could do nothing to help Cyla and Temar. His guts coiled and churned unhappily. Cyla was a beautiful woman, willowy and pale, with a sharp tongue and sharper temper. She was a second cousin to Lilian's granddaughter, and the two shared the same ethereal look.

Temar was the same, and as a boy, the look was even more striking. He had blond hair and blue eyes and very long fingers. When Shan had been no more than ten or twelve, he had seen Temar's mother hold up her young baby's hand and declare that he would be the church pianist one day, with hands like that. Shan remembered being envious of that child because, back then, the thought of living in the church had seemed like a wonderful and impossible dream. But now, Temar's life would not be one to envy.

No, Shan had failed to protect them. He wondered if he would sit and listen in confession as they whispered about anger and shame and a weariness that wore at their souls or if they'd avoid the church and carry this burden alone. And one day, what happened at Blue Hope would happen in Landing. When that day came, Shan wasn't sure if his vows to protect his people or his vow to protect the sanctity of the confessional would win out.

chapter
three

TEMAR SAT in the feed shed that served as a temporary prison, trying not to lose himself to the panic that soured his stomach and made his mouth dry. Standing in Young's muddy field, Cyla had done all the cursing for them, repeating all their accusations about Landholder Young stealing their father's water and ruining his farm. She hadn't convinced anyone. No, work-hardened hands had grabbed them, and Temar didn't have any illusions about what would happen now.

If he'd had any doubts, the fact that the council had ordered their shoes taken and then had him and his sister locked in separate sheds spoke volumes. They had no hope of escape now, not that there was any place to escape to. Unlucky stars. Sometimes Temar thought he'd been born under the unluckiest of all of them.

He heard a voice outside the shed and jumped. His heart pounded so heavily that his chest ached with the force of it. Part of him wanted the guards to come. They'd either sentence him to slavery or exile him. Either was better than waiting in the dark. If the sentence was exile, he didn't have a lot of illusions. He'd only last a few days out in the barchan dunes. In the deep valleys, shielded by massive rock walls, humans could build farms and thrive. In the towns, with their windbreaks and houses, humans could survive. Out on the open desert, humans died. If the sun didn't kill him, the sandcats would. Temar would die before he could walk half the distance to the next town.

Pressing himself back into a corner of the empty shed, he breathed the grain dust and considered the distances between Landing and the surrounding territories. Sadly, he knew enough math to calculate the loss of his body's water if he walked across those hot sands in the day, and he knew the probability of running into sand burrs or pipe trap plants if he walked them at night. He actually wished he hadn't excelled in school. Right now, a little ignorance would be bliss.

Cyla might get more mercy. Ever since the medicines had run out, so many women died in childbirth that they would have to think twice before exiling a young woman. The thought of Cyla being exiled made his stomach clench. His butt was going numb, so he shifted his weight forward and pressed his forehead to his knees. How did this all go so wrong? His eyes burned with tears. This was all his fault. He never should have followed her out into that field. He should have stood firm, and maybe she would have backed down. Then again, maybe she would have gone out on her own. Would that have been better?

"We need proof," she'd insisted. Cyla's words echoed through his memory. She had sounded so desperate, like she might break if he refused to help her. He was an idiot, because he should have known to run the other way when she looked at him with that expression.

If only he could have convinced her to stay home, the two of them would have been safe. Instead, they were about to be either exiled or contracted out to the highest bidder. Their slave prices would go to Landholder Young, and then that excrement of a sandcat would finally be able to say he had destroyed the entire Gazer line.

Temar couldn't stop the tears. He tried to. He knew they could open that door and drag him out any second, and he didn't want anyone to see him cry. But no matter how much he wanted to put on a strong front, his nose insisted on stuffing up and his head ached and his tears slipped out. He tried to push aside the fear and pain by focusing on another emotion—anger. Temar conjured the image of Landholder Young, his blotchy skin with whole patches of gray that stained his dark neck and chin, his balding head with another blot of gray and scaly skin, his fat fingers and his squinty eyes. His eyes were set so deep in his face that he looked like someone had taken him as a child and shoved their thumbs into his eyes, pushing them way back into his head.

Instead of helping him control his tears, the anger only made him cry more. When the crying grew so bad that his breath came in ragged gasps, he tried distracting himself by calculating square roots or counting the number of interplanetary governors he could remember. It wasn't enough to cut through the terror. Landholder Freeland was the eldest, and she would want him sold or exiled. His crime was against the land, and since he and Cyla owned land, they should have understood the horror of that. They weren't townies who had done some accidental damage while goofing around.

Temar's chest tightened as he realized that they probably didn't own land anymore. Their father's land was a poor strip between two larger farms. One of them would happily pay for the land, poor though it might be. If the council exiled him and Cyla, Landholder Young might even get his father's land to repay him for the lost water.

At that thought, his mind darted off in another direction, and this time guilt washed through him at the thought of all Young's water spilling out onto the dry ground in heaving surges. The memory made Temar sick to his stomach. He turned away from that thought as quickly as he could. Maybe when he wasn't so terrified for himself, he could take more time to stop and feel guilty about the damage they had done.

The priest might speak for them—argue for slavery over exile. That was one vote Temar was almost sure he could count on.

And his brother, Naite, spoke publicly of the need for more young people to be taken in hand as slaves. Pretty much any offense sent him talking about how those who weren't raised well needed the training slavery provided. He might be equally ready to keep them in the territory.

Dee'eta Sun…. Temar thumped his head against the shed wall. He had so badly wanted to purchase an apprenticeship with the woman. Glass sang for her, twisted into impossible shapes and revealed colors that no one else could duplicate. He'd had fantasies of her seeing his own sad attempts and inviting him to her workshop. Instead she was, right now, discussing what a failure he had turned out to be.

Getting to his feet, Temar ordered himself not to think about any of it. Unfortunately, that only made the thoughts and the fears and the lost fantasies all crash in around him. He felt like he was in the middle of a glass shop, and he'd dropped one piece, but in trying to catch that piece, he had clumsily knocked over a half dozen more. And as he turned and turned, desperate to save some piece of falling glass, he was destroying everything, and he couldn't find a way to stop. He should stand still and let the glass fall to the ground around him. That was the only logical way to prevent himself from doing even more damage, but he couldn't not try to save something, and the more he tried to save some small piece of the beauty he'd wrecked, the more pieces were shattered by his flailing.

Maybe the town should exile him while they still had some glass on the shelves. Maybe if he wasn't around to be such an idiot, Cyla would have given up her vendetta before this happened. Maybe if he understood people, instead of books, he could have found the words to convince her to let go of her anger. He sighed. Maybe he had no control over any of it. That last was more than an unlucky star. That was a whole constellation of unlucky.

Something scraped against the door, and Temar retreated across the empty floor. A moment ago, he'd wanted to get this over with, but now he wanted nothing more than a few more minutes in this dusty and dim room. In here, he was still Landholder Temar Gazer. He wanted to be able to claim his name this last time, because when they pulled him out, the council would strip him of his land and probably strip him of his last name and sell him as a slave. If the stars truly hated him, they would allow him to keep his name and turn him out of the settlement to die in the sand. And right now, Temar didn't want to know.

"Time to hear judgment, young water thief," Naite Polli said. He was a dark shadow blocking the door, so that the light streamed in around him. Motes of dust danced in the beams, and Temar swallowed, not sure whether the title of "water thief" or fear of his sentence kept him from walking forward willingly.

Worker Naite stepped into the shed. He was a huge man with a hawk nose that dominated his face and gave him a dark, predatory look. In his hand, he held a rope, and Temar couldn't take his eyes off that length of yellowed cord.

"I know this is hard, boy." Naite gave a wry chuckle. "I remember this very shed, and I remember Kevin Starwalker coming in to get me. I nearly pissed my pants, I was so afraid. I was sure someone would be writing a song about how many mistakes I'd made. In your case, though, they really might write a song, but you'll survive that too." Naite ran a thumb over the rope and stood looking at Temar silently for several seconds.

Temar knew Naite was waiting for him to do something or say something, but fear had turned his insides to stone, so he couldn't move at all.

"I know what you're feeling, but you need to face the consequences of what you've done," Naite said firmly.

Temar caught his lower lip between his teeth and fought against a terror that would make him throw himself on Naite Polli and beg forgiveness—or make him dash for the door to run through the sands until he fell into a pipe trap plant and broke his ankle. Then sandrats could mob his body. He wanted desperately to do anything except stand still and let the man put that rope on him.

"You'll live, Temar. Your pride may take a few hits, but if you're so full of yourself that you don't mind spilling two tanks of water, your pride needs to take a few hits."

"I didn't mean—" Temar cut himself off. Worker Naite didn't want to hear his excuses or his apologies. His father and Cyla had both gone to the council, claiming that their farm's water had been stolen, and all they'd gotten was a reputation for being a little hotheaded and a lot crazy. In Cyla's case, the hotheaded part was actually true, and after a few years of drinking pipe trap juice, his father's sanity had certainly been in doubt.

However, Temar wasn't foolish enough or angry enough to make his own situation worse by being one more raving fool, accusing others of the very crime he had committed. He hadn't meant to steal Young's water, but he had. He hadn't meant to damage the equipment, but again, he had. He had no proof that Young had ever hurt his father, but the proof against him and Cyla was stacked up like bundles of grain.

"You aren't the first to do something he never meant to," Naite said, his voice far gentler than Temar had ever heard it. Usually Naite was the sort of man who bellowed orders to workers across fields. Naite stepped forward, and Temar mirrored the movement by stepping back. His back hit the wall of the shed, and he had no more room to retreat, so he could only watch as Naite closed in on him.

Naite reached for him with a work-roughened hand, and Temar neither helped nor fought as he watched Naite wind a length of rope around Temar's wrist. Naite reached for his other hand and repeated the complex patterns of knots and loops, so that Temar was tied with intricate bindings. A long leash trailed from the knots around his left hand, and Naite took that in hand and pulled. Temar had no choice but to step away from the wall. His eyes felt sore and swollen, and he could feel the tears threaten to start, once again.

Naite slapped him on the shoulder, as one man might do to another. "You'll be fine, boy. You'll be better off than those seedlings in the field you washed out. It's been a lot of years since anyone on Livre has seen honest mud, and hopefully after this, we won't have any more young people decide to play these games with water."

Temar wasn't a boy even if he had acted like one and even if part of him wanted to cry like some half-grown child. Temar set his teeth deep into his lower lip and stared at his bound hands. Whatever he said would be seen as an attempt to justify what could not be justified, and if he railed against Landholder Young, the council might well decide he was mentally unbalanced and potentially unsafe.

Knowing no other way to mitigate the trouble he was in, Temar waited as Naite stood in front of him. Temar's bare feet looked tiny next to Naite's heavy, leather boots, and Temar amused himself by imagining himself so tiny that he could walk along the folds in the leather. He could shrink down so small that he could walk out between the cracks in the door and vanish from sight. He could slip between grains of sand and live in the shade of a wind tree leaf.

The rope tether pulled tight, and Temar followed out into the sun as Naite led him to the squat council building. It had once been a huge complex, but most of the metal had been bastardized for equipment, leaving only one small structure with thick glass windows standing in the center of town. Most buildings in town had steeply leaning walls, built to shrug off the wind, but this one was a box, with upright walls that defied Livre's winds instead of bending to them.

The sand was hot under his feet and slid between his toes as he padded after Naite. A woman with a young girl at her side sat against the council building and wove, her fingers twisting and braiding rope, like the one binding him. She watched from the sides of her eyes, her gaze darting from him to her work and back to him. If Temar were a townie, he would know her name, but he only knew those he had schooled with. Like Tith Starson, who leaned against a parked sled and watched him. Temar could feel his face heat, and not from Livre's sun.

Naite pulled open the door to the council building, and their feet tracked sand inside. With his eyes on the floor, Temar couldn't see much, but that was a blessing. He didn't want to see the condemnation or the pity. All he wanted was the answer to one question.

"Cyla?" Temar whispered his sister's name. Naite hesitated and raised his hand that held the leash. Temar tracked the movement as Naite's hand stopped just short of his arm. He watched the loop of the rope between his bound hands and Naite's fist. Oh gods. Don't let them have exiled her, he prayed. He tried very hard not to think about his sister's body lying in the sand with the sandrats and wind pulling flesh from her bones.

"No one may know a judgment that hasn't been given," Naite said. He pulled his hand away and dropped it.

"For God's mercy, Naite, you could at least reassure the boy."

"Shan." Lilian Freeland's voice rose above the two Polli brothers'. Temar closed his eyes and struggled to breathe. They were going to exile them. His legs turned so weak that, had his knees not been locked, he would have fallen to the ground.

"Young Temar, your sister will get no worse punishment than you." Lilian stepped up in front of him, and Temar studied her feet and the worn cuffs on her jeans. His father had always spoken so highly of Landholder Freeland, of her ability to run a farm and command respect and ride a tractor through a sandstorm. She'd risked her health with no fewer than seven children on a world where water and medicine were both far too rare, and she was like a sandrat that kept living, no matter the odds against it.

However, he suspected her opinion of him was not as high.

Bracing himself for the certain death sentence they were about to pronounce, Temar raised his chin and tried to find some lingering wisps of dignity. He'd fall on the floor and beg if it would help, but they had already voted, and his begging wouldn't improve matters now. Lilian looked him in the eye, and Temar felt a warm tear roll over his cool cheek.

"Your crime is too serious to ignore. We have decided that you are responsible for 800 square rods of seedlings being ruined, the loss of two tanks of water, and a measure tap being damaged." When she lined up all his crimes so neatly, Temar felt nauseous. It was half a lifetime's wealth that he had destroyed in one night.

"You are sentenced to slavery for no less than ten years, unless, in the testimony of your master and the determination of this council, your service is so exemplary or substandard to warrant amending your sentence."

For a second, Temar thought he had heard wrong. They were enslaving him and not exiling him. True, he had never even heard of a slave being sentenced to ten years, but it wasn't death. It was a hope for life and for eventually regaining his freedom. Temar was so surprised that he swayed, as if the emotional blow had physically knocked him off balance. Bringing his hands up, he had to catch himself on Naite's arm.

Naite's hand came up under his elbow and steadied him. This time, the tears that slipped out of Temar were of relief instead of fear. He wasn't going to face exile, and since Lilian had promised him that his sister's punishment wouldn't be worse than his, that meant she was going to be safe too. A month ago, he would have railed against ever being enslaved, but right now, it felt like a great stroke of luck.

Not all of the faces in the room looked particularly happy, though. Dee'eta Sun, a woman with shoulders almost as wide as Worker Naite's and a white streak in her black hair, watched him with a guarded expression. Any chance he'd ever had to be an artisan was gone. By the time he'd earned his freedom, he would be too old to apprentice, and he'd likely be an unskilled worker for the rest of his life. That was still better than exile.

The priest, Shan Polli, didn't even bother to hide his unhappiness with the judgment. Shan was a smaller version of his brother. Where Naite was a monster of a man, Shan was tall and sinewy... and intimidating. His leaner frame made his beak-like nose and sharp eyes more frightening, even though Naite had the same features.

Sometimes, when his father was well and truly drunk on pipe trap juice, Temar had used church as an excuse to walk into town and sit in the quiet and listen to the sound of the wind whispering through the cracks in the boards. He'd been young when his mother died, but he remembered sitting in her lap and listening to the hum of the church. It was a rare and cherished memory—one that he clung to after his mother had died and his father slowly turned into a drunk. Many times Temar had sat in the last row, listening to the wind against the roof and Shan's voice, watching the man move with a precision and grace and power that Temar had rarely seen in anyone.

"Don't think this will be easy. You're going to learn to work and respect the land that you seem to have so little regard for." Naite's words were gruff as he pulled his hand back, leaving Temar to stand on his own feet.

"I know," Temar whispered. Now that the fear of exile had passed, the fear of slavery was creeping in. As long as they didn't sell him to Landholder Young, he'd survive. He just wasn't sure anyone would pay a slave price for him, and without a buyer, his papers would go to Young to repay him for the damage.

"I very much doubt that you do understand." Shan spoke for the first time, and Temar ducked his head, eager to avoid the disapproval in that voice. He should get used to it. Even after his slavery ended, he would likely be known as a water thief for the rest of his life.

"Two landholders have requested your papers." Lilian quickly filled the silence left in the wake of Shan's comment. "I don't think you'll be surprised to know that Landholder Young filed a request."

Temar looked up, horror drawing his gaze to the councilwoman's face. Lilian gave him a small, crooked smile. "I think our reaction was similar to yours," she said, humor in her voice. "He's angry, so I think we can all agree that you are best placed somewhere else."

"Yes, ma'am," Temar agreed. The thought of Young having rights over him was enough to make exile sound pleasant.

"Ben Gratu has offered a fair price."

Temar closed his eyes as relief flooded him. Ben owned the farm on the other side of his father's land. He was a fair man who had always gone out of his way to offer the family a few kindnesses or a spare flat of seedlings. "Thank you," Temar managed to say. His legs felt like jelly, like the time he'd fallen from the valley cliff wall, only to be caught by the safety rope at the last minute. That sudden burst of fear and then the realization that he hadn't been crushed into a bloody mash left his body limp with relief. That's how he felt now.

Shan took a step forward, his sharp eyes focusing, so that Temar felt uncomfortably trapped inside the man's gaze. "Should you need anything, you know you have the same right to come to the council that anyone else has, correct?"

Temar frowned, not sure why Shan would imply that Ben Gratu would ever do anything that warranted coming to the council. He answered as politely as he could. "Yes, sir."

Shan sighed, clearly not happy with the answer.

Naite looked angry enough to chew glass. "Brother, we are not Blue Hope, and I hope you are not suggesting that Ben Gratu is anything like that pig shit they had hiding in their territory."

"I am not suggesting anything." Shan snapped the words out, and the two brothers glared at each other. "I am simply reminding Temar that slavery does not mean that he loses all his rights."

"Any rights he loses, he loses out of his own foolishness."

Lilian held her hands up. "Enough!" she commanded. She was a tiny woman, shorter even than Temar, and he was small compared to most people on Livre, but both brothers stopped at once. She looked from one to the other in clear disapproval.

"There are days that I question the wisdom of having both of you on this council. Were it in my power, I would ask your groups to name another." She turned away from them and walked to the table. Sitting down in a chair on the near side, she studied the whole room, like an artisan considering her supplies and finding them lacking. Finally, her gaze settled on him.

"Temar, you do keep your right to speak to the council. You have a right to food and water. You have a right to be safe from injury or danger. All other rights and names that once were yours now belong to your master. Do you understand that?"

Temar nodded. He didn't trust his voice, not when his emotions were pressing so hard against him.

"You will work where ordered, live where ordered, and obey your master. You will be restrained however your master determines." Temar went cold at the thought of being tied and tethered like a beast, the way he was tied now, but he also knew that would be Ben Gratu's right. He nodded again.

"Child," Lilian said softly, "if Ben restrains you, it will be to keep you from making an even more disastrous mistake. If you damage your master's property maliciously, show recalcitrance in following orders, or attempt to escape, the only punishment remaining will be exile. If you are placed under exile, your name and image will be sent to all the territories, and no settlement will share water with you. Do you truly understand that?"

"Yes," he agreed. His voice cracked halfway through the word.

Naite pulled the rope leash tight. "It's not that bad, boy. I got fairly good at plowing a field when chained to the wheel." Naite almost made the experience sound amusing.

"Naite, take the boy to his master," Lilian said. "I suspect we will need more time to speak with his sister."

Temar's head snapped up at the mention of Cyla. "Could I…." He looked around the room with a desperate hope that they would allow him to see her. Bari and Kevin studied the papers in front of them. Dee'eta watched with that same impassive face she'd worn the entire time, and Shan had an expression that Temar couldn't hope to interpret, but it wasn't good. It was Lilian who answered him.

"You were told to go to your master, and you are ready to disobey already. You need to remember your place." The matronly warmth she had shown seconds ago had vanished, and she frowned at him.

"It's not so easy to give up your freedom," Naite answered for him. "He'll learn." Naite gave a sharp tug on the rope leash, and Temar had to stumble forward to keep his balance.

"Naite!" Shan said sharply.

"You'll learn to weigh your words before you assume that your needs are more important than the rules," Naite said to Temar, ignoring his brother. He strode out of the room with long strides, and Temar was forced to trot after him, his arms stretched out in front of him as Naite half dragged him out of the building and to the waiting sand sled.

Silently, Naite threaded the rope leash through the handle of the door, pulling Temar's wrist close to the polished wood before tying the rope off. Given a few hours of privacy, Temar might be able to use his teeth to free the knots, but with a few townies standing around and watching, Temar was going to be forced to stand by the side of his new master's sled, tethered and waiting.

He blinked and turned his head away from the hot wind. For long seconds, Naite stood next to him, his body making a long shadow against the sand. "I know how hard this is, boy."

Temar glanced up, not sure what he was supposed to say. Naite made no secret about having been enslaved himself, but he hadn't faced ten years.

"It does get easier. And the ability to think before acting is a skill worth developing. Work hard to please your master, and Ben will give you credit for it. He's a fair man, and you could shorten your sentence by earning his respect." Naite gave him another slap on the arm, and then he was gone.

Temar watched Naite walk toward the line of storage sheds, lined up along the edge of town to keep the worst of the winds off the houses. As he walked, his footsteps made divots in the ground that slowly vanished as the wind shifted the sands. Out of some perverse need to test his bonds, Temar pulled against the leash, but he didn't have more than an inch of room, and the bindings were far too well tied for him to free himself, even if he put in an honest effort to do so.

Instead, he watched Naite go into another of the empty feed sheds. Before Naite could come out with his sister leashed and ready to hear her sentence, Ben Gratu came out of the general store, already slipping his sand veil over his hat as he walked toward the sled. Time to learn to be a slave to his master. Temar's stomach was knotting already.

chapter
four

SITTING IN the passenger seat, Temar held tightly to the handgrip. With his hands still tied, he was having trouble keeping his balance as the sled lurched and bounced over the sand slopes. The engine whined as it pushed them up to the top of an enormous dune. For a second, they balanced on the ridge, and then the sled tipped over onto the downward side. Temar braced himself as the engine cut out to allow gravity to drag the sled down the far side.

"I have to admit, I'm a little flummoxed about what to do with you," Ben Gratu said, once the noise of the engine had fallen. Only the wind answered, whistling past them as the sled slid down the sand. Clouds of dust followed them. Temar coughed. His sand veil had come off when Landholder Young's men had grabbed them, and the sand stung his eyes and made his throat burn. "We'll be home soon enough. We need to get you a veil. I thought you were smarter than to wander around without one," Ben said, but then the engine kicked on as they reached the bottom of the dune, and they couldn't talk over the scream of the machine as it shoved them up the slope of the next dune.

In the past, Temar would have insisted he was smart, but now that was somewhat questionable. His wrists ached, not as much from the rope as from instinctively trying to pull his hands in different directions as the sled listed from one side to the other. A smart man wouldn't have ended up a slave, and a smart man would stop fighting the bindings. Obviously, he fell a little short of the mark.

With a final lurch, the sled reached the top of this new dune, and the rocky ridge that marked the beginning of Spence Valley appeared. His father's farm was a narrow strip pressed up against the west rock face, with Young's farm on the far end and Ben's farm on the near end. Temar had driven past Ben's place dozens of times, but now he'd be living and working there. The sled's engine cut off again, and Ben deployed the sails from the sides to guide the sled toward the south entrance to the valley.

"I know you're not the best on a plow, so maybe we can find some other work for you," Ben offered. Temar wasn't sure what he was supposed to say. He'd work wherever he got assigned. "Your father always bragged about your math. He thought you'd join the skilled workers and take up pipe work, or maybe electrical or engine work."

"I liked glass work," Temar answered.

"He'd mentioned that," Ben agreed. His hands were huge, and for a second, he concentrated on pulling on the yoke of the sled, forcing it south of the rock without slowing at all. Ben wasn't as dark as most men, but his arms and hands were tanned as dark as Naite Polli. He wasn't like George Young, who ran his farm from inside his house.

"He'd wanted you to have an apprenticeship." Ben pulled the levers that retracted the guide sails as the sled finally slid to a stop near the south gate to the valley. Temar's father had always made big promises about buying him an apprenticeship when they got a big crop in, but they'd never had a crop of anything other than pipe trap plants. Temar would probably spend the next ten years pulling weeds grown from seeds blown over from his father's old farm.

Ben stopped, sat behind the yoke, and stared out at the heavy gates that protected the valley from wind and sand. The gates could only be opened in the afternoon, when the sand drifted south and the blowers could clear the gates. Open it in the morning, and sand would blast through the gate and bury good farmland. The blowers on the gate had only recently kicked on, and dust devils twirled and danced in the air as the machinery cleared the area.

"It's going to be a long ten years if you don't plan to talk to me." Ben's voice was gentle and soft, and that fatherly tone made Temar's guts tighten. His own father had emotionally left them long before the pipe trap juice had finally killed him.

"I'm not trying not to talk," Temar offered. They weren't even at the farm, and he'd already disappointed his new master.

Ben reached over and put a hand on Temar's knee. "Your father sometimes…." Ben grimaced. "Sometimes he talked bigger than he could carry through."

Temar blushed. He knew he didn't have a right to tell Ben to shut up about his father, but none of that made this conversation any less uncomfortable. Ben sighed.

"I don't say this to make you silent again. Your father was a kind man, and the way he was at the end—that was more pipe trap juice than any choice of his. I'm asking if you're as good with math and equipment as your father always claimed. Based on your adventure over at George's place, I wouldn't call you mechanically talented."

"That was an accident."

"I didn't think you had done it on purpose. If I had, I wouldn't have paid your slave price. What happened, Temar?"

While Temar was quiet by nature, he could feel Ben's concern seep down into him. Pulling his bound hands into his lap, Temar stared at them and wondered how he could have ever been such an idiot. He should have gone to Ben Gratu for help in the first place—then he would be sitting, talking to him, landholder to landholder, instead of slave to master.

"Landholder Young was siphoning father's water," Temar said softly, fully expecting Ben to order him to stop making such wild accusations. Instead, Ben leaned back in his seat and studied him.

"What proof do you have?"

Temar looked up in surprise at the interest in Ben's voice. "I built my own flow meter and installed it on the irrigation system. Water was taken from our pipes. And I tested the soil on Young's land and ours. If it was leaking equipment, as Young claimed, I would have found saturated patches of ground where the water was escaping." Temar looked up, encouraged by the surprise and belief on Ben's face.

"I did tests every ten meters, over the full length of the irrigation pipe, and there wasn't any leak. I would have found a leak and fixed it. And the pipe trap plant absorbs a steady four to seven jignots a week, more than that and the plant splits. The plants on our land show signs of wrinkling, so they're getting three to four jignots a week, and we have a plant density of twelve per square rod, so that doesn't account for the missing water, even if you assume there was a leak somewhere. Water is being stolen." Hope swelled in Temar, pulling his words out faster and faster. Ben was staring at him in clear shock.

"Have you shown these results to the council?"

Temar shook his head.

"Great gods, boy! You have proof of water thievery, and instead of going to the council, you trespass on another's property and destroy two tanks of water? What were you thinking?" Ben slapped the sled's yoke.

"I wasn't. Cyla wanted—"

"Cyla has a temper like a sandcat. I would think you had more sense."

"We had gone to the council last harvest end," Temar defended himself, feeling stupider by the second.

"With the evidence?" Ben leaned forward, his face tight with anticipation.

Temar shook his head. "I started collecting the data after the council dismissed father and Cyla when they made their accusations." God, he was stupid. "Cyla thought we would find something conclusive. She thought I could find how he was siphoning the water from the system." He should have talked Cyla into waiting a couple of months and going back to the council with all his calculations. They might not have taken his word for it, but he had detailed enough notes to get them to send someone to check his work.

Ben turned and stared out the front of the sled at the huge gates. The blowers had cleared the sand from the area, but he didn't move.

Slowly, he began to shake his head. "Your father always said you were far too bright to be a landholder. He should have found a way to buy you an apprenticeship." Ben reached down to the floorboard between their seats and pulled the lever to release the wheels. The sled jumped and jerked and then settled on its fat, wide tires. "Boy, you sit put. This may not be as bad as it seems," Ben said before he got out of the sled and headed for the main gate. For the first time since being grabbed, hope outweighed Temar's despair.

Once they were through the gates, the sled rolled through the valley. The tiny green crops were pushing up toward the sun, and the sun filter offered some shelter from the oppressive heat.

The moment Ben passed the boundary onto Gazer property, the neat rows of seedlings gave way to clumps of pipe trap plant. The plants grew in a circle around a bare center. A newcomer might mistake one for a dozen different plants, but the real plant was underground, inside that ring of green leaves, waiting to trap anything heavier than a grasshopper that stepped on it. Of course, a person was far too heavy and big for a pipe trap to eat. A person's foot would go right through the fleshy meat of the plant's stomach and probably kill the plant. Falling into a pipe trap was also a good way to break a leg.

Ben stopped the sled in front of Temar's home—what had been his home. Ben reached over and let his hand rest against Temar's shoulder. "It's infested with pipe trap seeds. They'll more than likely burn all of this." His voice was sorrowful, but Temar imagined he'd be glad enough to get rid of the source of so many weeds. "So, where do you have these notes?"

"My room." Temar started reaching for the sled door, realizing a second too late that he needed permission before running off. He looked over at Ben.

"Go on, get them." Ben waved him on, and Temar pulled the door open, the movement awkward with his hands tied. Hurrying through the house and trying hard not to look at all the possessions that would soon be stripped by whomever the council chose to give the land to, Temar reached his room. The sloping wall created a small niche on the floor, where he kept all his work, and he pulled out the box with all his carefully detailed records. Picking the box up might be a problem with his hands bound, however.

"Let me," Ben said from the door. He walked in and picked the box up and settled it on the bed. "Did you show anyone these records?" Ben asked as he pulled the top off and started looking at the first notebook. Each page had observations that Temar had recorded as carefully as if he had done the work for class or for an apprenticeship application.

"My father." Temar gave a lopsided shrug. By the end, his father hadn't been able to comprehend much more than a child. The pipe trap juice made him high and happy by killing the brain cells that reminded him what a miserable life he had. From the time their mother had died, he'd been slowly killing himself. It'd taken nearly fifteen years, but he'd finally accomplished his goal. "I showed Cyla, but I'm not sure how much she actually listened to. She was angry." Angry didn't even cover it. Temar had actually been afraid of her temper, for the first time in his life. He didn't think she'd hurt him, but he didn't know how far she would go in her fury. Clearly she'd gone too far.

"She should have listened to you." Ben sounded distracted as he flipped though pages of observations and calculations. "If anything, your father underestimated your math skills. Come sit here." Ben patted the bed next to him, and Temar obediently sat down, resting his tied hands on his knees. His hands were tingling, but he didn't want to distract Ben from his intense concentration. His father and Cyla had never taken his notebooks very seriously, but Ben clearly did. "Do you have more?"

"No, that's it. Isn't it enough?"

"Oh, it's enough. This could have been disastrous."

"Could have been?" Temar asked, a bit of his old humor returning as he realized Ben wasn't dismissing his work.

"Yes, it could have been. If you'd shown these to someone…." Ben shook his head. "I'll take these home to burn." He dropped the notebook into the box.

"You'll… what?" Temar started to stand, but Ben grabbed his bound hands.

"I'll burn them, and you won't mention this to anyone."

Temar's chest tightened so that he could only take little rabbit breaths. Oh shit. He wasn't just an idiot; he was the chosen high idiot of all idiots.

"You stole our water." Temar's voice was trembling, but he managed to get the words out without stuttering.

"Watch your mouth, slave."

"I'll tell. The minute anyone sees me, I'll tell." Temar scooted away so that their hips no longer touched, but Ben was so much stronger that he couldn't pull his hands away from Ben's grip.

"I doubt that." Ben's smile had turned feral, and Temar suddenly found his voice. He screamed as loud as he could. If one of Ben's or Young's workers heard him, there would be questions. They would have to get the council. They would have to stop Ben from burning his work. Temar hadn't even finished his scream when Ben lunged at him, pressing him flat to the bed, so that his weight pressed down on Temar, forcing him to gasp for air. With his bound hands pressing into his stomach, Temar felt as though he were suffocating and his weak struggles couldn't move Ben's massive body off him.

"Since you won't be quiet, I'll have to quiet you," Ben said. He reached over and pulled the pillowcase off Temar's pillow. Ben's forearms corded with muscle as he pulled at the fabric until it finally came apart, with a ripping sound. He pulled two long strips of material off the pillowcase and dropped the rest of the torn thing back onto the bed.

"No," Temar begged, his eyes stinging with tears as Ben wadded one strip up. Temar squirmed and pinched Ben as hard as he could. He got a heel into the bed, straining to turn his body. He did everything he could, but nothing helped. Ben held the wad of fabric against his lips, and Temar tightly closed his mouth.

"Boy, you're making this far harder on yourself," Ben warned. His voice had a paternal tone that turned Temar's stomach, and he only pressed his lips more tightly together. Bracing his fingers behind Temar's head, Ben pressed his thumb into the soft of Temar's jaw. Tears escaped and rolled from the outer corners of Temar's eyes, the pain forcing him to open his mouth. Ben pressed the fabric in.

"For someone so smart, you have some things to learn about life." Ben placed the second strip over his mouth and pulled it around to the back, tying it tightly. Between the gag and Ben's weight on him, Temar struggled to get air into his chest. Gray blurred the edges of his vision until Ben finally rolled off him.

For a second, Temar could only lie in his childhood bed and gasp air through his nose as his body tried to get oxygen back into all the places that needed it. Ben's strong hands flipped him over to his stomach, and Temar was too weak and trembling too badly from fear and lack of oxygen to argue. The leash that dangled from his bound wrists was brought up between his legs and then tied tightly to the back of his belt, so that when Ben flipped him over again, Temar could only blink up helplessly.

His breathing still came in ragged gasps, and Ben reached over and pinched his nose shut. Temar panicked, flopping like a dying sandcat caught in a pipe trap. The hand released him, and he gasped for air again.

"Listen, young idiot!" Ben shook his shoulders, and Temar stared up at him in terror. He'd throw up, only he was afraid Ben would leave him gagged, choking on his own vomit. "Take one deep breath," Ben ordered.

Temar tried. He got some air in, but just when his body demanded that he push it out and gasp for more, Ben pinched his nose shut again. "I won't have you hyperventilate. Slow down. When I let go, breathe out." The fingers released his nose, and Temar blew the air out, hurrying to get more in right away, but Ben pinched his nose shut too quickly. The gray started fuzzing the edges of his vision again.

"Deeper breath this time," Ben said, letting go. For long minutes, Temar lay on the bed with Ben pinching and releasing his nose, until Temar finally figured out he could only get enough oxygen if he breathed as Ben ordered him to. His vision cleared, and his breathing evened out, but the terror still clawed at him.

"I knew you were trainable," Ben said with a friendly slap on the arm that made Temar flinch away. Immediately, a hand was around his neck. "You don't ever flinch away from me, understand?" Ben's eyes were hard, and his fingers pressed into the soft of Temar's neck painfully until Temar gave a small nod. All he had to do was play nice until he could talk to someone, ask them to send word to the council. The farms might be isolated from the town, but there would be unskilled workers on the farm all the time. Young's workers would pass by on the road to get to town, skilled workers would have to come out to calibrate solar equipment and test water. He could get word out somehow. Right now, he had to keep Ben happy.

Ben smiled down at him and then used the hand he had wrapped around Temar's throat to pat him on the cheek. "Good boy."

Ben sat up, and then, as if testing Temar, patted him first on the arm and then the stomach and then the thigh. "You never flinch from me, boy," Ben said again, but this time he sounded far friendlier. Of course, this time Temar had held himself still as Ben did as he liked.

Reaching into his inner vest pocket, Ben pulled out a communicator and slipped the listener into his ear. Temar's eyes went wide. At one time, communicators had been common enough, and most people had grandparents or great grandparents that still grumbled about missing them, but very few still worked. The search team at White Hills had two and the council at Landing kept one for emergency searches, but no one owned one. Ben pulled one out as casually as one might pull out a handkerchief. A few taps, and someone on the other end must have answered.

"The Gazer boy has evidence. A lot of it." He waited as he listened to the answer. "No, he was such a good little boy that he didn't tell anyone other than his sister." Ben smiled down and gave Temar another pat on the cheek.

For a second, Temar really thought he was going to throw up, gag or no gag.

"I think he's under control. I do want a little insurance, though. No one was bidding the slave price on that sister of his, and the council is not going to like the idea of turning her over to George Young. Why don't you come in and make a bid on her. If she's in another territory, I think our boy is going to be very careful to cooperate. He doesn't want to see his sister hurt." Ben gave him another pat on the cheek and a smug smile.

Temar had to hold himself stiffly still under that touch, because there was nothing he wanted more than to rip Ben Gratu into tiny little shreds. If he hurt Cyla…. Temar snuffed, struggling to clear his nose as more tears escaped.

"No, I don't think killing them should be the first choice. If Temar gets free, I'll call you, and you can kill the girl. Between his father's insanity and his sister's death, any madness he spews will be dismissed as more paranoia from the Gazer family tree. God knows the family doesn't have a great reputation." Ben listened to the voice on the other end, and Temar realized Ben was right. Without the notebooks, without proof, he would be no different from his father, accusing neighbors of terrible crimes with absolutely no evidence.

"The plan's still safe. We move forward," Ben told the person on the other end, and then he pulled the listener out of his ear, ending the conversation.

"So, let's get this crap and my new slave back to the farm," Ben said in a voice cheerful enough to make Temar wish, for the first time in his life, that he had the power to kill another human being. "We can discuss a few ground rules as we head back to the farm." Ben stood and pulled Temar to his feet. With his hands tightly bound and his mouth gagged, Temar couldn't do anything except walk in front of Ben. All around him were the artifacts of his childhood—the old worn couch where he'd bed down his father when he'd staggered home, the picture of his mother with the yellowing edges, the red streak on the wall where Cyla had dropped the stain when she'd tried to apply sealant to the ceiling. But Temar wasn't part of this life anymore. Temar's life had taken a definite turn for the worse.

chapter
five

BEN'S HOUSE was four stories, tall and narrow and pressed tightly against the cliff wall. The area above the house had been blasted and then reinforced with metal struts to keep the rock wall from threatening the structure. They had done that in the early days of the terraforming. Back then, the drop ships with their weak engines would be cannibalized for parts, as soon as they got the settlers safely down-world. Metal had been far more common then. Now that the inner planets were too busy warring with each other to finish the job of terraforming on Livre, such huge metal struts would never be used for the benefit of one lone farm.

Temar shifted in the seat, pressing his bound hands down into his lap to take the pressure off the rope as he studied the farm that was going to be his home for the next ten years, unless he had a brilliant idea sometime in the next five minutes. The edges of his mouth stung, but at least he had managed to stop crying. Crying wasn't helpful. Of course, it didn't hurt anything, and Temar thought he was justified in feeling a little self-pity. As soon as those records were burned, he had no proof that anything illegal was going on. And after seeing Ben Gratu's darker side, he wouldn't be surprised if the man went out and broke some of his father's pipes to cover up for the water theft.

The sled bounced to a stop, and a bald worker stuck his head out of the main door of a three-story barn that sat on the far side of a well-tended and well-watered garden.

"Boss?" He stepped out into the light, and Temar recognized Cardan Smith. His face heated with shame even as a little flicker of hope burned, deep inside. Cardan was a good man. He'd helped Temar and Cyla replace a fallen fence and had undercharged them by quite a lot. No way would he go along with water thievery. Temar glanced over at Ben Gratu. Maybe. Temar was starting to suspect he wasn't a particularly good judge of character.

"God's luck, but I did pick up an interesting purchase this morning," Ben said in a friendly tone as he got out of the sled. Cardan, however, was looking at Temar with a frown, and Temar could feel his face heat. Sometimes he hated being so different, and this was one of those times. With his fair skin, he knew his blush would be turning his face bright red.

"You bought his slave papers?" Cardan asked. His voice was cautious, but Ben pulled Temar's box of test results out of the back and then stacked a load of purchased goods on top of that.

"I thought I was getting the even-tempered Gazer," Ben said with a dismissive snort that suggested he'd been wrong. He stood and looked at Temar with great sorrow. "I know your father has told you these lies, boy, and I understand how hard this is. If I open this door, are you going to kick?" The false sympathy and the suggestion that Temar was some sort of wildcat made Temar blush harder. He closed his eyes tightly and focused on breathing.

"He give you trouble?"

"None that I couldn't handle," Ben said, his voice clearly suggesting that yes, Temar had given him quite a lot of trouble. He reached through the open window and patted Temar on the arm. "I know it's hard, boy. You're stronger than you think you are, though." After that bit of unctuous advice, Ben shook his head and turned to his worker. "He's a teenage boy, and he's had a lifetime of his father telling him how everyone else is out to get them. Between his father's paranoia and his sister's quick temper, I'm surprised the boy has the common sense he's managed to show, up until now. He'll settle in as soon as he calms down."

Cardan leaned on the front of the sled and looked through the glass at Temar. "I always thought the boy had inherited all the common sense in that family."

"After hearing him go on about Landholder Young, I can safely tell you that he inherited all the foul language, that's for sure. If Young hears half the accusations this pup is spewing, he's going to demand a few labor days, at the very least. I would just as soon we keep George away from our young fool, at least until he grows up and learns to control his mouth." The suggestion that Ben was trying to protect him made the tears press up in Temar's eyes again. He'd been such an idiot for thinking Ben would want to help. He'd been such an idiot for thinking anyone would go out of their way to help him.

"George has the sense of humor of a pipe trap plant."

"That's an insult to pipe trap plants," Ben countered. "Can you escort him up to the house? Watch out, because he's one to kick and bite at the most unexpected moment, and the first day of a ten-year slave sentence would test the common sense of anyone, even without the Gazer family temper."

Temar sat through the exchange with his face hot and his guts twisting. "No worries. If I can work with that bad-tempered boar of yours without getting gored, I can handle one wisp of a boy." Ben turned away and picked up the box from the dusty ground. When Cardan opened the sled door to release the restraints, Temar tried staring desperately at the box. If the box went into the fire, he had nothing, no chance. He needed to get someone to look at his papers before the council could sell his sister to Ben Gratu's friend. He needed Cardan to notice that box.

Without fighting the tight grip, he stared first at Cardan and then the box in Ben's hands and then back to Cardan. He'd give twenty years off his life in exchange for five minutes of telepathy. Unfortunately, Cardan pulled Temar into a small room with a couch and several chairs made of windwood branches. A rock arch led into a second room with the mechanics. Temar strained forward. The incinerator and recyclers would be in here. He couldn't let his work end up being recycled into fertilizer.

"Boy's about white eyed with fear," Cardan said, his hand tightening around Temar's arm. Temar felt another tear escape, leaving a cold trail over his cheek.

"Slavery would leave even me white eyed with fear. Give him a little time to come to terms with this." Ben set the box down on a long sorting table. A cooling unit, a recycler, and an incinerator all stood side by side, thick insulation between them, and Temar tightened his jaw. A small trail of spit escaped from his gag, and Ben leaned over with a rag in his hand, gently wiping Temar's face, from his chin up to the corner of his mouth.

The touch made Temar's body stiffen in terror. "He's handling this about as well as such a young man could," Ben said kindly. That kindness was a slap in the face that made Temar hold his breath, as he waited for the choking grip around his neck or the affectionate pat on the face. The fact that he didn't know which he would get was actually far worse than the casual cruelty he would have received from the hand of Landholder Young.

"You're having remarkable patience with him," Cardan said. Ben lifted the supplies off the top of the box with the notebooks, and Temar stared in desperate hope at those piles of notes that he had collected and maintained so carefully. Ben lifted the first out of the box and smiled at Temar.

"I think young fools deserve a little patience. After all, the whole point of the slavery system is to help those who have been handicapped by poor parenting. Isn't that what Naite Polli is always saying?"

Ben pulled the heavy door of the incinerator open and put the first notebook in. Temar made an inarticulate cry behind his gag, but Cardan merely patted him on the arm, the way someone might soothe an anxious goat about to be castrated. And the image wasn't far off. His power was in those notebooks, in his carefully kept records, and Ben piled them inside the heavy machine.

Ben changed the subject. "So, any word on that south field?"

"Still underwatered. I was hoping that, with the Gazer farm shut down, we could start watering our seedlings their full allotment."

"If there's a broken pipe, the pipe traps are still getting half our share," Ben said with a weary sigh. Temar frowned in confusion. Ben should have all the water he needed if he was stealing, so why did he feel a need to play these games?

"We should get out there and find that broken irrigation pipe. You should have gone to the council and complained about the Gazer farm years ago. So, whose land is that now?"

"No doubt George Young will get the land to repay him for the Gazers' tricks, because the slave prices weren't enough to replace the water and the damaged crops." Ben paused with Temar's last notebook in his hand. If Temar had evidence that implicated him in his hand, he would be panicked and sweating, but Ben only looked thoughtful. "Honestly, I don't know that George is going to care about a leak any more than old Erqu Gazer did. Maybe we should petition the council to cut the Gazer farm off the irrigation system altogether."

Cardan rubbed his bald head. "George'll protest that."

"George protests everything. The council is going to engrave a chair for his butt." Ben shook his head and leaned against the incinerator, the notebook still in hand. "He can get the land back on the system after he's done a few burns and gotten those pipe traps ripped out... and after he's found that damn leak. But it's a waste of water, and it's keeping us from getting our full share. Erqu was... lost... after his wife's death. I wouldn't have taken that man to the council for all the luck in the stars. He was a good man."

Ben fell silent, his sorrow appearing so real that Temar had trouble believing his eyes. Then Ben pulled himself out of his grief as he pointed a finger. "But George had better be ready for a fight if I don't get my full water share. If he takes one drop from me, I'll petition to have him doing labor days." Ben poked his finger in Cardan's direction, and Cardan smiled.

"George Young doing a hard day's labor prepping the ground?" Cardan outright laughed at that thought. "That would mean moving his own sorry ass or hiring out the work."

"Or getting Cyla Gazer to do it." Ben made an unhappy face. "There wasn't anyone bidding her slave price when I left town, so the council might be forced to hand her over to Young." Ben practically threw the last book into the incinerator and then slammed the door with far more force than it needed. "I don't like the idea of her over there with that man. He's not one to show anyone human respect, and he definitely wouldn't respect a slave."

Temar almost choked on the irony of that. Right now, Temar would far rather have himself and his sister in Young's hands. He might take his fury and frustration out on them, but Ben frightened him far more.

Cardan patted him on the arm again. "Don't think that we'll let him do poorly by your sister," he offered reassuringly, his voice deadly serious.

"Perhaps we can retire the northwest corner from pasture for a few seasons, turn the goats loose in there."

"It's not scheduled for livestock for another four harvests."

Ben's mouth curved into a slow smile. "Ah, but if we have goats so far from the house, I imagine some would get through that old fence on a fairly regular basis."

"Which would lead to us having to ride up to Young's place, looking for our missing stock. I wouldn't mind catching that bastard being a bastard."

"Me too." Ben sounded so honest in his desire to protect Cyla that Temar thought, for a moment, that maybe he'd imagined the whole scene in the bedroom; maybe he'd hallucinated the entire hellacious week. How could a man appear so honest one moment and—Temar's thoughts froze in a white storm of horror as Ben turned the incinerator on. The heavy machine thunked and hissed and then gave a mighty roar as it devoured all his work and then sent the ashes down to become fertilizer.

"We may lose stock to the pipe traps." Cardan continued the conversation, never knowing he was witnessing the end of Temar's hopes. His father would forever be remembered as a fool, and he and his sister would be water thieves for the rest of their lives.

"Don't you think it's worth a few stock animals to make sure that Cyla doesn't end up like that girl in Blue Hope?" Ben asked.

Cardan's face hardened. His jaw bulged, and he pulled his lips back so the white of his teeth shone against his dark skin. "They should have done more than exile that man. What he did was an abomination."

"Let the sandcats eat him. Some people are born wrong." Ben pressed his lips together into an angry line and shook his head. "I won't have that happen here. If Young gets that girl, we will be keeping a close eye on her." Then Ben turned to Temar and gave him another of those fatherly smiles that turned Temar's guts to ice. "Don't worry. We'll make sure we keep tabs on your sister."

"That we will, boy," Cardan agreed, slapping Temar on the arm. "We'll keep an eye out for both of you."

Ben's smile suddenly looked far more dangerous. Temar fought an instinctive urge to run away, because clearly he wouldn't get far. Even if he'd been free and ungagged, he'd never convince people that Ben Gratu was a water thief and monster. "It looks like Temar has calmed down some. Why don't you head back out to the barn, and I'll see if I can't get our hellion settled in some, before the field crew comes in."

"You got it, boss. Behave, boy," he said with a final friendly slap on Temar's arm, and then he wandered out of the mechanical room, leaving Temar alone with Ben.

Ben ran a finger over the door handle to the incinerator. "Do I need to explain the futility of screaming?" Ben asked, with an amused twitch pulling at the corner of his mouth.

Temar shook his head. Clearly, Ben had won this fight. Temar's family was gone, his land was gone, and his sister's life was in the hands of a monster.

"Such a trainable boy," Ben said, his expression widening into a big grin. He stepped forward, his body trapping Temar against the table as he reached around to pull at the knotted strip of fabric. Ben was taller, so when he leaned in, Temar was eye level with his chin and had a close-up view of the tiny, rough hairs pushing out of his face. Temar focused on the stubble, tracing patterns in the miniature forest of hair rather than look up into the mocking friendliness in this monster's eyes.

With a last tug, the tie came loose, and Ben pulled it off, leaving Temar with a mouthful of fabric that he wasn't sure what he was supposed to do with. He looked at Ben, wondering if he dared to spit the soggy mess out or if that would bring back the anger. His throat still ached at the memory of those strong fingers wrapped around it as they threatened to strangle him.

Ben's smile grew larger as he considered Temar. Bringing a finger up, he traced from the edge of Temar's mouth to a spot under his ear. Temar suspected he was following the red line made by the gag pressing into his skin. "Such a trainable boy." Ben retraced the mark, pressing on the corner of Temar's mouth. Temar sucked air through his nose as the pressure made the skin heat and sting.

"Ten years is a long time, but your life would go much smoother if you would yield to reason… if you're a good boy and yield to me. There's no cause to fight, because there is nothing to be gained."

Temar watched with wide eyes, not sure how he was supposed to react.

Ben traced the edge of Temar's top lip with a fingertip. "Do you want that out of your mouth?"

With a small nod, Temar watched Ben, feeling very much like the birdbug about to be pounced on by a sandcat. For a second, Ben didn't do anything but run his work-rough finger over Temar's lower lip and watch Temar with a predatory eye. Temar held himself perfectly still, his hands helpless and fisted between them.

"Such a *very* trainable boy." Ben pressed down against Temar's lip, and he allowed Ben to open his mouth and reach in for the soggy cloth. "You are so much brighter than your father even knew. You see the sides of the trap even now, don't you?"

Temar dry swallowed, fear stealing his spit so that his lips and tongue tried to stick together. Ben tossed the cloth aside and pressed so close that Temar's back had to arch against the hard edge of the table. "What would happen if you told your story to Carden?" Ben was back to sounding friendly and helpful.

For a second, Temar wasn't sure whether Ben really wanted an answer, but then the hand that had been stroking his lip gave him a light slap across the face. "He'd think I was just accusing you because I'm angry. He wouldn't believe it," Temar blurted.

Again, Ben reached up, but this time he patted Temar on the cheek. "Good boy. You aren't coming across as particularly reliable right now. And the less reliable you are, the less I have to worry about you, and the safer your sister is going to be. Guess what game we're going to play." Ben wiggled his eyebrows, and Temar watched him, terrified because right now anything that came out of Ben's brain was not going to be good.

"We're going to go out there, and you're going to play good slave until someone mentions water or George Young. Guess what you're going to do then." Ben reached up and fingered a lock of Temar's hair, stroking it with his thumb. After a second, he gave that same lock such a hard yank that Temar gasped. "I asked you to guess, boy." Suddenly he didn't sound as friendly.

At first, Temar was too afraid to guess anything. He wanted Ben to tell him what to do so he knew how to navigate this shifting sand he'd found himself walking. He felt as if, any second, the winds would change, and the dune would move under him, and he'd be buried under two tons of sand. However, his mind spun an answer out of Ben's words.

"You want me to prove how unreliable I am." He whispered the answer.

He'd hated giving answers in school because he never wanted people staring at him. They whispered about his father or about how Cyla had gotten in trouble again or about how he came to school in clothes that were too large because he had to take whatever handouts others would give him. And as time passed, the number of handouts others had been willing to offer had dwindled. He didn't want anyone to see any of that. Even when he'd had the right answer, he had preferred to remain in the back, unnoticed and uncommented on.

Now Ben was asking him to make himself the center of a scene, like his father when he was so drunk that he flung accusations as easily as clods of dirt.

Ben rested his palm against Temar's cheek and stroked his thumb over the corner of his mouth, where it was still sore. "Good boy. I'll never trust you until you show me you can earn that trust by doing what your master says. My friend wants to kill your sister, so you know that I'm the only one standing between the Gazer family and death."

Ben's expression softened with worry. "Your father was a good man before your mother died so young, and I've wanted to do something to help you. I just always worried about drawing attention to myself. But now, I can help you. I can protect your sister, and I can make sure that these next ten years are easy for you. But you have to show me that you know how to appreciate my protection." Ben's hand paused, and he brought his other hand up, so that he cupped Temar's face. Temar held himself perfectly still. He didn't know the rules to this game, but he knew he had no power in it.

"I think you want to scream and rant and accuse George Young of stealing your water and setting you up and ruining your farm. Hell, you can throw in something truly outlandish, like a suggestion that he killed your mother. What am I going to do?"

Temar's gaze darted to the table where the clump of damp cloth lay. "You'll gag me."

"That I will. After all, as your owner, it is my job to teach you control, and I would never allow you to publicly slander George. That would give George the right to demand days of labor from you, and everyone knows that I'm too good of a man to want George near you or your sister. That man values land and money and wringing fourteen hours of labor out of a twelve-hour day. I wouldn't give him the right to overwork my young Temar. So, what will the others think of me for gagging you?"

"That you're protecting me." Temar choked on the words, but there was a twisted logic to them.

"And what will they think of you?"

Temar closed his eyes and took a deep breath as his guts knotted at the idea of all those men staring at him, judging him. "They'll think I'm mad. The council will strip me of adult rights." His chest ached with fear.

"I doubt they'd go that far." Ben patted both his cheeks and laughed. "No, I'll be sure to protect you. I'll explain how your father's words have poisoned you. I will take care of you, Temar. You only have to obey. You can do that, right?"

Ben took his hands away, and Temar's warm cheeks suddenly felt cold. He looked up as Ben took a step back. "Will you follow orders?" Ben asked.

Temar's mind darted through his options, a rat caught in a pipe trap, running and running, but always running in circles and feeling the poison sinking in through his skin. He had no evidence. He might get the men to take him to the council, but he couldn't get anyone to act before Ben would make a call to whoever had purchased his sister. People were all too ready to believe that a Gazer was mad with paranoia, and his word against Ben Gratu would lead to only one outcome. No matter how he turned, he couldn't find an escape. Exile or death waited at every turn—every turn but one.

"Yes, sir," Temar whispered.

Ben beamed at him. Reaching over, he slipped his hand behind Temar's neck and pulled him in for a hug. "Such a good boy you are. Let's get you some water and some food before the others come." Ben slapped him on the back and then turned to the refrigerator, one arm still draped over Temar's shoulders. "I fear I don't trust you enough to untie you yet, but you point out which foods you like, and I'll feed you."

chapter
SIX

"YOU'RE UP late." Div settled himself down on the pew next to Shan.

"Thinking."

"Didn't think you were praying," Div said. From the senior priest, those words could have been sharp with rebuke, but instead Div sounded almost amused. Shan took a moment to glare at the old man.

"I often pray; however, God helps those who help themselves."

"The Gospel according to Ben Franklin." Div nodded slowly, his skepticism showing in the twist of his mouth. "Is that not the man who whored his way through Europe after escaping an apprenticeship with his brother? I'm not sure I would trust him for spiritual advice. I would rather turn to Proverbs. 'Whoever trusts his own wit is a fool; anyone whose ways are wise will be safe.'"

"I've been called worse than a fool," Shan admitted. He stared up at the stylized cross, metal strips and windwood branches artistically woven together to create something stark and beautiful and mesmerizing.

Div settled next to him, pulling his glasses off and perching them on his head before he leaned back in the pew and crossed his arms over his chest. For long minutes, they sat in the dark of the church, the wind scraping over the sloping sides of the building.

"Are you going to sit here all night?" Shan finally asked.

"That would depend," Div answered without opening his eyes.

"On what?"

"On how stubborn you are being tonight." Cracking one eye open, Div silently challenged him. Shan sighed. He knew full well that if the obstreperous old man insisted on talking, he would not be placated until Shan talked. As a teenager, he'd tried testing Div's patience and stubbornness, and he'd lost every time.

"I'm bothered by the things I see around us."

"Oh, wait until you're my age," Div promised. "You'll be absolutely terrified by them. I think God measures our lifespan in how much change we can take before our heads explode."

Shan smiled. As a boy, Div had always been his safe haven, a man who would speak his mind without the need to belittle others. He'd changed little in the years, except that his chin drooped lower, his nose was bulbing, and his thinning hair had turned white. He was still the blunt man whom Shan could count on for some honesty.

"So, what is threatening to make your head explode like an overwatered pipe trap?" Div pressed back in the pew, and the wood groaned under the force. Shan mentally added the pew to his list of repairs around the church.

"Meid is pregnant again."

"Which is not a reason to sit in the dark and brood."

"I'm not brooding."

"Of course not. You only sit in the dark and stare at the cross and blame yourself for the flaws of the universe. I stand corrected." Div paused. "Actually, I sit corrected, and I would like to be lying in my bed, asleep and corrected."

Shan frowned, bothered that he was keeping Div awake. The man was getting old, and the doctor didn't hold out much hope for his heart. He needed rest. "And I've made you brood more." Div reached over and rested a hand against Shan's leg.

"Your heart will overfill and explode long before your head, son. What's truly bothering you?"

"I wasn't lying. It bothers me that Meid is pregnant again. We nearly lost her to her last pregnancy. The doctors can't do much without medicine and equipment."

"Both of which are in short supply," Div agreed, his voice growing solemn. "People have lived without technology before. We will survive this. 'The spirit of those who fear the Lord can survive.'"

"Jeremiah?" Shan asked, curious as to where Div had pulled that quote.

"Book of Ecclesiasticus."

Shan nodded. Div carried entire libraries in his head, so he trusted the man's memory, even if the doctors doubted the reliability of his heart. "But that was on Earth. Are we as sure of Livre? This place was not built for humans. The pipe traps and sandcats and sandrats are designed for this world, but we aren't."

Div didn't answer immediately. He turned his gaze to the cross. Even in the dim light that filtered in through thick glass, the metal gleamed. "Sometimes we don't know where faith and foolishness meet. Do you think our great-grandparents were fools for coming here?"

"In my case, it was my great-great-great-grandparents," Shan corrected the man. Div reached over and softly backhanded him across the arm. "And I don't know. They believed the inner worlds would support them until the world was terraformed."

"And now the universe has changed." Div continued to look up at the cross. "Had they remained on the inner worlds, the odds are that you would now be on a ship, ordered into battle."

"A priest is not much good in battle," Shan quickly disagreed, but Div only turned his head and gave him a long, searching look. "And I know that playing a game of what-if helps no one. I'm just not sure that the changes we're making to this world are the right ones. We sent Cyla as a slave to another settlement. How can we move people around—take their rights—as if they're pieces on a chess board?" Shan's voice had slowly risen to a near shout, and he snapped his mouth shut. Div didn't deserve his anger.

Div patted his leg. "Love uprightness you who are rulers on Earth, be properly disposed towards the Lord and seek him in simplicity of heart."

"I'd rather have guidance than platitudes." Shan turned to Div, begging his mentor to lay out some choices as simply as he had when Shan had been sixteen. His brother had recently been sentenced to slavery, and his father's temper had turned from Naite to Shan. After the first beating, he had come to Div and cried in the priest's arms. Now it was others who came to Shan and begged for guidance, but he never felt like his words reached people like Div's had.

"The Bible is full of guidance, and if they sound like platitudes, it's because we don't want to listen," Div corrected him, the censure clear even if his voice remained mild. Shan grimaced as he realized his slip. "I can't tell you anything that you don't already know. You aren't a child whose feet I can put on the path. You're a little heavy for me to lift, these days." Div patted him on the leg again and then crossed his arms over his chest once more.

"You should return to the council," Shan said softly. The church members would vote Div back on the council in one second if he showed any willingness to serve.

Div laughed. "Lilian would gut you for even suggesting that. As much as I adore that woman, we risked homicide more than once being in the same room. So, what are you going to do? I assume that you already know that sitting in the dark will not solve any of your problems."

"I don't know." Shan wouldn't have admitted that to anyone but Div, but the fact was that he wanted to do a lot of things. He wanted to dismantle the slave system before another Blue Hope. He wanted to throw every resource behind the doctors so they could do their jobs. He wanted to send a message up to space to tell the inner worlds to stop their stupidity before everyone on Livre slowly died. He wanted to rip the whole world apart out of sheer frustration. But in the end, he didn't know what to actually do.

A Bible verse floated to the top of Shan's memory. "For trampling on the poor man and for extorting levies on his wheat: although you have built houses of dressed stone, you will not live in them; although you have planted pleasant vineyards, you will not drink wine from them."

"You think someone lives in a house of stone?" Div asked.

"The lords of the inner worlds," Shan immediately answered.

Div chuckled. "I have great faith in your ability to change the world, but that is a little far for even you and your passion to reach. Is there anyone closer... someone who you might actually reach?"

Shan thought about that. Temar came first to mind. The boy used to slip into the back of church during service, and every slave had the right to come to church, but he hadn't shown up since Ben Gratu had driven off with him a month ago. Likely the boy was using Sundays to sleep, and in reality, he was far more concerned about Cyla. However, Temar was the easiest to reach.

Div used the back of the pew to push himself up. "I can already see you have a mission in mind. So, go. Do something useful that does not include staring at the cross and waiting for God to act."

"I thought you didn't believe in God helping those who helped themselves."

"I don't. But I do believe that the Book of Ecclesiasticus also says, 'The sinner will not escape with his ill-gotten gains nor the patience of the devout go for nothing. He takes note of every charitable action, and everyone is treated as he deserves.'"

Div rested a hand on Shan's shoulder, and for a second, he leaned heavily into Shan and wobbled slightly on his legs. When he stood too quickly, sometimes he would have to grab at something to avoid falling. Right now, Div's fingers pressed into Shan's shoulder, and he could feel the warmth between them. Everything his father had denied him, Div had offered, and seeing Div struggle this way worried him. That was one more battle Shan didn't know how to fight.

Div cleared his throat and caught his balance again before patting Shan on the cheek. "You need to fix fewer pews and read more Bible verses. So, go… take some charitable action."

Shan smiled up at his mentor and rested his own palm against Div's, so that Div's hand was, for a moment, trapped between Shan's face and palm. "Thank you."

"It's in the job description," Div said, with a touch of mockery in his voice. "I have to pretend to be wise and have something useful to offer." After dismissing his own words, Div turned and walked toward the back where a narrow passage connected the church proper to the parish house next door.

Shan waited as the door closed. Div would move slowly through the narrow passage and up the stairs to his room. If Shan timed it right, he would give Div enough time to get to his own room before he followed. That way Div wouldn't hurry to try to get out of Shan's way, and Shan could make sure Div got safely into bed before he went to his own room. And when tomorrow came, he'd check on Temar and visit Cyla in Red Plain. Maybe he'd feel better if he faced a few of his fears and proved to himself that he was only seeing boogeymen in the dark.

chapter
seven

THE SAND cycle, with its oversized tires, lost traction again, and Shan found himself sliding down the dune face faster and faster. Wind tore at his sleeves, and dust clouded his vision, but his muscles knew this game. He closed his eyes and felt the bike between his legs, the warm metal and plastic veering first right and then left as the engine powered down during the long fall, and all Shan concentrated on was holding his own weight directly above the machine. The sand cycle would go where it would go, and riding down a dune was an exercise in trusting the Lord to keep you from breaking your neck.

The angle of the fall changed, and Shan opened his eyes enough to see the bottom of the dune rise up in front of him. The cycle bucked and wobbled from side to side as it slowed, and the engine finally sputtered to life again. For a half second, the fat wheels spun and threw the sand. Then Shan settled his weight back, and the extra traction allowed the back tire to finally push against the sand and send the cycle darting forward toward the giant gates to Spence Valley.

This was the oldest and most terraformed of all the valleys, so Shan imagined the farmers were more than a little pleased to burn the weeds off Erqu Gazer's land. Ben might even have Temar doing that, although if he was kind, he wouldn't ask the boy to burn his father's home. Then again, Ben might not want to do anything that might help George, considering what a small-minded and arrogant man that one could be. Ben might let the weeds choke the land.

If someone didn't clear the weeds out, eventually Chad Dura or Mara Kelligan or Tepah Starcharter or even Tom Sulli would complain. Their farms were farther from the old Gazer place, but seeds traveled, and not even walls and stone could keep the Livre wind out altogether. Ignoring the large vehicle gate that was still blocked with sand, Shan guided the bike through the narrow walkway. It was a tight fit, but the cycle was designed to make the narrow turns as the passage led a winding way through the rock into the valley.

He finally reached the top of the passage, and the valley opened below. This route took him high into the cliffs behind the Gratu farm, which was why so few people used it, but Shan enjoyed the narrow paths, steep cliffs, and dangerous turns. He turned his cycle toward the valley floor and, for a time, concentrated on not falling to his death. No doubt Ben would not appreciate a priest and his bike falling though the barn roof.

The green fields were dotted with unskilled laborers. Naite would be working over at the Kelligan or Sulli farms, not that Shan had any desire to track him down. The cycle bounced over a low ridge and then onto the rock shelf where the Gratu house and barn sat. Sua Smith was sitting in front of a table in the sun, pipe fittings in front of her. No one could miss the wild tattoos scattered across her back.

"Sua!" Shan called. The woman turned, a pipe torch in hand, and frowned.

"Shan? Who's dying, that we need the priest out here?" She pulled her weld mask off and set it and her torch on the table.

"Hopefully, no one. I've just been missing a parishioner, so I thought I would see how Temar is doing."

Sua snorted. "That boy has his sister's temper."

Shan blinked in shock. "Temar?"

"Temar," she said firmly. "Let someone say the wrong word around him, or let him be in the wrong mood, and the anger flies out of that boy."

"Temar?" Shan repeated. He felt a little like a man who had stepped off a ship into a new world, where all the rules of the universe changed. To claim that Temar had a temper was a little like expecting water to fall from Livre skies. It did not happen.

Sua laughed, but it was an unhappy sound. "You wouldn't think to look at him, but he has a mouth." Sua straddled the sawhorse she had set up next to the table and pulled up the pipe she had just welded, holding it up against the sun and squinting at the joint. "Ben's been patient to no end, but if he requests an extension on that boy's contract, I'll be testifying for him. Ben has less time to work his own fields, and Temar is not all that useful, even when he is in a mood to work."

Shan could only blink as he tried to figure out if this was some odd joke on her part. "Temar?"

Sua smiled and shook her head. "The boy fooled you with that sweet look of his, didn't he?"

"Obviously, he did." Shan swung his leg off the sand cycle and crossed the dusty yard. "I feared he'd be beaten down by his slavery. It can't be easy on a man, knowing that his rights are gone."

Sua put the pipe down on the table. "Sometimes I think that's true. He'll walk around, creeping from shadow to shadow, always looking for Ben and staying two steps behind him."

Shan flinched at that description. Sometimes even those with short-term services lost their confidence. In Naite's case, he had come through with plenty of ego, but then he'd had extra to spare before he started his term. But some slaves became shells of themselves. They'd come into confession, practically asking him to tell them what to confess to.

That lack of power grated against Shan's conscience and made slavery feel unnatural to him. He hadn't wanted that for Temar. But the flares of anger—he wasn't sure if that was a healthy and normal reaction to having so much taken from him or if Temar was in some sort of trouble. He'd like to think that Temar would know to come to him or Ben if someone on the farm was doing something, but the young man's habit of shadowing Ben did suggest that he feared something, real or imagined.

"Where are they now?"

Sua jerked her head to the north. "Out working fields. The guys are weeding today. Considering that Ben hasn't come back with Temar bound, the boy must be in a mood to work."

"Bound?" Shan's mouth went dry. He never thought Ben would be the sort to chain a slave.

Already, Sua was nodding her head. "The boy's first day here… you should have seen the fit he threw. About as quick as Ben untied him, Cardan made a poorly considered comment about the boy's sister. Temar went near mad. To hear it from him, Cyla is a saint, and George Young is a water thief who murdered his mother in order to steal the Gazer land, and the rest of us are in on it all. He knocked over a pile of feed, broke two lanterns, and led the men on quite the chase before Marcos pinned him. And when Marcos finally got hands on him, Temar all but collapsed, trembling and flinching. The boy caused havoc."

She pulled the leather tie out of her hair and ran her fingers through dark curls before retying the strip. "Ben has his hands full. He had to take the boy up to the main house and keep him there for three days before he trusted the boy not to go wild. And even now, let the wrong word fall, and he'll curse you back seven generations."

Shan's stomach soured. The helplessness and the flares of anger—the fear and the fury—that was a pattern he knew well enough, and he'd only seen one sort of betrayal that caused a person to react so wildly. Shan closed his eyes and cursed himself for never trying to reach out to the boy before. "Lord have mercy on Erqu Gazer's soul, because right now I am not feeling charitable toward the man," Shan whispered.

While Sua didn't answer, her nod and her grim look made it clear that she agreed. So Shan wasn't the only one to suspect the boy had been abused by that sandcat of a drunken father. Only, Temar wasn't a boy now. He was a young man who'd been stripped of his rights, very likely because he'd been hurt and confused and no one had stepped in to protect him when he'd needed it. If Shan could dig Erqu Gazer up and bring that man back to life for one minute, he'd have more than a few words for that old drunk.

"I should go and talk to him."

"I know Ben would appreciate someone reaching out to the boy. His patience has to be near an end." Sua touched his arm. "You'll help?" Shan suspected that this had to be hard on everyone at the farm. No one liked to see a young man hurting so much, but to know that he'd been your neighbor and you allowed that to happen.... Shan mentally made a note to spend a little more time out here.

"I'll certainly try," Shan promised her before he turned his steps toward the north field, where he'd seen people working. Sua nodded and turned her attention back to her pipes.

The paths here were narrow, and Shan chose to walk rather than risk his tires taking out the plants on the edge of the field. Ben ran a careful farm. Most of the fields were well watered, but the paths were so dry that puffs of dust rose with his steps. The first workers Shan saw were straddling the line of half-grown plants and pulling tiny weeds before they could steal too much water. The small intruders were collected in bags for the incinerator, so that their nutrients would end up back in the soil. Men and women nodded to him as he passed. Not everyone in town attended church, and few of the farmers or farm workers found it worth their time to make the trip every week, but he knew them all from weddings and funerals and Landfall celebrations and council business.

Ben was working the edge of the field where the weeds were worst, his broad back burdened with a large bag. Temar was the small figure working beside him. Shan regretted this whole situation. The young man was remarkable, and even without a parent to buy him an apprenticeship, he would have found a skilled worker to sponsor him if he hadn't attacked George Young's water supply.

His deep blue eyes had always haunted Shan when Temar had come to service. He'd watched with an expression Shan could never quite understand. He was a beautiful boy… rather, he had been a beautiful boy. Now he was a beautiful man who could have made an enviable future for himself. He had a giving soul and had always been the first to lift a burden or open a door for someone in need. Shan had seen the eyes of most of the unmarried women and half the unmarried men following Temar with longing, either because of his physical beauty or his inherent goodness. Now, he was likely facing a lifetime of unskilled labor.

"Ben!" Shan called out. Ben turned, an awkward movement with his legs straddling the row of plants.

"Shan!" he called out in obvious pleasure. "What, have you come to see how honest workers make a living?"

"Considering how often I have to repair pews after your honest workers break the joints, I think I already know," Shan teased right back as he closed the distance between them.

A frown crossed Ben's face. "There's not something wrong, is there?" His eyes darted over to Temar. Shan got his first look at Temar. He was sweating and he had put on more muscle, but the only thing Shan saw at first was the leather gag covering his mouth. Shan stared at it until Temar dropped his head and blushed, and then Shan tore his eyes away and looked at Ben for some sort of explanation.

"I know what you're thinking." Ben stepped clear of the field, his hands held up as though to hold off an attack.

"You should let him hear the boy, then he'd know why he's on four days' restriction," one of the other workers called from the next row. Shan vaguely remembered her from a wedding. "The boy needs to learn to think before he says things that will make others demand work days from him to compensate for his slander."

"He's slandering you?" Shan asked Ben in a shocked voice.

"Me? God no." Ben shook his head. "But if George catches wind of half the lies that have been flying around this farm, I doubt I'll be able to keep him from demanding a month of work days from the boy. I know you're on the council, Shan, and I hate putting you on the spot, but we need to make sure that, no matter what happens, we keep the young fool separated from George." That shocked Shan, but now that he thought about it, it shouldn't. Those who were abused often turned their anger somewhere… on a neighbor or even themselves, but the human body couldn't hold that much hate without it spilling over.

"George would work him half to death and go out of his way to find tortures for the lad," the woman in the next row agreed. "Which we're not going to let happen." The look she gave Temar was full of sympathy, but he ducked his head lower, so that his face and the gag vanished behind a veil of blond hair.

"The workers have been great," Ben nodded. "We're all trying to keep a lid on this young one." Ben didn't say anything more, but from the worried expression on his face when he looked at Temar, it was clear he'd come to the same conclusion Shan had. Ben reached over and put a hand out for Temar, and Temar took it, allowing Ben to help balance him as he stepped over the plants and took his place next to Ben.

"And I thought Cyla was the one with the temper," Shan admitted. He'd actually been quite worried about her, but maybe he'd been worried about the wrong Gazer the whole time. At the mention of his sister's name, Temar's head came up. Ben immediately put a comforting arm around the boy's shoulders and pulled him close. Shan watched in concern as Temar leaned into the other man, obviously seeking safety and comfort. Certainly, Temar was young, and after the death of his father and the loss of his freedom, Shan expected to see the psychological damage of slavery, but this needy fear went beyond what he had expected.

"I think the temper was inherited by both." Ben looked down. "Sometimes I'm quite amazed at the fury that comes out of him, but he's learning to control himself, and when he can't, he's learning there are consequences." Ben reached up and brushed a bit of hair back from Temar's face and at the same time touched the gag.

"I actually came out to talk to Temar, since he'd missed services," Shan said, hoping Ben would catch his hint, but it was a workday, and if Temar's owner had imposed a punishment, Shan had no business interfering. If this were anyone other than Ben Gratu, Shan wouldn't even suggest that he make an exception for him. But Ben was already reaching for the latch on the leather strap that went behind Temar's head.

"I think talking is healthy for the boy, if he can control his mouth." Ben pulled the gag off, and there was a mouthpiece that went inside Temar's mouth and then connected to the strap that went around his head. It was dark with saliva. "Can you control your mouth? Can you honestly think about what is going to come out of your mouth and weigh the potential consequences of your words?" Ben put a finger under Temar's chin and pushed up so that Temar had to make eye contact with him.

"Yes, I can," Temar agreed quietly.

"Good boy." Ben smiled and gave him a pat on the back. "He's still under restrictions because his mouth is really quite remarkable, so when you two are done, put this back on before you return him," Ben said, holding out the leather gag. Shan instinctively took what Ben offered, even though it sent a shiver of revulsion through him to do that to another human being. The leather was soft in his hand, and Ben had clearly had a worker spend a lot of time and effort to make something that wouldn't hurt the boy, but it still made Shan's heart ache. "Go show Shan what a mess I have on my north border, Temar. I think the council will be hearing about that soon enough."

Ben gave Temar one last slap on the arm before he stepped back into the field and turned his attention to the weeds. The other workers who had slowed to watch the conversation returned to their work.

Temar didn't say anything, but he set off for the north border, and Shan watched him for a second before hurrying to follow. The young man looked in good enough health. He was walking with a stiffness in his gait, but even good workers had trouble keeping up with Ben Gratu, and Temar wasn't physically prepared for heavy farm work.

"I've missed seeing you in church," Shan offered. He fingered the edge of the gag, feeling the soft leather and trying to ignore his deep sense of disquiet.

Temar's step faltered for a second, but then he continued his steady walk toward his father's old farm. George owned the land now, but no doubt he was using the water ration on his own land, without tilling the weed-infested Gazer farm.

Shan frowned, not sure how to start this conversation. Normally, slaves would come to him in confession, and when they sat down, they wanted to talk. They were hungry to sit in the dark and let their fears spill out. They wanted him to solve their problems, to tell them how to fix lives that had spun out of control. Shan had told the story of Job so often that, for all of his shortcomings in Biblical history, he could recite that book verse by verse. However, he wasn't sure how to get a reluctant slave to start talking.

"I thought I might travel to Red Plain next week and visit Cyla." Shan hadn't been planning that up until now, but looking at the tentative hold Temar had on his own psyche, now he was concerned about how Cyla might be reacting in a new town.

Temar stopped and looked at the ground in front of Shan. He chewed on his chapped lower lip and seemed to be weighing something in his own mind, but he didn't say a word.

"Would you like to send her a message?" Shan asked.

Temar's gaze came up to meet his for a second before those bright blue eyes darted off to the distant cliffs. "Can you tell me if she's well?" he finally asked, his voice whisper soft.

"I will come back and tell you everything she says and how she looks," Shan promised. Temar swallowed nervously and then turned toward the Gazer place again.

Shan followed. He'd never felt so helpless in his life. Div would know how to approach this, but Shan never felt the guiding hand of God the way Div had. Oh, God had helped him more than once, but God hadn't given him Div's talent to read wounded souls.

"Has Naite come to see you and tell you his inspirational tales from slavery?" Shan finally asked. Temar shook his head, his blond hair flopping to the sides. He should cut it, but maybe Ben hoped long hair would protect the boy's neck from sunburn.

"Naite loves to tell slaves how this can be a chance to fix your life. I'm not sure whether it helps or if it makes people feel more trapped and resentful, but he does mean well. Our father was not what you might call a paragon of fatherly love, and sometimes I suspect that Naite inherited our father's ability to completely ignore a person's emotional needs. He'll tell that tale, even if the slave he's talking to is nodding off with sleep or trembling with anger."

That made Temar look over his shoulder, his eyebrows lowering in confusion, but he still didn't speak. For someone Ben had accused of talking too much, Temar was remarkably silent.

"Our mother died young, just as yours did." Shan watched the boy, studying him for some sort of reaction. Looking at the similarities in their lives, Shan was an idiot for not suspecting abuse. A man, alone with two children, isolated on a farm and not hiring in workers. Erqu Gazer and Yan Polli could have been twins.

Temar stopped and reached up to rest his hand on a line of windwood posts that marked the boundary of Ben's land. Looking out, Shan studied the clumps of pipe trap weeds and the trailing vines of creepweed covering the land. "God's mercy," Shan breathed. The farm was ten times worse than he'd expected.

"Cyla and I always worked to keep the fields clear," Temar said softly, and Shan believed him. One month without the two young Gazers trying to control the weeds, and the farm had exploded into a full crop of pestilence.

"Given this evidence, I dare say you and Cyla had been working hard to control the problem." Shan bent down and tugged on a creepweed that had crossed into Ben's property. Even though the plant had only put up two leaves, the roots were so deep Shan couldn't pull the whole plant up, and the green of the plant broke off in his hands. "They've put in roots. Come harvest end, someone will bring this to the council." Shan grimaced at the thought of dealing with George. He'd throw a fit, but if he didn't burn off this land and bring in the deep-till equipment to rip out the weeds, he'd have to forfeit it.

"I suppose it's hard seeing the land go to ruin like this," Shan offered gently. Temar stood by the windwood post and shrugged as he stared out at his old home.

"I should go back now." Temar glanced over, but he didn't meet Shan's gaze—he stared at the leather gag in Shan's hand. Shan closed his fist around the soft leather.

"I want to help you."

Temar took a step back as though afraid, and for a second, he searched Shan with suspicious eyes. Shan's heart broke. Why hadn't he ever noticed how lost and broken he was? "Please," Shan said, offering his empty hand.

Temar's eyes went from his face to his outstretched hand before darting off to the side and settling on the distant cliff. "Stable water levels were part of the terraform process."

The change in topics mystified Shan, but the Lord did work in mysterious ways, and sometimes abused young men were even more mysterious.

"The sun-net captures enough moisture from the air to replace what is lost from the ground, so yes, the system is stable." Shan shrugged. "Or the system would be stable, if the inner worlds had finished the terraforming. Right now, we're holding our own, though, and we aren't losing enough to threaten our lives or the lives of our children." Shan didn't say that if the inner planets continued their wars, their grandchildren would be on dangerously tight water rationing, and their great grandchildren would be dying of thirst, but that was an open secret on Livre. As soon as children were old enough to study planetary ecology in school, they could complete the equations for themselves.

Temar nodded and looked out onto the fields.

"Is there something that worries you?" Shan asked. He risked taking a step closer.

"Many things." Temar sounded so lost that Shan wanted to make a promise that he would make things better, but there was no "better" to be had. The emotion vanished from Temar's face. "I need to go back." He looked down at the gag again. Shan followed his gaze and found himself looking at the strip of leather, but he couldn't bring himself to fasten the gag around Temar's face. He was so devoid of words now that it seemed cruel to take the rest from him.

Temar reached out, and Shan allowed him to take the gag. Shan watched while Temar slipped the flat flap into his mouth and then buckled the strap around his head. He took a second to pull out wisps of hair that had been caught under the leather, and then he started walking back toward the field where Ben was working.

Shan followed from a distance, oddly bothered by Temar's willingness to put that thing back on himself. Actually, he was bothered by many things, starting at the wary look in his eye and his obvious need of Ben's protection and ending with that odd, disjointed bit of conversation about water. It was almost as if Temar's mind had slipped for a second, thoughts tumbling down into illogic.

Unfortunately, this visit had done nothing to ease Shan's worries, but he couldn't think of anything else to say to young Temar, so he followed him back to the field where Ben and the others worked to pull weeds that had obviously seeded from the Gazer place. With the whole Gazer farm going to seed, they would soon have more. Everyone in the valley would suffer, but with his farm next door, Ben would catch the majority of the trouble.

Ben looked up when they came close and shifted his bag of weeds from one shoulder to the other. Ben held an arm out, and Temar went immediately to his side, leaning into him as though seeking to soak up the other man's strength. Shan had never seen a man weakened so much by slavery, and he'd never seen the psychological damage take hold so fast.

For a second, Ben held Temar in a one-armed hug, and then he gave him a slap on the arm. "Take this up to the incinerator, will you?" He held out his bag. Temar nodded and took it in both hands. "Are you in control enough to do this?" Ben asked, and again he brought a finger up under Temar's chin, pressing his head up. Left on his own, Temar did spend a lot of time staring at the ground. Temar nodded. "Good boy," Ben praised him and then patted him on the arm.

Temar headed toward the house with the bag clutched to his chest, and Ben leaned backward, cracking his back and stretching. "So, you've seen the mess on my north border? I used to like Erqu Gazer, which is why I didn't make complaint about the water that would go missing from my share—it was never enough to publicly humiliate a man who had already lost so much. But I have no qualms about humiliating George. I'll lay claim to workdays from him and have his fat ass out here pulling weeds blown down from his farm if something isn't done."

Shan nodded, his attention still focused on Temar's retreating figure. "It's your right," Shan agreed. Really, what else was there to say?

chapter
eight

CYLA WAS sitting under the sloping eaves of a windbreak with large vats set out in front of her. "See? She's fine. I don't know why you'd assume she wasn't." Ista Songwind was angry. Angry might be too strong of a word, but she definitely didn't like Shan.

"I always assumed she would be well cared for, Worker Songwind," Shan said mildly. "I would not have signed off on the slave fee otherwise, but as the priest, she is still my responsibility, even if she's in another territory." Shan was stretching that a little, but he assumed God would differentiate between a lie and a stretched truth told for the greater good. If not, he could always confess to Div later. The man would love a chance to have Shan reread "Ecclesiasticus" for penance.

"She hasn't asked to go to the church, or I would have let her. I know the law."

"I have no doubt you do, Worker Songwind," Shan agreed. "I have heard people speak very highly of you, both your skills with computers and your fair temperament." Shan didn't say that he was beginning to doubt the latter. Their conversation was cut short when Cyla looked up from her work.

Her blonde hair was pulled back in a ponytail, and the wisps that had escaped were plastered to her face with sweat, but she didn't look emotionally or physically beaten down. She frowned when she saw Shan standing at the edge of the windbreak.

"Shan? Did something happen?" After pulling a sheet of computer chips out of the mild acid wash, she set them to the side and started to stand.

"Neutralize the acid before you even dream of it, girl!" Worker Songwind didn't sound particularly cruel with her order, but she made it clear there was no room for debate. Cyla gave her an unhappy look, but she took the sheet with the computer chips attached, and she moved to a second vat.

Putting the sheet on the wire netting over the mouth of the vat, she picked up a spray bottle and started spraying the cloudy solution onto the board with an even hand. Before Shan went into the priesthood, his father had purchased him an apprenticeship with a mechanic, and Shan still remembered enough to know that Cyla had been carefully taught this skill. After ten years, she might be able to challenge the mechanics' council and claim a title as a skilled worker.

"Is Temar okay?" she asked, her hands still working their task.

"He's fine," Shan said. Physically the young man was fine, and Shan was not an adequate judge of his mental state.

Cyla paused for a second before finishing the spraying. Shan glanced over at Ista Songwind, hoping she would get the hint and give them some privacy, but the woman was standing with her arms crossed in a pose that suggested she was not moving. Shan turned his back on her and moved closer to Cyla.

"I promised Temar I would see how you were doing. Worker Songwind says you aren't going to church."

Cyla frowned and put the board to one side. Now that the acid had washed away the impurities, someone would have to go over every circuit board to remove any residue left by the base solution. But that residue would be large and crystalline and easy to remove, compared to the tiny impurities that would coat a computer surface after any time exposed to Livre's atmosphere.

"Church was more his thing than mine."

"Maybe he needed it more," Shan suggested, trying to give the girl some opening to explain what might have happened. However, if she didn't know about her father's abuse, he didn't want to tell her. Cyla carried enough burdens now, and he knew the guilt that came with having been ignorant when a loved one had suffered.

"Maybe he just liked to sit in the back and pretend that his life wasn't fucked up from the time he was born," she said with bitterness.

"Not that anyone did anything to help either one of us." She looked him up and down with disgust, making it clear that she considered him one of the people who should have done something. Shan leaned back in surprise. Okay, slavery had not dulled her tongue.

"You seem to be learning a good trade." Shan changed the subject, hoping a more neutral topic might put her at ease. After all, few slaves had the advantage of learning a trade, most, like Temar, labored at unskilled jobs. "Are you washing the circuits, or are you learning to scrape crystals, too?"

Songwind took a step forward. "That work's too delicate for someone who can't remember to neutralize the acid immediately."

Shan sat silent for a moment, not wanting to return barb for barb with Ista Songwind. At least Cyla had found an owner who could match her, sharp, bitter comment for sharp, bitter comment.

"No doubt, after ten years under such a capable woman, you'll know skills enough to either become a skilled worker or easily earn an apprenticeship to finish your training," Shan said with a smile.

"And Temar?" Cyla demanded. "What skills will he learn in some farmer's fields? Tell me that George Young didn't get his contract, because if he did, I'll trade with him right now. Hell, Temar would be better with this crap than I would, anyway," she said with a wave of her hand at the table of circuits.

Shan looked at the worktable. The circuits were lined up by type. A wide control panel circuit was on the far end, its pink glass structure winking in the sun. A half dozen small circuits were attached to a board that had been covered with a dust shield, and the panel Cyla had just finished had a dozen more small-scale circuits. Obviously, Red Plain had suffered some storm that had required them to pull many of their circuits for cleaning. The loss of this many computers must have the town functioning on minimum resources. Shan was surprised they hadn't asked Landing or Blue Hope for some equipment to tide them over.

"Ben Gratu bought his contract. He's as well as he can be," Shan reassured her. "Worker Songwind, if you have need of assistance with so many computers down, Landing can send a few trained workers or some equipment over to assist you," he offered.

Worker Songwind scowled at him, but that seemed to be her most used expression.

"We're fine."

Shan didn't have an answer for that, so he turned his attention back to Cyla. "Is there anything you would like me to tell your brother?" For the first time since Shan had seen her, Cyla looked honestly remorseful. Her lips pulled down into a frown, and her pale face pinked.

"Tell him that it's my fault. Tell him that I'm sorry, and I'm glad that Ben got his contract and not George. Tell him…." She took a deep breath. "Tell him I should have listened to him."

"I'll carry the message," Shan promised as he stood. Cyla was still unabashedly Cyla, so he didn't think she was carrying any deep wounds, and her questions had focused on Temar's contract, so he didn't think she knew about any abuse Temar might have suffered before his slavery. This had clearly been a false trail. Whatever was wrong, he would only get the answers from Temar.

"If you need to talk, consider going to the church, or ask for me. I'd be happy to come back down," Shan offered.

Cyla gave him a distrustful look. "You'd cross seven thousand rods of deep desert to talk to me again?"

"I would," Shan promised her.

Instead of looking grateful, she rolled her eyes. "You sure didn't go out of your way for us before. But if you have any spare time, spend it tracking George Young's water use," she suggested. Clearly Cyla still had all of her ego and confidence intact. She was a beautiful woman. She had the same blue eyes, the same high cheekbones and long fingers as her brother. On him, the features were ethereal. He had a beauty that made people look twice. On Cyla, the same beauty was sharp and almost uncomfortable to look at for too long, as though her personality was leeching out through her skin.

"I think George Young's water use is a subject you had best avoid," Shan advised her before he turned to leave. Ista Songwind was watching him as he passed, but then perhaps Shan had offended her. Cyla's work certainly depended on timing, and Shan had not called ahead to ask when he could see her. No, he'd allowed his suspicions to guide his actions, and he'd shown up at Worker Songwind's door with no warning. Cyla was not the only one who needed to work on being a better neighbor.

"Is your valley gate disabled?" Shan asked.

"What?" Songwind looked at him with far more alarm than the question warranted.

Shan tried to give her his most charming smile. He'd been told that he could be quite a charmer when he put his mind to it. "The control panel circuit… I noticed you're having to do repairs on it. If your valley gates are down, Landing really would be happy to send some skilled workers over. You have quite a large task ahead of you with so many computer chips to clean."

"We don't need help," Songwind said sharply. Shan decided she was in an unpleasant mood, either that or she was an unpleasant person. For Cyla's sake, Shan hoped that the first was true. Then again, it wasn't like Cyla was some helpless child who needed a soft hand. She'd give back as good as she got—slave or not.

Ignoring his growing dislike for Songwind, Shan smiled. "If you change your mind, I'm on the council, and I know we would be happy to help. After all, the day may come when we need to ask for help in return." When her weathered face remained just as hard, Shan decided a change in topics was in order. "I hope the calm holds until I get home. The winds made the trip slightly more exciting than I would prefer." He stopped near his sand cycle, but Songwind looked at him, her expression hidden behind a dark, wrinkled face.

He nodded respectfully. "Thank you for letting me pass on Temar's message."

"Next time, call before interrupting my work," Songwind said without a bit of grace.

"I will," Shan promised. Throwing a leg over the sand cycle, he gave the woman one last smile that she didn't return. His engine whined to life, and Shan tightened his dust veil over his face and settled his weight back onto the seat. Then he guided the bike carefully out of Songwind's area. The woman was badly misnamed, and Shan suspected that if he threw sand up or dislodged a windbreak post, the woman would demand labor days from him. It'd been a long time since he did mechanical work, and he really didn't feel like doing it under Ista Songwind's eye.

Before he'd quit, his own apprenticeship had been under a white-haired man named Holmes who had chewed a reed and watched silently as Shan made his own mistakes… well, unless Shan was working on something like computer circuits, which were both sensitive and rare. Then Holmes had become a sharp-eyed taskmaster, so Shan could hardly blame Songwind for being equally sharp. Cyla had only been working for a bit over a month, and computer chips were too valuable to have an apprentice ruin a whole board of them. Ista's willingness to teach her at all was a boon that none of them could have hoped for, yet something felt wrong.

Shan guided his cycle past the low, slanting roofs of the town and toward the open desert. The guidance system in his bike beeped to tell him he was off path, but he ignored it as he steered around a ponderous scoop hauler that slowly trundled over the sand toward town. Holmes would never have allowed Shan to tend so many circuits without watching, and Shan had been talented with machines. The computer command boards were too rare and too important. With the inner worlds off on their ridiculous wars, the promised tech had dried up as quickly as spilled water on the sand.

The cycle's back tire spun as Shan leaned too far forward, his weight uneven. Shan settled back and let his mind chase random thoughts as he turned his front tire toward home. The facts were like a broken piece of glass. Parts fit, but other edges wouldn't marry up, no matter how Shan considered things. It was like some piece was missing, and he couldn't figure the shape of the whole.

The first deep desert dune commanded his attention, and Shan leaned back and focused on guiding his machine up the shifting sands. The feeling of it under him was familiar, and the task at hand demanded all his attention. For a time, he allowed himself to feel the cycle and the desert and the rhythms of life on Livre. The sand sparkled, red and gold, the patterns shifting as the gentle midday wind tugged at the surface of the dunes. About an hour into his long journey, a whining hiss made Shan tilt his head and focus on the straining engine. He could come up with a hundred reasons for a straining engine to whine in protest, but none would have that high-pitched tone that cut off so suddenly. The second whine came a half second before a tuft of sand spurted up from the ground, right in front of him.

For a half second, Shan couldn't figure out what was going on. He looked over his shoulder, and a sand hunter was roaring toward him. The wide vehicle had one driver and a second person standing on the sideboard with a weapon on his shoulder. The cycle started sliding out from under Shan, and his body shifted instinctively to correct the balance. At that moment, the gun flashed, and another whine warned Shan a half second before a bullet hit the sand next to him.

God's mercy. Surely there was some sort of confusion or perhaps a great bout of drunkenness. Nothing else made sense.

However, rather than debate the senselessness of the situation, Shan aimed his bike toward the top of the dune and opened the engine. The cycle screamed to life and lurched madly under his grip, but Shan rode it to the ridge and then felt the cycle fall out from under him as he hit the backside of the dune. Normally, Shan would fishtail the back of the bike to slow his descent, but this time he threw his weight forward as he went into a near free-fall down the front of the dune.

Sand whipped by his face so fast that individual particles worked their way through his sand veil, and his eyes started to sting. More sharp, whining cries warned him that his pursuers hadn't given up. As he reached the bottom of the dune, Shan threw his weight onto the back tire and opened the engine to full throttle. It screamed and then sent the cycle roaring toward the next dune.

Since the pursuers now had a clear shot at his back, Shan pulled the control yoke right and left and took a winding path up the face of the giant dune. No bullet had yet torn through his back, so clearly his strategy had worked so far, but a number of bullets hit so close that a cold panic rolled through Shan's guts. He had almost reached the ridge when his cycle bucked under him, and the smell of burning metal stung his nose. The cycle pushed him up to the ridge of the dune, but already the engine was sputtering and failing.

Pushing his weight forward, Shan let gravity pull him into a near free-fall as he studied the land around him. Livre was full of deep valleys and ravines and rock ditches that made travel difficult, so he needed to find one deep enough to hide in. And then he needed to find a way to get rid of his pursuers. And then he needed a set of mechanic's tools to fix his cycle.

He needed a lot.

When he spotted the ridge of rock that marked the mouth of a valley, Shan sent up a quick prayer of thanks and aimed his cycle toward the opening.

He'd gained ground on the sand hunter, which had to slow on the downslope, but he didn't have much time. Shan studied the ridge for any narrow break in the rock that would let the bike through but block the wide sand hunter. As the bottom of the dune approached, Shan slowed, and the engine on the cycle sputtered under the strain.

In the desert, size and distance could trick the eye, and Shan realized the stone ridge was both farther away and far larger than he'd thought at first glance. The rocks cast long shadows over the sand, and small whirlwinds of sand and air swirled at its edges. Sanity dictated that Shan slow down and approach such a large valley with caution, but the armed attacker behind him made that rather difficult. More tufts of sand rose in front of him, and Shan steered toward the bullet marks, hoping the shooter would assume he'd turn the other way and overcompensate. A narrow gap opened in the rock, and Shan steered the cycle toward it.

At this point, prayer and not falling off the cycle filled Shan's mind, and he focused on both with a determination born of fear. The bike smelled of hot metal and burning plastic, the frame shivering between his legs, but the gap in the rock grew closer. Dust blew up like a curtain rising from the ground, and Shan realized this was a major valley he was about to fly into blind. If he was coming out at the top of a cliff, he would only have seconds to regret the decision. However, given a choice, Shan would rather fall to his death than take a bullet in the back.

The engine made the squealing death cry of broken belts, but Shan focused on the rocks ahead. The whine of a bullet went past his head and then ricocheted off the rock with a dull ringing sound. Shan ignored the instinctive need to slow down and aimed for the gap. The cycle bounced as it hit the rocky ground, and the fat tires made it fly into the air. Shan had a half second of warning before he realized that he was heading straight for a drop far too steep and too deep to survive.

Shan had thrown all his weight backward to get the last bit of traction out of his dying engine, and now he instinctively pushed back from certain death, scrambling to throw himself off the back before the cycle crashed to the bottom of the valley. Something blindingly hot touched his leg, and the pain flashed through his whole body, so he could only see the whiteness of agony, and then his fingers brushed rock, and Shan clutched the ground. His legs went over the cliff with the bike, and Shan almost followed it.

Instead, he twisted so that his stomach was to the ground and he could grab a half-embedded boulder. It held, and Shan slowly pulled himself back up onto the cliff top until he could hug the boulder. He honestly never thought he would let go of the blessed thing. He'd be happy to kneel in the dirt and hold the boulder for the rest of his life. Shan might have done just that except the sound of another engine was approaching. The sand hunter had slowed to a crawl, the engine rumbling as the driver carefully approached the rocks Shan had so recklessly crashed into.

Shan pushed himself up onto shaky legs and hissed when his left leg nearly collapsed under him. Looking down, Shan saw a hole in his pants, with black edges. Underneath, his calf had a raw, red burn that was already weeping that clear fluid that gathered under blisters. His skin had stuck to the cycle, so the leg wept openly.

"God, I appreciate the help, but I wouldn't mind a little more right now," Shan said softly before he limped south, searching for somewhere to hide. If he got shot now, after all this, he was going to show up in heaven and accuse God of having a very nasty sense of humor. About fifty feet down from the opening, Shan found a small hollow where two boulders met, and he pressed himself into the shadowed space and tried to breathe very, very quietly.

The engine stopped, and Shan heard footsteps against the rock.

"He went over."

"I noticed." The second male didn't sound amused. He also didn't sound drunk, so that destroyed the theory that this was some mistake made by a couple of hunters with too much pipe juice in their blood. "We should check the body."

"Do you see a way down?" For a minute, there was only silence. No one willingly wandered the desert, not even in a sand hunter, and Shan sent up a quick prayer that these two would consider the danger too great.

"We could drive to the end of the valley and backtrack," the second voice suggested.

"Which would take a whole day." The first male clearly considered the matter closed, and Shan could only offer a prayer and a promise to God that he would spend more time reading his Bible if the first guy won this argument. If they backtracked and didn't find his body, he'd be in trouble.

Footsteps came closer, and Shan stopped breathing altogether. "Should we call Landing?" the second voice wondered. Shan blinked. Landing? Someone at Landing had wanted him dead? Okay, so he had angered a few people in his day, but he'd never done anything to inspire this level of hatred. Actually, other than accidents and drunken fights, Shan couldn't remember the last murder around Landing, although Hope Valley had had one about six years past. For the most part, people on Livre were too busy to get up to nonsense like murder. They left the inner worlds to play that game, and they focused on bringing in crops and feeding the children and not getting blown away in the afternoon winds.

"Yeah, let's see what he says. He'll be able to tell us if the priest shows up, but the chances are that he's dead as a rat in a pipe trap."

The voice grew softer as the person walked away. Shan started breathing again. His leg throbbed in time with his heart, he had no water and no cycle, and someone in Landing wanted him dead— someone with enough connections to know if he showed up in town again. Things were not looking good.

Shan looked up at the endless blue sky. "God, do you remember how I said last week that the priesthood didn't have challenges enough for me? That I missed the puzzle an engine could provide? God, you do know that I lied, right? I could do with far less mystery and challenge in my life right now." Shan looked up at the blue sky. His sand veil dimmed the brightness of the sun, but other than that, it was only sky above him. God rarely gave such direct answers. This time, Shan figured he would have to get himself out of this mess.

chapter
nine

SHAN MEASURED the drop with his eyes before easing himself over the edge of the rock ledge. Getting out was going to be far harder than climbing down, but he needed some supplies, or he wouldn't last a day on the open desert.

The desert lied. The dunes looked like gentle slopes, and the sand gave a golden haze to the world that made Livre look like an inviting jewel. In reality, the dunes were mountains of sand that would slip under your feet, and the shimmering sands offered very little in the way of food and water.

Pipe traps settled wherever the barchan dunes didn't follow their migrations. They preferred stable sand. Chokeweed moved with the sand dunes, their long roots and stems getting pushed around like seaweed in the oceans of Earth. One offered poisonous water and food. The other offered very little at all, except for long lines of sand burrs that would cripple a man. Shan needed the cycle, or even the parts he could scavenge from the cycle, or he'd die out here as surely as if the attackers had shot him.

He dropped down, and his injured leg gave way, sending Shan crashing to the ground. By the time he got himself out of this, he was going to be one giant bruise. He was going to be one giant, thirsty bruise, and the way his leg kept leaking clear fluids wasn't making him feel better about his situation. A burn might not kill him, but losing body fluids sure as hell could.

He tried to stand, and the pain in his leg made him curse colorfully. "I'll make that up to you later," he promised God as he walked to the edge of this new ledge and searched for a path down. He was so close to the bottom that he could see the twisted remains of his cycle, so he knew it was a lost cause, but he might be able to activate the emergency beacon, and the emergency kit on the back held water.

A sharp wind raced down the center of the narrow valley, and Shan turned to the side to shield the burned leg. It stung like battery acid anyway. When the wind died down, he started moving again. Unfortunately, the physical demands of the climb weren't enough to keep his mind out of trouble. Thoughts crashed through his brain. Who would want him dead?

Okay, so his father probably had a few thoughts about killing both him and Naite. After all, the two sons he had groomed so carefully had both turned on him. Naite had been condemned to three years of slavery, and Shan had walked away from his apprenticeship with a mechanic to go into the church. Yep, his father had their lives all planned. Naite would follow him as a landowner, and Shan would get all the training required to run the farm machines, and the two boys would make their father the envy of the Spence Valley. It hadn't exactly worked that way. Their land had been sold to pay his father's debts, Naite was an unskilled worker, and Shan... he wasn't sure who he was anymore.

The next drop was farther, and Shan braced himself for the pain when he fell. Yep, it hurt. He limped through a low ridge of broken rocks and fallen debris.

Whoever wanted him dead, the two hired killers thought that he would know the second Shan got back to town. That definitely wouldn't be his father, not unless someone had dug up the old man and found some magic potion for bringing the dead back to life. In terms of alibis, death was a fairly solid one.

Shan stopped and leaned against a warm, copper-stained rock for a second. White spikes of borax crystals stuck up from the surface like an embedded crown, and Shan studied the tiny shadows formed by the rock, focusing on the stark beauty rather than his pain. Everything ached, and his leg stung with a vengeance, and a little part of him wanted to lie down until the pain passed. He wasn't about to participate in his own murder, though. That meant he needed to force his body to keep moving, and he needed to force his mind to solve this puzzle.

Naite was the next to come to mind. When Shan's cycle went missing, Naite and Div would both be called, and if Shan showed up, they'd be the first to hear. True, as children, Naite and Shan had enjoyed a hate-hate relationship, but would his brother truly want him dead?

Naite had always been their father's favorite, and he got all the gifts and the attention and the praise. As a child, Shan hadn't understood the price his brother paid for that favoritism. Shan had been devoured by jealousy, and he'd hated his brother with a passion born of loneliness and need. So, when Naite had started acting out, Shan had gone out of his way to get his brother in trouble.

Once, Naite tried to slip out to steal some fruit from a neighbor's field. Shan broke into one of the panel boxes and hit the water alarm, raising everyone in the valley, so his brother got caught. After Naite had finished a week of labor for a neighbor in return for fire damage to the man's barn, their father had ordered him to stay in his room. The old man had gone as far as to set nails in the shutters to imprison Naite. But Shan had hated that their father still spent long hours in with his precious firstborn. It was like he loved Naite more, no matter how much Shan tried to be the perfect son. So, Shan had gone and pulled all the nails out of the shutters, knowing their father would blame Naite.

Now that Shan was old enough to understand exactly why their father had favored Naite, Shan suspected that Naite had a whole lot of reasons to hate both their father and him. Their father had made Naite's early life miserable, and Shan had been an unwitting accomplice to that torture. However, Shan couldn't imagine his brother trying to kill him. Their hate was a more familial sort of hate.

Shan reached the twisted cycle and pushed those thoughts and memories aside in favor of checking his resources. The emergency beacon in the yoke was a total loss, but the survival kit was in one piece. Unfortunately, the water container had only a few milliliters in the bottom of the warm, plastic container. Pulling the container out, Shan felt along the smooth plastic, looking for the crack that had allowed the leak. He found it near the neck of the bottle, where the side curved into the lid.

"God, I wouldn't mind things being a little less of a challenge," Shan told the sky. He really didn't like the choices this left him. He drank the tiny bit of remaining water and then turned to the medical supplies. A spray derm kit covered the burn, but Shan didn't want to take any pain medicine—not with the ordeal he had ahead of him. If he slipped and put a foot into a pipe trap plant, he could break an ankle and be dead before morning. Sandcats weren't particularly aggressive, but they would go for the injured. And sandrats were twice as dangerous when they gathered in numbers.

People had come to this world and assigned names to native plants and animals, deciding to call the small, nearly hairless hunters that burrowed under the sand "sandrats" and their larger, more furred cousins "cats." The truth was that the two species were closely related. Both were ferocious omnivores that would eat anything organic, and they had no problem waiting until a larger animal was lying helpless on the ground before attacking in mass swarms that gave the victim little to no hope of survival.

Turning to the cycle, Shan salvaged what he could. Lengths of plastic tubing and metal washers and long pipes—he slipped them all into pockets. A corner of a fender had been torn and bent out of shape, and Shan wrapped his shirt around his hand to protect himself from the sharp edge, and then he pulled the hunk of metal loose. It would have to serve as a knife.

Shan missed the days when, as a mechanic in training, he'd gone everywhere with a full toolkit on his belt. The weight of it had made him feel important. After all, Holmes, a man famous for making machines sing, had chosen him as an apprentice. His father's apprenticeship fees had also helped Shan get in with the master mechanic, but Holmes never took on an apprentice who wasn't good with the work, no matter what fee was offered.

He missed that tool belt right now. A half dozen tools, and he could have converted parts of the cycle and his thermal blanket into a wind glider, but now it looked like he was going to have to walk out.

Since he couldn't climb up and out, he followed the bottom of the valley south and hoped the end sloped up to the desert floor. Otherwise, he was going to have to retrace his steps and try to find a north end escape from this long gash in the face of Livre.

He had walked almost an hour, and the sweat had made the inside of his sand veil misty with perspiration, before he found a pipe trap large enough for his needs. Going stiffly to his knees, Shan used his hands to scoop the sand away from the top of the plant. The leaves shivered in the wind, and the sand swirled around him, but eventually, he uncovered the pipe of the plant.

It was a large, circular ring of hollow stem. The tufts of leaves would attract insects to the pipe, which promised moisture and food. The pipe trap's exterior even smelled fresh and clean, like a field after a particularly heavy watering. However, the insect would fall down one of the funnels hidden within the leaves and into the hollow pipe. It would drown in the poison the plant hid inside its buried base. This pipe trap was large enough that it would digest sandrats and sandcat pups without difficulty. Shan carefully slit the top of the pipe trap and then leaned back to avoid the stench that rose. Why people drank diluted pipe trap juice for pleasure, Shan would never understand.

Erqu Gazer came to mind. After his wife had died and then his baby girl had followed, not more than a week later, he'd taken to drinking watered-down pipe trap juice with reckless abandon. Shan was a little surprised that he'd had the energy to abuse Temar, given how much he would drink.

Shan's father only started drinking it after Naite had been taken for his three-year sentence. After that, things changed. Their father had started paying attention to Shan, and the glass jars with cloudy juice from pipe traps started appearing on the windowsill of their house. Shan prayed for the nights that his father drank the pipe trap juice because it made him slow and lethargic. On those nights, Shan didn't have to fight him. He only had to suggest that his father would rather go to bed, and he would blearily agree, tottering off down the hall like one of those children's toys that rocked from side to side without ever falling over.

It was the nights when he hadn't been drinking that Shan would have to flee out into the night, out to ride the sands through the dark, out to risk death on a cycle, flying downslope in the dark of the night. If he stayed home, things would get far more dangerous.

When the wind had taken the worst of the stench away, Shan slipped a tube down into the pipe trap and uncoiled the full length. Bracing himself, Shan sucked on the end of the tube, just until he could taste the foul liquid, and then he quickly pinched off the tube and spat the poison out. Pure pipe trap was more likely to kill you than satisfy any thirst. Putting the end of the tube in the water bottle, Shan loosened his hold on it and let the yellowish fluid trickle down. When the bottle was almost full, Shan pulled the tubing out and shook it to get the poison off as much as he could before he tucked it away.

"God, if it doesn't interfere with your plans too much, do you think you could keep me from killing myself with this? I mean, I've had bad plans before, but this one is pretty stupid. I know you protect the simple hearted, and I'm hoping the simpleminded can slip in with that group." Shan finished his prayer and considered the bottle in his hand. He'd heard stories of early explorers surviving this way after sandcat attacks and windstorms that separated them from their space ships. He never thought he was going to get a chance to test such an idiotic contraption.

Attaching the tube so that it was above the level of the poison and would capture only the water that evaporated out of the juice, he taped it carefully in place. Then he taped the bottle to his good leg. If it worked, he would get small amounts of water in drops that clung to the sides of the tube. If it didn't, he was about to poison himself. Of course this way, if he was going to die, he'd die happy and lethargic. Looking down the length of the valley, Shan set his sights on a distant spire of rock and started walking.

The sand pulled at his feet, and his body was stiff with injuries, but all he focused on was moving one foot in front of the other. The leg with the pipe juice felt heavy, but his other leg ached, so it was about even. The sand sloped up toward the surface, so Shan thought he was probably going to be able to reach the top of the crevasse without backtracking, but as the cliffs grew shorter and the sun rose higher, the shade clung to the sides of the rock, leaving Shan exposed.

Hour after hour, he walked slowly and sipped carefully of warm and foul-tasting water that gathered, drop by drop, in the tube that ran up his leg.

"Pretty stupid. You'd have been better taking over my title," his father said. Shan might be drunk enough on pipe to hallucinate, but he wasn't drunk enough not to notice that his father was a hallucination. Of course, the way his father's center kept wavering in and out of existence, making him look almost donut-like in the middle—that was a big clue.

"I didn't want to own land. Besides, I'm not going to be a replacement for Naite," Shan told his father. He figured he didn't have anything better to do than to talk to hallucinations. His father shimmered in the sun, the illusion of water washing him away so that Naite stood in his father's place. Naite looked like their father. They had the same olive tone to their skin, and the same sharp nose and imposing figure with wide shoulders.

"Like you could replace me." Naite's words were sharp and sarcastic, but the tone was almost friendly.

"You didn't try to kill me, did you?" Shan asked. He wondered if confessions given through hallucinations would be valid for the council. Naite turned his head to the side and looked at him out of one eye like a buteo, one of those large birds that rode the winds for hours, looking for life on the open desert. Shaking his head at his own stupidity, Shan closed his eyes for a second, blocking out the blinding glare of the sun.

"I'm going to fall on my face if I don't sit," Shan whispered to no one in particular. He moved to a spot right next to the cliff and carefully sat, propping his burned leg out in front of him.

"Do you really think I'd try to kill you?" Naite asked, crouching down in front of Shan. It was annoying the way his face kept blurring into the sky along the edges.

"Don't know. Don't think so, but…." Shan shrugged.

"Idiot," Naite said. He sat on the pointed top of a boulder and pulled his legs up under him.

"You hate me."

"No I don't. I think you're an idiot, but that's not the same as hating you."

"I wasn't nice to you when we were kids," Shan pointed out. He wasn't sure why he was trying to convince Naite that they hated each other, but it seemed like the right thing to do.

Naite had to think about that one for a while. "Kids aren't nice," he finally answered with a shrug.

"I didn't know." Shan closed his eyes and leaned back into the warm rock. "I promise you on my vows, I didn't know."

"You should have."

Shan opened his eyes at the unfamiliar voice. Temar stood there, his arms crossed over his stomach and his blue eyes staring at Shan accusingly.

"Yep, I should have," Shan admitted. "I never paid enough attention."

"You didn't want to look at me too long. You didn't want to admit how you felt when you looked at me for too long." The light haloed through Temar's blond hair, and his face was almost angelic. "You're so busy trying not to do something wrong that you didn't do anything right. You didn't protect me."

Shan stared at Temar, his guts suddenly cold. "No."

"I'm your hallucination. I couldn't say it if you didn't already know it was true."

Shan reached down and pulled the pipe trap juice bottle off his leg. The liquid inside the bottle had turned a dark urine yellow as the water evaporated out, and Shan opened the mouth of the bottle and poured it out onto the rocks. Tiny rivers and rapids and waterfalls and tributaries appeared as the juice flowed over the ground and soaked into the white sand. A yellow stain, shaped like an upside-down tree, remained.

"Doesn't make what I said less true," Temar pointed out.

"I need to change the pipe juice more often," Shan answered. Of course, that wasn't an answer, but he had grown skilled at avoidance and obfuscation over the years. He remembered those months after Naite had left the house. He'd grown very skilled.

Naite rose up out of the yellow tree stain like a pale ghost of himself. "I was a stupid kid. I shouldn't have left you with Dad, but I really didn't think he'd go after you. I thought I had done something to lead him on. I thought it was my fault, and that if I was out of the house, things would be better for you. God, Shan. You know this. You know that I've always loved you, even if I don't know how to say it. And you still think I would kill you?" Naite looked so hurt. His face twisted in despair, and Shan reached out for him, only to have Naite's form explode into dust and swirl away like a sand devil.

As the sand devil vanished, Temar was left standing in the sun. "If you would have looked at me… if you would have let yourself admit that you were attracted, then maybe you would have noticed how much trouble I was in."

Shan closed his eyes and tried to focus on his thoughts and not the sluggish desire that rolled through him. "I'm a priest. We give up attraction and marriage and children. A married man, a man who is courting someone, he is worried about this world, about his future, about making his life better, here and now. I'm supposed to worry about the next life, about people's souls, about pleasing God."

"So, how is that working for you? Did you save my soul? Are you avoiding thinking about the needs of this world?" Temar's voice was suddenly bitter, but then considering how Shan had failed him, he couldn't blame the man for a little hatred and bitterness.

"I'm still going to try to help you," Shan said. He didn't mean to sound defensive, but he did. Silence answered him. When Shan opened his eyes, Temar was gone. The white sand and the red-stained rock and the crystal borax jutting out all waited silently. The yellow tree stain and the hot sun mocked him, and Shan found he couldn't summon the energy to care.

chapter
ten

WALKING THROUGH the open sands, Shan had learned to focus his mind on one landmark, clearing everything out, so that reaching that landmark became the only goal that existed. For almost three days, his landmark had been the heavy Livre moon. The sand-sculpted mountains and valleys around him shifted and reshaped themselves, hour by hour and minute by minute, but the larger moon, pale and barely visible in the daylight, pulled him in one constant direction.

His father shadowed his steps sometimes, Naite too. The specters didn't hold actual conversations with him anymore, not like they had that first day. His most constant companion was Temar. The young man varied between gazing at him with wide, injured eyes and spitting hate at him. But it was like watching a vid because nothing Shan said interrupted his ravings. Sometimes the endless, silent accusations wore at him. Once Shan had stood in the middle of a dune and screamed at them all to leave him alone. They hadn't, and part of him was glad. They offered an odd sort of companionship, and that was better than the solitude of the white sand.

"You should have reached the valley, Shan. I don't like this," Naite complained. Temar had temporarily vanished, and Shan walked in the illusion of shade his brother's image provided.

Naite's voice turned into the throaty pitch of Shan's year six history teacher lecturing about the political systems in the inner worlds. The other planets wanted Livre's purified borax deposits and white sands and arsenic and, more importantly, the optic-circuit quality glass that could be made from such unusually pure forms of the basic glass ingredients. When they'd destroyed enough of each others' jump ships that they needed huge quantities of high-quality glass for optical circuits, they'd be back.

Of course, Shan knew this version of Naite was an illusion, because the real Naite complained about chokeweed and rusting water lines, not politics. Shan pulled the tube up and sucked at the warm, hallucinogenic and plastic-tasting drops of water. It was never enough to quench his thirst, and once again he eyed the pipe trap juice in the bottle. This latest batch was clearer than any he'd collected yet, and he was tempted to gulp it down. His tongue felt like it was glued to the bottom of his mouth with thick slime, and his lips were cracked and painful. The pipe juice sloshed against the sides of the plastic bottle so invitingly.

"Try it and you'll be sorry," Naite warned.

"You think I don't already know that?" Shan shoved at Naite, and his hand went right through his brother's middle, scattering his body like motes of dust in a sunbeam. One of the little sparks twirled and hovered and then sank down until it rested directly above the sand dune to his right. Shan frowned at the steady light, waiting for the hallucination to waver, but it seemed remarkably constant for a pipe-induced vision.

"Check it out," Naite suggested.

"I can't just start wandering the desert," Shan told Naite, but he couldn't take his eyes off that small and constant point of light.

Shan looked up at the oversized moon that hung in Livre's sky, hiding the smaller moon that orbited in its shadow this time of day. The blue of full day was slowly fading into the purple of evening, and the storms on the face of the moon were evident in the barely visible swirls of color.

"I'm so dead." Shan breathed the words. Up until this moment, he hadn't wanted to admit it, but right now, it was not looking good.

Temar's ghostly figure rose from the sand, and Shan turned his head to avoid looking at him. In real life, he'd tried so hard not to pay too much attention to the young man that he hadn't paid nearly enough attention to him at all, and so now, given the chance to stare at him—to watch Temar's delicate fingers play with a button and to look into that unusual shade of blue eyes—Shan felt guilty. He had no business indulging himself, especially not when the real Temar was suffering for Shan's lack of judgment. Besides, he was distracted by that same light winking at him from the same spot on top of the same dune.

Shan had to consider the possibility that he had passed Spence Valley. And Landing was a small town, perched on the edge of a rock shelf, and he had no chance of finding it in the middle of all this shifting sand. If he stopped to think, he would be tempted to sit down, drink as much pipe juice as it took to finally quench his debilitating thirst, and then lay on the hot sand and go to sleep. That plan had been slowly fermenting in the back of his mind, and he was trying hard to keep it shoved as far back as he could.

"What would it hurt to investigate?" Temar asked.

"Potentially? Potentially it could cost me my life," Shan answered truthfully, but he held his life by such a slender thread that it no longer sounded like much of a threat. He'd counseled people facing death. He'd sat by bedsides and in the clinic, and he'd held people's hands. He'd watched people face death with calm grace or with terror and denial and fury, but he couldn't seem to feel anything at all for his own death—nothing but a vague, nagging regret. High on that list was the regret that his murderer might get away with this. He was a priest. He was supposed to forgive. But right now, he didn't feel like forgiving anyone. Give him a gun, and he would seriously consider shooting someone… just as soon as he figured out which someone he was supposed to be shooting.

Naite appeared, and for the first time in a while, he decided to have an actual conversation with Shan. Of course it started with threats. "I'm going to shoot you if you don't pull your head out of your ass and investigate the damn light," Naite said.

Shan glared at his two ghostly companions before he took a ninety-degree turn and started walking. As he got closer to the base of the huge sand dune, the top of the dune swallowed the point. "This is so stupid," Shan muttered to himself when the light slipped below the horizon. Not even his hallucinations wanted to try to climb this monster with him, so Shan set his feet into the rippled sand, sank in up to his knees, and started wading up the uneven surface.

A half dozen times, he had to stop and lay on his stomach, his arms outstretched as he let his trembling and burning legs rest. A dozen times, he fell and tumbled down the steep slope. Each time he stopped, the wind dusted him with sand, but Shan kept climbing until the sharp and rippled top edge appeared, white against the blue sky. When Shan's hand reached the top of the dune, clawing at it, the ridge collapsed, and sand showered down on him. Only then did the twinkling light reappear, this time attached to a sharp point of metal that rose high into the sky.

"Oh Lord." Shan's heart pounded in relief. "Thank you, God." He'd found the signal tower for Spence Valley.

chapter
eleven

TEMAR SHIFTED in the bed. Ben's body was hot and heavy against his side, and his skin crawled at the contact. Only now, in the night, when darkness hid his face, did Temar let himself truly feel the emotions washing through him like a giant sand dune, shifting in the wind and threatening to bury him under his own hatred. He hated Ben.

Before his slavery, he thought he'd known hate. He'd hated the pipe trap juice his father would carefully funnel into old juice bottles and then hide, as if his children wouldn't notice he was drunk. He hated George Young, who would drive past and look at them with disgust. He hated the slow encroachment of poverty and despair, the way he couldn't afford the nails to fasten down the roof boards to keep the dust out.

At least, he thought he'd hated those things, but he hadn't. What he'd felt then were soft little emotions that tickled at him and annoyed him until he wanted to strike out. But what he felt for Ben Gratu wasn't soft or little. Temar shifted slightly, hungry for some space.

Ben threw an arm over Temar's stomach, and Temar froze. He wished he still felt the need to recoil from Ben's touch, but the fact was that he'd grown used to Ben's heavy, hot hands on him.

"Going somewhere?" Ben asked, his lips so close that his breath tickled Temar's ear.

"I have to use the bathroom," Temar answered. If he stayed in bed with a fully awake Ben, he had no doubt where that would lead. His hips and thighs were still bruised, and he wanted some time to heal. He wanted to walk down to the bathroom and spend ten minutes pretending he wasn't trapped in the middle of a nightmare. He'd lie to himself for that long.

"Without permission?" Ben asked, and that was his mock patience. That was the tone that suggested Temar was about to be bound or gagged or leashed or pushed down over a table and a belt taken to the backs of his thighs, all in the name of teaching him a little discipline.

"No, sir."

Ben pushed himself up on one elbow, his hair sticking up and his eyes blurry with sleep. "Do you really want to lie to me?"

"No, sir," Temar quickly answered. "I wasn't going to leave without permission. I just…." His mind blanked out with fear as Ben frowned.

"Yes?" Ben's voice was the voice of an imperious ruler, annoyed by some subject about to get beheaded, like in one of those old vids of Earth history.

"I was squirming. I have to pee, but I didn't know if it was bad enough to be worth waking you up." The words tumbled out. Temar fisted the sheets as he waited to see if it was enough, if he had placated the monster inside Ben Gratu.

Ben's frown slowly faded, replaced by a look of sympathy. "You know I'm always here for you. You should have woken me." Ben put his hot palm on Temar's chest, and his hand slowly drifted down until it rested over Temar's abdomen. Then he started slowly pressing down. The urge to pee made Temar squirm and hiss. He tried to control the reaction, because he knew pain made Ben more curious, more voyeuristic. It was as if Ben drank up Temar's despair and pain like a dying man in the desert drank water—greedily. Temar only wished the analogy was complete and that Ben would get stomach cramps and vomit from ingesting so much.

After a second, Ben gentled his touch. With one calloused finger, he traced a pattern over Temar's stomach. "Such a very good boy you are to worry about what would please me… or displease me. But I don't ever want you to hold back when it comes to your needs, Temar. It's my job to take care of you."

Temar swallowed. He hated that his body was reacting to Ben's tone. Ben was happy, so for one second, Temar was safe. He felt like glass that was cooled too fast, like he could hear the creaking that came right before the glass shattered.

He'd been in a glass shop once when that happened. A wind had picked up the edges of the tent where the glassblower had been working, and Temar had been about six, so he'd sat in the sand, watching. The artisan had pulled the orange-hot glass out of the oven, blowing it into a giant bubble and twirling the blow rod. But he'd gotten the shape he wanted too quickly, and he tried to save the piece by putting it under the cooling fans. The glass creaked, and even though it wasn't a loud sound, every artisan in the tent had stopped. Men and women had looked around, and then the glass bubble shattered.

He still remembered the thin red trails up the artisan's arms, tiny scores made by the passage of glass fragments. Sometimes Temar fingered the bruises Ben left, the purpling finger marks and the straightedge belt scores, and he felt like that glassblower. Other times, he thought he was the glass bowl, ready to shatter.

"May I go to the bathroom?" Temar asked quietly. Ben didn't answer immediately. He traced patterns in Temar's skin, his warm hands sliding over the curve of his hip and his thigh. Fingers brushed Temar's balls, and he felt a warmth start. And he hated himself the most for this. Ben chuckled and leaned down to kiss Temar's shoulder.

"Such a good boy you are. My colleagues were so certain you were a threat, that I should do to you what they did to that priest, but they don't understand you at all, do they?"

Temar thought it was a rhetorical question, but Ben pulled at his nipple, and sharp pain flashed through him.

"No, sir, they don't," Temar hurried to agree.

"You just need a strong hand to guide and shelter you. You aren't anything like that priest, are you?"

Temar didn't need to even think about that. "No, sir, I'm not." Shan had been a strong man. He wouldn't have lain under another man's hands and let someone abuse him. He would have killed Ben Gratu before yielding to him. But Temar wasn't that strong. Nope, he had a warm bed and good food, and that's all it took to make him lay still while Ben tied him spread eagle on the bed. He even helped by being as unstable around the others as Ben wanted. When Ben raised his hand a certain way, Temar threw a fit and cursed and spit until Ben kindly restrained him and slipped a gag in his mouth to save him from slander.

A little voice whispered that Temar didn't have a choice in any of this. Maybe he didn't have a choice when it was him in Ben's bed, with Ben's hands around his thighs, bending him in half so that Temar's ankles were around his ears. However, he didn't have any doubt about his own culpability in Shan's death. He'd only said what he'd said to Shan because he'd wanted to fantasize about rescue. He had his stupid little dreams, and making that comment about water—that was so he could lie in bed next to Ben and dream about the council breaking in and confronting Ben with the evidence of his water thievery. Temar wanted his fantasy, and Shan had died.

And the worst part was that, even knowing Ben's group had been involved with Shan's murder, Temar still climbed into bed with the man every night. He stayed quiet while Ben's hands caressed and pinched and held him against the white sheets. He got hard when Ben stroked him, and he wanted release. In the past, he'd always thought of himself as a good person. Never before had Temar realized he was weak and disgusting.

"What are you thinking?" Ben ran a finger across Temar's forehead, brushing hair back, away from his face.

"That I want to have you happy with me." Temar thought for a moment that he'd said the wrong thing. Ben frowned and studied his face by the light of the double moon that shone through the window set high in the bedroom wall.

"You are such a beautiful boy. Such a prize. The others are fools, who crash around like panicked sandcats in a glassblower's shop. If I'd had a choice of partners, I would pick men and women who had the insight to see how beautiful it is when someone bends to your will. They could have taken that priest and molded him into something useful to the cause. Instead, they destroyed him. No matter, though. I've saved you from that kind of reckless action. I've saved you and your sister, haven't I?" Ben ran a finger over Temar's lips, and Temar could only nod.

"So, you have to go to the bathroom." Temar nodded again. Ben smiled, a look that made Temar nervous. "Gag yourself, boy."

Temar tried to slip out of bed, but for a second, Ben kept his arm over Temar's chest, easily holding him down, not that Temar tried to fight. He yielded as soon as he recognized the game. That made Ben laugh.

Slapping Temar on the hip, he repeated the order. "Go on, then. Gag yourself." There were two gags Temar knew intimately. One was a small mouthpiece with a leather strap that Temar often wore in front of the others. The workers all agreed that it was good for Temar to learn to control his mouth, and even when he wasn't gagged, the others listened carefully for him to say a word out of line so they could go and get Ben and have Ben put the gag back on. The second one Ben only used in the house. It was large and thick, and it made Temar's jaw ache. Even though he hated that gag, it was the one he reached for.

He turned as he buckled it in place, and Ben was smiling at him. Truly, Temar was weak, because the man's approval soothed some gibbering, terrified animal, deep in his chest.

"When you get back, I think we should take advantage of the fact that we are both awake at such an early hour." Ben crooked his finger, and Temar stepped close. Ben's hands encircled his wrists, holding him still. "Get the rope." Ben's smile wasn't reassuring, but Temar also knew Ben was more likely to be gentle when Temar was restrained and compliant, and so he moved to get the rope the second Ben released him.

He still needed to pee, but he stood patiently while Ben looped and knotted the rope in complicated patterns, tying his wrists together. The rope made his wrists itch, and the sweat gathered where the insides of his wrists were pressed together. Leaving the two ends of the long rope hanging, Ben put his hands on Temar's hips and turned him.

"We'll have so much fun that we may need to sleep in tomorrow." Ben laughed. "After all, I'm the boss, so I think we can get away with it." He pulled the two ends of the rope around to the back and knotted them. Temar had some room to move his hands, enough to be able to hold himself while he peed. But the second Ben dropped him, stomach down, on the bed, the loose loop of rope would make him totally helpless.

Once Ben was done, he pulled a nightshirt off the headboard. Pulling it over Temar's head, he smoothed the fabric with his palms.

His gaze traveled up and down, and he reached down and traced the bare thigh under the hem of the shirt. "Be quick," Ben said, and then he gave Temar a kiss on the forehead and a slap on the hip. "I'll be waiting."

Temar's eyes grew warm, but he blinked the emotion away and turned. So much for wanting to escape the feeling of being trapped, for even one moment. Temar walked slowly down the narrow stairs to the first floor and the small bathroom next to the kitchens. He would have been better off lying in bed, turning his back, and pretending that he had some lover behind him. Maybe he could get really good at pretending… good enough to see someone else's face when Ben stroked him until he came.

When Temar came out of the bathroom, the double moons were shining through the back windows. On the other side of the house, the side that faced the workers' area, the windows were set high into the wall or were covered for privacy. But on this side of the house, the windows overlooked fields with long, green lines of crops. Temar wandered to the window and leaned against the cool glass. The heat from the day had lifted, and now the night breezes made the plants sway.

Letting his eyes lose focus, Temar turned the world into a swirl of colors. Green plants and brown soil, gray rock and deep blue sky, all merged into a blurry world. He leaned his forehead against the glass, letting the cool surface leech Ben's heat from his skin, and for a second, he considered standing there until Ben came to find him. He'd pay for it, but right now, looking out onto this world of color, Temar just wanted to slip away into it and never come back.

But something wasn't right in this world. Temar looked at the far corner of the field, near the waterline spigot. A shadow was moving along the edge of the field, crouching low to the ground and moving slowly. While Temar could imagine a dozen reasons for a worker to be out in the field—checking the ground temperature, night watering, slipping away from the workers' quarters to have sex somewhere with a little privacy—none of those excuses matched the shadow's movements.

Temar glanced up toward the bedroom. Ben would start looking for him soon. But if he went up there, he had no way of telling Ben there was a problem in the fields. Experience had taught him that once

Ben had tied him up, he didn't want to hear anything from Temar until he had finished.

The shadow reached one of the tanks and stood near it. It was a man, and he was tampering with the water tap. Temar remembered the feeling of the tap under his fingers as he'd tried to check the pressure on George Young's lines. The gear had jammed, and then, as Temar had tried to pry the broken piece free, the seal had broken, and water had gushed over his hands, more water than he had ever seen.

The part of Temar that had worked the land never wanted to see water wasted like that again. A darker, weaker, more corrupt shadow self whispered tempting thoughts about how Ben would have someone else to torture if another thief tried to steal his water. To his shame, Temar wasn't sure what dissuaded him from that thought—the immorality of wishing his life on someone else or the fact that it wasn't likely to work. Anyone condemned to a few workdays or weeks for a little thievery was going to see Ben's charming side, not the monster within.

So, he would scare this thief away. Temar moved to the door. He had to shift around awkwardly to lift the hem of the nightshirt enough to reach the door, and even then he had to stand on his toes to work the handle. Dropping his shirt back down to cover his bound hands, Temar moved far enough out onto the porch where the stranger could see him, and clearly he did. The shadow froze.

Instead of running away, the figure slowly stood, his face turned toward the brightest moon as he looked at Temar. Clearly, Temar was either dreaming or insane, because the man looked like Shan. He was dirty and had days of beard growth, and his torn clothes hung loosely, but he was the image of Shan Polli. Shocked and more than a little confused about seeing a ghost in his owner's fields, Temar took a step forward, out of the eaves of the porch and into the moonlight.

Could the figure be Naite Polli? Naite worked for the council and might be checking for illegal water use, particularly if George and Ben had started suing each other, as each threatened. But Naite was larger. His shoulders were so wide that Temar could identify the man from three fields away. This stranger had Naite's features, but he had the smaller body of the priest. Actually, he was smaller than Shan. This man looked like a scrawny younger brother to Shan, and for a half second, old stories of ghosts drifted through his memory.

"Temar?" the man asked as he started walking toward the house. He moved like Shan Polli, the same sharp, deliberate steps that Temar would often count when Shan gave sermons. He always took six steps toward the choir and then seven steps back to the pulpit. Temar could never quite figure out why he took more steps one way than the other, but he'd never taken more than six steps away from the pulpit, and never less than seven back to it.

"Temar?" the man asked again, and now he was quickly closing the distance between them. Only then did Temar realize he was half-naked, tied, and gagged. Horror vids were made out of scenes like this, and Temar would have been shouting at the main character's stupidity by this time. He stumbled backward toward the house—better the devil you know than the ghost you don't. But his tied hands kept him from pushing the door closed.

Shan-ghost's boots thudded against the heavy plastics of the porch, and Temar didn't have time to do more than wonder about the probability of a ghost wearing boots when he was pulled back outside. Having already learned what happened when you fought and lost, Temar stood staring at the ghost and smelling the sour breath of someone drunk on pipe juice.

"I hate seeing you in that." Shan stared at Temar, his mouth a thin, hard line. The gaze made Temar feel even more naked than the short nightshirt did.

"Boy, hurry up," Ben's voice called from upstairs. Shan was weaving, and he was obviously using his tight grip on Temar's arm to keep his balance. So, when Ben called, Shan twisted around so fast that his knees went out from under him, and Temar got pulled down on top of him.

"Oh God," Shan said. Temar looked down and realized the nightshirt had lifted, showing hand-sized bruises on his thighs. "That's not right. I never saw that, or I would have done something. But I didn't see that, and I never did anything." Shan babbled before he traced the edge of the bruise with his finger. Temar forgot to even breathe for a second.

Temar blinked. This wasn't quite his fantasy rescue. Shan was clearly drunk—too drunk to take on Ben. Up close, Temar saw he was half-starved and red from sun exposure, and if he said one word, Ben Gratu was going to call his friends and have them kill Temar's sister. Shan might have survived an attempt to kill him, but Cyla wouldn't.

Awkward and still off balance, Shan climbed to his feet only by hanging onto the doorknob. "You could have told me, Naite. You wouldn't have been as blind... or as determined to not look at him too long." Shan's words didn't make any sense. He was looking at the doorjamb as if he expected it to talk back, and he was blinking fast. Temar's father sometimes did that when he drank too much and the world wouldn't focus.

Again, Temar shook his head, and this time he climbed to his feet and tried to push Shan out. The man was no match for Ben. But Shan clung to the doorknob, and Temar couldn't do much with his hands tied.

"Boy, if you make me come down, my plans will change," Ben called again, and Temar knew Ben's plans had already changed. He was probably fingering his belt right now—trying to decide whether to whip the back or the thighs. Desperate now, Temar took a step back and practically charged Shan, hitting him on his shoulder. Sure enough, Shan wheeled around and stumbled out the door. If Temar could have run for the stairs, for Ben, for the safety of a known world where his misery bought his sister's place learning a skilled trade, he would have. Ben was sick, but he did offer a type of protection. Temar hated the price he paid, but he wouldn't jeopardize the balance they had reached.

However, life never treated Temar fairly. With his hands tied, he couldn't balance much better than Shan with his pipe-juice-addled brain. Temar stumbled out after Shan, falling to one knee on the back porch.

"Damn." Shan clung to one of the porch posts. "And I am not saying that in a profane manner. I am praying. I hope God damns any parent who could do that. And that's not very priestly of me, but I think it anyway." Shan started stumbling back toward the open door, and Temar stood, putting himself into the drunk's path. Temar had already put Shan in danger's way once, and he wasn't going to let the man throw his life away after escaping Ben's friends in Red Plain.

"I really don't have time for this," Shan muttered. Considering how drunk he was, Temar was surprised Shan had managed to stay focused for this long. But now he looked around, like he was searching for something new to capture his attention. Temar carefully and silently backed up toward the house. If he could kick the door closed, he was guessing that Shan would wander away in a drunken haze. And maybe, if he sobered up, he could defend himself, because if he confronted Ben, he was going to have to defend himself.

Temar was almost to the door when Shan repeated his words. "I really don't have time for this." Turning to face Temar, Shan caught Temar's arm, and pulled him back out onto the porch. Captivity had taught Temar not to fight, but he couldn't resist kicking as Shan bent over, put his shoulder in Temar's stomach, and lifted him. Thinking of his sister and nearly blind with fear, Temar kicked and squirmed, but Shan put an arm around Temar's legs and then started running for the fields. Temar could only sag helplessly and grunt as Shan's shoulder dug into his stomach and get annoyed by the small trail of spit that was dribbling from the side of his gag.

chapter
twelve

SHAN HAD run nearly the length of the farm before he stopped and fell to his knees. Temar tumbled off to the side, unable to catch himself. Behind the gag, he grunted and nearly choked on the smell of pipe juice. While his father always had a sour smell that lingered under the scent of dirt and sweat, Shan stunk like he'd soaked in the juice.

"Sorry," Shan said, his voice bleary. "You're right. I keep hurting you. No wonder you get so frustrated with me. Wait, I've never been able to touch you before. I don't think this is a good sign." Reaching over, Shan caught Temar by the arm and pulled at him. Shan's inability to engage with reality made Temar's stomach tighten in panic.

"And I wish you would take that gag off. You have a right to be angry. God. If Div had still been doing the sermons and shaking the hands, he would have noticed what was going on." Shan's face twisted with some dark emotion Temar didn't understand, but then he didn't understand most of what Shan was saying. He'd seen people drunk on pipe. He'd seen his own normally quiet father screaming at the sky and waving his arms in the air. He'd seen Cyla drunk once, and the entire house had suffered for that binge as she flung half their belongings around. But he'd never seen anyone this drunk or this lost in his own delusions. It was like reality didn't even exist for him.

Shan threw his hand up in the air, like he was trying to stop someone, but there wasn't anyone else in the field with them. "Enough. If you want to give me the silent treatment, I accept that. You have reason enough to blame me, but you don't have to wear that gag. The Lord knows you shouldn't suffer because others failed you." Shan reached for him so fast that he couldn't control the jerk of surprise, and a small part of him expected punishment. Instead, Shan pulled at the buckle. The edges of the gag dug into the corners of his mouth, and Temar grunted in pain, but Shan finally managed to fumble the buckle loose.

"Metaphor is one thing, but you don't need to rub it in." Shan's voice was soft as he reached up and touched his thumb to the corner of Temar's mouth. Temar's lips burned at the touch, the sore skin protesting the salt from Shan's sweat, but it was a small pain, and Temar endured.

Shan jerked back, his eyes wide with panic. "We need to hurry. I can't let them find me. Do you think they found the cycle?" Shan reached out, and Temar held himself stiffly still. His mind spun with a dozen different arguments, but he wasn't sure any of them would get through. Clearly, Shan's brain was pickled in pipe juice, and Temar couldn't defend himself if he turned violent.

Looking over his shoulder, Temar could swear he saw a glimmer of light in a third floor window. The house was a long way off, the length of a full field, but if he could convince Shan to let him go back, he could lie and tell Ben that he'd panicked, but that he'd decided to come back. A small imitation of a laugh escaped because it was a little ironic. Ben would probably enjoy the chance to punish Temar for something real. Normally Ben had to order Temar to act up and then punish him for it.

"Shan," Temar said softly. He felt like he was trying to tame a boar, which was one farm skill he'd never mastered. Well, one of many. "Shan, I need to go this way. You should go that way." Slowly, Temar started backing up. Under the nightshirt, his fingers curled into fists, and he prayed. It felt a little hypocritical, praying. He'd spend the last couple of months cursing God, when he bothered thinking about him at all. However, right now, he needed a little luck. He needed Shan's delusions to keep him distracted.

"No!" Shan twirled around, panic clear in his face. "We've made it this far together, the three of us. You didn't think we'd make it, back at the bike. I could tell from your face. You don't hide things well." He frowned. "Or you do hide things. Or I was so busy not looking at you that I never saw the obvious when you came to church. How could I not even notice your pain? Do you really think we're in the valley, or is this God's mercy, letting us die thinking that we managed to save ourselves?" Shan caught Temar's arm, pulling him forward.

Clearly Shan had hallucinated some version of him, but Temar was at a loss as to why he'd do that. While Temar would often go to church, he was never particularly close to either of the priests. The church was simply a place of quiet and peace, when Temar hadn't been able to listen to Cyla's anger or his father's insane rambling. If Shan were going to hallucinate, surely he could find someone more important to hallucinate about. However, until he changed hallucinations or sobered up, Temar didn't have much choice.

He followed down the long dusty path that led to the opposite side of the valley and away from Ben and George Young's farms. A rise in the ground caught Shan off guard, and he fell to one knee, his fingers clutching at Temar's nightshirt. With his bound hands, Temar couldn't do much, but he did reach for Shan's elbow, struggling to help him back up to his feet. As drunk as Shan was, Ben could kill him with a single finger. After being the cause of so much trouble already, Temar wasn't going to let that happen.

"Shan, you need to hide," Temar said.

"You and Naite need to stop teaming up on me" was Shan's nonsensical answer. Temar obviously needed to wait until Shan sobered up a little more. Wobbling a little, Shan got to his feet and started down the path again.

A line of fence posts with no wire marked the boundary between Ben's place and the Sullivans'. Their farm was long and followed the slight curve of the valley floor. Temar stood in the moonlight and eyed the path back toward Ben's place. If he went back after this long, Ben was going to make him pay. The memory of Cyla running through the rows of rye on their farm rose up so vivid that Temar imagined her racing between the beans and the rhubarb. She'd die. If he made the wrong choice, she'd die. Of course, if Ben was nervous, he would have already made the call. That thought nearly sent Temar to his knees. The only thing that kept his legs from buckling was the belief that Ben was too arrogant to ever get nervous. He wouldn't make that call about Cyla until he thought he had to, or until he thought he didn't need leverage anymore.

Leverage. Temar had to take several deep breaths as he remembered what he had allowed that man to do because he had leverage. And if he went back now, Ben would have all the time in the world to make Temar regret his few stolen moments of freedom. Maybe it was fear of that pain, and maybe it was fear that Shan would get confused and follow him back to Ben's place, but for whatever reason, Temar turned his back on Ben's farm and started walking after Shan.

The Sullivans grew vegetables and rhubarb that provided both food and the oxalic acid the early settlers had used to leech the iron out of the glass sands to make optic quality glass that the more developed planets envied. Of course, there wasn't much demand for that type of glass these days, but the rhubarb kept growing, even when the farmers had to cut back on irrigation. The already reddish stems looked even more red under the light of the moon, so that the wide green leaves looked like they were drifting on top of red sands.

"Hurry up," Shan called.

"Coming," Temar answered. Clearly, Shan was used to his hallucinations disagreeing with him, because he turned and looked at Temar with a bewildered expression, but he didn't say anything. Awkwardly kneeling down, Temar strained against the rope leash until he could grab the red stalks and snap them off.

"What are you doing?" Shan wandered closer, stumbling now that he didn't have Temar to lean on.

"You need food, or the pipe juice is going to rot your brain."

"It already has," Shan pointed out. Temar stopped for a second to really look at Shan. Wearing his black clothing and standing in front of the congregation, Shan always looked imposing and regal, and with his sharp features, a little intimidating. Now, he looked smaller.

"Just help me steal some food." Temar waddled a few feet down the path and broke off more stalks. Hopefully, the theft was small enough that no one would notice it. Then again, the council couldn't do much more to him… not unless they exiled him, and at this point, Temar thought that might be the better fate.

"Thou shalt not steal," Shan announced grandly, his voice sounding like a sermon as it boomed in the darkness. Of course, he also started snapping off rhubarb stalks. "I don't like rhubarb."

"It's the only crop that's ready to eat." Temar had several fat stalks in his hands, but as he stood, he could only hold them by the green tops and let them hang low. "Take these, and then we can go." Temar awkwardly swung the red stalks out toward Shan.

Shan stared at his bare legs for a long time. "You aren't wearing pants."

"No, I'm not."

"The sandrats will get you if you aren't careful."

"We aren't on the desert. We're in the valley, remember?" Temar tried to keep his voice even. When his father was like this, anger would either make him cower in fear or, on rare occasions, strike out. Temar didn't intend to find out how Shan would react.

"We're in the valley?" Shan looked around. "Ah. I stole water from Ben, but I don't think he'll mind too much. He's a good man."

Temar's guts tightened in immediate hatred. He knew it wasn't Shan's fault, no more than it was the fault of the workers who would tell Ben how wonderful and patient he was. The sound of people praising Ben Gratu still made his stomach sour. "Take the food or don't," Temar said as he flipped it onto the path near Shan.

"You're angry because I noticed your legs are bare. You're right." Shan bent over and grabbed the stalks and started snapping off the poisonous leaves, throwing them farther into the field where rows of bean plants were starting to get bushy. "I never looked at you long enough to see your father was hurting you, and now I act like I have some sort of right to stare, just because I'm hallucinating."

"You… what? My father never hurt me."

"Naite used to say that to people too." Shan nodded and turned back toward the far side of the valley, but the turn put him so off balance that he stumbled sidewise, got tangled in a rhubarb plant, and fell with a heavy grunt.

"Shan." Temar hurried over, but tied he couldn't do much except crouch down near him. Shan was staring up at the stars, not even trying to move, one hand fisting the base of a rhubarb crown.

"What kind of a priest stands at the pulpit and doesn't notice that people are in trouble?"

"Who's in trouble?"

"I suppose I should forgive myself for Naite because I was too young and idiotic to know any better. But how could I let Erqu Gazer hurt you? Why didn't I ever walk up to you in church and tell you that you could stay? That's what Div did for me, you know. I was sitting in the back of the church one night, after a day interning with Holmes, and he sat next to me and asked if there was something I needed to talk about. I should have done the same for you." Shan reached out so fast that Temar didn't have a chance to retreat. Shan's hand caught him right above the knee, and he held on tightly, his thumb pressing into one of the purpling bruises decorating Temar's legs. "I'm a poor excuse for a priest. I should have been a mechanic."

Shan's hand was close enough for Temar to reach, and he worked his fingers between his leg and Shan's hand, struggling to make Shan release his painful grip.

"I never needed saving until recently. Shan, please, you're hurting me."

Immediately Shan let go. "I do that too much." The fatigue seemed to settle over Shan like a sudden weight, and he let his head fall back onto a bean plant so that the teardrop-shaped leaves covered part of his face. "You should go on."

For a second, Temar couldn't form words, with the panic growing like a bubble in his stomach. Oh no. Shan couldn't drag him away from Ben just long enough to get him in real trouble and then abandon him. True, this wasn't the rescue he'd imagined as he lay in bed or as he'd walked the rows of neat crops on Ben's farm, pulling weeds and picking off bugs. However, if this was the only rescue he was getting, he didn't want the rescuer passing out where Ben was sure to find him.

"Shan, you have to get up."

"No, I don't. If I'm in the valley, then someone will find me, and if I'm imagining the valley, then maybe it's time to let the sandrats have me. 'The upright have God for their Savior, their refuge in times of trouble.' Not that I am all that upright. I tilt to the side, but I swear that I never meant to hurt you, Temar. I never meant to let someone else hurt you." Shan rolled his head to the side and looked up with such agony that Temar could feel his anger give way to the same sort of exasperation he'd always had for his father when he'd been drinking.

Sometimes pain was more than a person could bear, and they had to either drink or hear their own hearts cracking like glass cooled too fast. But Temar couldn't understand why Shan would drink. The man had, until now, always appeared so confident.

"Shan," Temar said slowly, trying to find the words to reach through the fog. "Naite wants us to hide," he said hopefully. If Shan wouldn't listen to him, maybe his hallucinations would have more power over him.

"I really want to lay here."

"If you do, the people who tried to kill you will come."

"They wouldn't dare." Shan smiled, but slowly his smile faded. "But they're already here. I heard them." Reaching over, Shan patted Temar's leg, and Temar's skin crawled at the familiar gesture. It was one Ben often used when he was in a particularly good mood. "They said he'd know."

"Who?"

"Don't know. Naite insists that he wouldn't try to hurt me, but I'm not sure I should believe a hallucination. I'm really drunk." Maybe Shan was sobering up, or maybe he had more self-awareness than Temar's father had had when he was drunk. He pushed himself up onto his elbow. "If I don't know who tried to get me killed, I should hide."

"Do you know a really good hiding place? We have to hide where nobody will ever find us," Temar said. He considered telling Shan that it had been Ben. Ben had left the bruises and tied him and had listened on the phone with his lips pursed in thought as his friends described how they'd killed Shan. He wasn't sure that Shan wanted to hear that. In truth, he wasn't sure that Shan could understand him—not now, with his brain inventing visions.

"I know a place that only Naite knows about." Shan grunted as he pushed himself back up to his knees. "But what if Naite is the one they called? They tried to shoot me. They missed."

"Naite wasn't the one," Temar promised. He held still as Shan used a shoulder to get back up onto his feet. The skin around the corners of his mouth had the shriveled look of someone about ready to drop dead. "Did you drink water when you were at Ben's place?" he asked. If Shan got food in his body before water, the man probably would drop dead.

"You and Naite are always ganging up on me," he complained.

Temar stood next to Shan and then took a step forward, urging him into motion. "I'll stop ganging up on you if you tell me whether you drank some water."

"Too much water," Shan said with a distant look in his eye. But whatever his destination had been before, he obviously remembered it because he started walking with purposeful steps, his arm around Temar's shoulders for balance. "I almost vomited, but that seemed like such a waste. I put more water in my canteen, but I don't like the smell of it. I'm sorry I liked you."

Temar shook his head and kept walking next to Shan. Hopefully morning would bring more answers, and hopefully he could convince Shan to untie him. For now, they simply had to find someplace to hide that Ben wouldn't find.

chapter thirteen

THE CAVE where Shan had led them was little more than a deep crack in the rock face. A pile of rock that had tumbled down from the cliff had piled up in front of the opening, and a giant wind tree with branches twisted into impossible shapes had taken root in the rock itself, so that a person could walk right by the mouth of the crack and never see it. Hopefully, Ben Gratu would walk past without seeing it if his search brought him this far. Logically, Temar knew everyone posed an equal threat, since anyone in the entire valley would turn him back over to Ben, but it was the idea of Ben finding them that made him afraid to sleep as he rested his head against the warm rock.

The night was a long series of half dreams and shadows and the sound of Shan snoring heavily in the deepest corner of the crack, and morning came with vivid streaks of red and orange that stained the sky. In the distance, a worker walked the rows, sinking a probe in every five or six feet, checking buried irrigation lines, and his long shadow followed him. Temar's wrists itched from being tied together, the sweat gathering between them, but he sat on the loose gravel and watched the distant worker.

As the morning sky brightened to blue, Shan groaned and shifted. He pushed himself up on shaking arms until he had his back to the wall of the cramped cave. He peered through narrowed eyes, and Temar was guessing he had a headache big enough to make his head fall off. Maybe his time with Ben had brought out his own meanness, but Temar was a little amused at Shan's misery. If the man was going to drag him out of his familiar despair, at least he got to hurt as much as Temar.

"Great," Shan said with tremendous disgust. "I'm brain damaged. I'm at least half sobered up, and I'm still seeing things."

"No, you aren't. Not unless you're still seeing ghost Naite." Temar shifted around awkwardly. His bound hands were trapped near his stomach, so he used his heel to push himself up a little straighter.

Shan frowned. "Temar?"

"Yes?"

Shan's eyes scanned him, and his eyebrows drew down with worry or confusion. It was hard to tell, but his color looked better, and his face didn't have that odd wrinkling and puckering that suggested imminent death. "But…." Shan stopped and then inched forward. "I imagined those."

Temar looked down to where Shan was staring. His short nightshirt couldn't hide the vivid, purple bruises with a rim of green where the skin was healing. He could feel the heat gathering in his face. Logically he knew it hadn't been his fault, but a little part of him wanted to hide the marks and hide the fact that he hadn't been smart enough to find a way out of Ben's trap on his own.

"No, you hallucinated a lot, but these are mine."

"I kept imagining you and Erqu on that isolated farm—"

"My father never touched me!" Temar froze, horrified at his own shout. Looking out through the curling branches of the wind tree, he watched the worker continue to walk the rows.

"Is someone out there?" Shan moved forward but grunted with each step he crawled.

"A worker. He didn't hear."

"Thank the Lord." Shan sagged against the rock, but he'd moved forward far enough that their legs touched, even though Shan pulled his knees up under him. "We have to go to someone on the council."

Temar's stomach rolled with panic, but he set his heels into the dust of the cave floor and pushed himself back. "No."

Shan jerked back in surprise. "Temar, he hurt you."

"Gods and stars… don't you think I know that? Do you think I'm stupid?" Temar pulled at his bound hands. Ben had done more than Shan would ever know because he had no intention of telling anyone. His suffering was his own.

Shan blinked his eyes a little more open. "Of course you do. I never suggested you didn't." Shan closed his eyes and let his head come down to rest on his knees. He was the picture of misery, and Temar felt wisps of guilt for verbally striking out at the man who had tried to save him. True, it was a disorganized and clumsy rescue, but it had worked… maybe. Temar still wasn't sure what they were supposed to do from here. If Ben didn't find him soon, he'd have his friend kill Cyla, and then he'd tell the council that Temar had run away, so that an exile order would go out. Three valleys and five towns. That was not a lot of room to hide. Shan moaned and tangled his fingers through his hair.

"You're recovering from pipe poison. You shouldn't be talking," Temar pointed out. His father always complained that his own voice echoed in his head, the morning after a particularly bad round of drinking. Before all this happened, Temar had wondered how his father could ever drink, but now he understood. If he had to face a life in Ben's bed, he would have happily lost himself in the madness of pipe juice. Ben wouldn't have liked that much, but that would have been a bonus. Temar never thought Shan would be one to drink. Temar wondered if the attempt on his life had driven him to drinking. Actually, now that he thought about it, Temar had no idea how Shan had survived at all. Ben said his friends had killed Shan outside Red Plain, and Temar hadn't heard of any rescues.

Shan sighed heavily and then spoke in a whisper. "I need to untie you."

"Hand me a knife and I'll manage," Temar suggested.

"If I had a knife, I would." Shan held up his empty hands. "The Lord provides, but he didn't provide a knife." Shan tried to laugh, but he strangled on the sound and cradled his head in his hands. "God, my head hurts."

"You need more water and food," Temar said. If he had a choice, he'd rather stay tied up than lift his nightshirt and let Shan see more of the damage Ben had done.

Shan nodded and pulled up the leg of his pants. He had a canteen strapped to his leg, but it was yellowed with pipe juice, and when Shan opened the top, Temar could smell the sour.

"You're going to drink pipe juice?" he demanded.

"God almighty, no. I rinsed the container the best I could, but I carried pure pipe juice in here, so this was the best I could do." Shan took a deep drink. Temar frowned at the implication. Sure, when he was a kid, his favorite vid character had walked off the desert by drinking water evaporated out of pipe juice, but no one would be stupid enough to try that in real life. No one would survive if they tried doing that long enough to walk from Red Plain to the Valley. That was too far, and the desert was too full of sandrats to survive something like that.

"You drank water evaporated out of pipe juice?" Temar's voice squeaked with incredulity.

"It worked," Shan said with a shrug as he bit off part of a rhubarb stalk. He made a terrible face, but he kept chewing until he swallowed. "There weren't a lot of choices." He held out a stalk to Temar, but Temar turned it down with a shake of his head. He wasn't that hungry.

"You could have killed yourself," Temar pointed out.

Shan laughed again, but this time it was a weak, thin laugh. "I just about died more times than I can count. I now understand why the people of Israel thought Moses was insane for wanting to cross the desert. I'm not sure I would follow him after this experience."

"But… why didn't you use the emergency beacon?"

Shan looked up with bloodshot eyes. "Because someone was shooting at me. I had to crash the cycle into a canyon, and I lost the equipment. Given a choice between walking off the desert or lying down and dying, I decided that even a stupid plan was better than nothing."

Temar couldn't come up with an answer to that. Fear curled around his stomach, fear that Shan would blame him, fear that Ben's friends would put Cyla in that situation, fear that he was going to end up walking the desert when he got exiled because, right now, he was technically a runaway slave. "I'm sorry," Temar whispered.

Shan lifted his head off his knees so fast that he hissed with pain. "Why should you be sorry?"

"I made that comment about water. I sent you over to Red Plain. I just…." Temar stopped. His mouth had gotten too dry for him to confess that he wanted to be rescued so much that he put other people right into Ben Gratu's path.

"You didn't do anything wrong. Ben Gratu is going to pay for what he did, but you aren't to blame for anything," Shan hurried to say.

"I'm not blaming myself for the abuse. I'm blaming myself for giving you enough information to get you involved without telling you the whole truth."

"Then tell me the truth now."

Temar frowned. He'd been willing to share everything with Ben… right before Ben had burned all the evidence, but now Temar could feel the fear, like a sandrat he'd swallowed alive. The men and women on the farm looked at him with pity, and he knew they'd never believe him, even if he tried to convince them the sky was blue. While he thought Shan would give him a little more respect, he wasn't totally sure.

"Please," Shan said. He rested his palm on Temar's ankle.

Looking at that dark, sun-roughened hand resting against his ankle, Temar blinked to clear his blurring vision. Ben had ordered him to shy away from any touch other than Ben's own, and the weight and warmth of a comforting hand wasn't familiar anymore. "It was Ben who was stealing water," Temar said, expecting to be interrupted. Instead, Shan watched him. "I had taken readings, and when Ben and I got to the valley that first day, I told him I had evidence."

"Why not bring it to the council?" Shan asked. At least he didn't openly doubt the story.

Temar shrugged. Looking back, that had been where the problem had started. "Cyla asked Naite for an emergency meeting of the council, and when he told her to wait for season-end…." He stopped and shrugged again, unwilling to blame his sister for their problem, not when Ben was the person behind it. "I told Ben I had months of daily moisture readings. I thought he'd help me with a case against George Young. Instead, he looked at them and then he…." Temar stopped again, his arms tingling with the memory of Ben's hands on him, holding him down on the bed Temar had slept in as a child. With Ben looking down at him, with Ben's heavy weight holding him down, he'd felt as helpless as a child again. A dark laugh slipped out before Temar could stop it. "I used to be better at telling stories."

"I'm a priest," Shan said. "I hear stories from people overwhelmed by their own emotions for a living. You're doing fine."

"He tied me up and called some friend in Red Plain—told them to come and get Cyla's contract and that if I did anything to speak out against them, they would kill her."

"His farm never showed signs of having extra water. If anything—"

"He was short of water," Temar interrupted. "I know. He mentioned that he was shorting his own water too, and then he was blaming it on my father. But all the missing water from my place and from his and from who knows who else's… it's Ben."

Shan pressed his lips tightly together and reared back. Even though Temar missed the warm touch on his ankle, he used the chance to pull his legs closer. "I'm going to kill him. I know that's not a priestly thing to say, but I really am going to kill him. He used that water theft to get his hands on you and…. What he did…." Shan stood in the narrow cave and turned his back to Temar. With his hands braced on the gray rock, he looked like he was trying to hold up the cliff. His fingers curled, the tips pressed to the stone, and his back arched. Shan might be a priest, but he was a strong man. Temar had watched him climb roofs and carry heavy parts as often as he'd seen him at the front of the church. Now that strength frightened him.

Temar scooted back toward the mouth of the small cave, uncomfortable around the gathering emotion. For the first time since the "rescue," Temar was aware of how much taller and stronger Shan was. However, when Shan spoke, his voice was small.

"Ista Songwind didn't like me. I thought it was because I had interrupted her work, but she was trying to keep me away from her hostage." Shan slapped a hand against the rock, hard enough that Temar flinched. "She's in on this, and I'm willing to bet that Ben is the man the two shooters mentioned. They said their contact here would find out if I turned up alive, and Ben is the center of gossip for the whole valley."

"Everyone trusts him," Temar agreed.

"We'll go to the council, and then Ben is going to regret all of this. He'll regret ever touching you. I promise you that."

The laughter that slipped out of Temar was wild and dark.

Shan turned around to look at him. Whatever he saw worried him enough that he crouched down. "Temar?"

"We can't go to them."

"I won't let Ben get away with—"

"Don't I get a say in this?" Temar demanded, cutting Shan off. "Are you going to tell me what to do? Maybe you like having me tied up so I can't disagree with you."

Shan flinched back, and Temar froze, all his anger draining as he watched Shan rear back like he'd reached for heated glass with a bare hand. The look on his face… Temar could see the horror, but he ignored the other emotions. He couldn't deal with Shan's feelings, not now. Cyla was in danger, and Ben.… Temar took a deep breath and tried to push the panic away.

"I should go." Temar kept his voice calm, even though the thought of going back to Ben made him want to throw himself off the nearest cliff. Actually, if he could get up high enough, that might be a solution.

"Go?"

"I should get out there in the open where I can be found before Ben has to look too hard. You have to get to Cyla. Ben is.…" Temar had no words to describe how everyone looked at Ben like they wished he was their father, their brother, their son. They loved him. Temar started edging toward the opening of the cave, but Shan caught his arm. Shying away from the touch, Temar slammed his head into the side of the cave and then recoiled, nearly into Shan. Temar flinched away, half blinded by the pain as his head throbbed. He wanted to curl up and not think at all, and he couldn't even reach up to hold his own throbbing head.

"I'm sorry. I'm sorry. I'm not touching you." Shan was on his knees, his hands held up in surrender. "I'm not touching you, and I won't touch you. I promise I won't."

"Promise." Temar snorted his disgust at that word.

"I just… Temar, I'm a priest, so whatever you tell me, I promise that it will remain between us. I won't even tell the council, if you order me not to. That's what the confessional means, that's what it means when you trust a priest and ask for spiritual help. I don't understand. You have to help me understand, because right now, I don't understand why you have to go back to him."

Temar got one leg under him and pushed himself back up to his knees. His head pounded in time with his heart, but he ignored that. "You'd hide information from the council?"

Shan answered slowly. "I wouldn't like it, but as a priest, it's my job to listen to confession and to offer advice to people who need it. What happens between a person and the priest can't go anywhere else. People have confessed all types of crimes, and I've never taken them to the council."

A thought crossed his mind. "If Ben Gratu had come to the church and confessed this, would you have kept that secret?"

Even with his face in shadow, Temar could see Shan's mouth come open and then close again a couple of times before he managed to find any words. "I would tell him that God knows we're weak and he will forgive, but only if confession comes with a change in behavior. I would tell him he had to stop hurting you and turn custody back to the council."

Temar laughed, but it turned into a sob, and for a second, he had to concentrate on controlling his breathing before his emotions overwhelmed him. "If he gave up custody, if I knew Cyla was safe, I'd turn him in."

"And he'd have to face the consequences of his behavior," Shan agreed.

"I've heard you speak, so I know you're an intelligent man. You can't really believe he'd do that."

"No, I don't. I'd tell him that was the only way to save his soul, though. I'd remind him that this life lasts a very short period of time, but that eternity is a long time to suffer, just because you refuse to face your own evil. I'd remind him that everyone makes a mistake eventually, and that he would be caught, so it would go easier on him if he came forward on his own."

"And when that failed?"

Shan leaned back and thought about that for some time. "I'd shoot him," he finally answered.

Temar didn't have an immediate response to that.

"Before I'd allow an innocent person to suffer, I would shoot him and deal with the damage I'd done to my own soul."

"That's not a very priestly answer."

"I'm not always a very good priest, but I try to be a good man. Right now, I'm feeling like a stupid man because I don't understand why you would suddenly decide to go back to Ben. If you wanted to kill Ben, that, I could understand. I would tell you that justice would be better left to the council or God, but I would understand."

Temar swallowed, hope and an overwhelming urge to run sticking in his throat, but he had to do what was right, not only for him but for Cyla. It wasn't like Ben could hurt him more than he already had. There was a limit to how much pain a body could take without it showing in the morning, and Temar knew Ben wouldn't cross that line. "I'm trusting you to get to Cyla, to protect her and find some evidence. But if I go with you, by the time you have evidence, by the time you convince anyone that the almighty Ben Gratu is a monster, my sister will be dead. I can't buy my freedom with her death."

"Ah." Shan sighed the word as he leaned back. For long minutes, there was silence. Temar didn't know why he continued to sit near the entrance of the cave. He should leave. He should do what he knew he had to. At least now he could lie next to Ben and wait for the coming rescue. That would make it much easier to endure.

"Temar," Shan said slowly, "you know Ben's smart. He's an immoral man, and while it's not very priestly of me to say this, I suspect he's condemned his soul to hell, but you have to admit he's smart. He's not going to do anything suspicious." Shan leaned forward and looked Temar right in the eye.

"I know that, but he said he'd kill her." Temar remembered Ben's joyful expression as he held him down and called to arrange Cyla's slavery… called to arrange her death, if Temar tried to fight.

"He probably will, but not yet. You're alone, you have no shoes and no equipment. He knows you aren't a threat unless you go to the council."

"And I could be doing that right now. He'll kill her before I have a chance to talk to them."

"If he had her killed, it would make the council suspicious. The thing he used to threaten you came true. Temar, stop and think. What would be the smarter play?"

Temar gasped as the reality came together like hot glass merging. "He'll keep her alive. If they ask her if Ben ever threatened her, she'll say 'no.' Her words will condemn me."

"You'll look twice as crazy," Shan agreed. "I made a promise, and I'll keep it, but we can't just sit here. We have to make a move. Now Div could get us food, water, and clothes, and given some time, he could get us some transportation over to Red Plain. We could make sure Cyla is safely back in council custody, and then we can start questioning people. We might even go to the communication relay station. If Ben is doing something with water, he has to move it. That means he has to be using the terraforming pipes, and the station will have the blueprints."

"What proof do we have? I'll end up looking crazy, and they'll say you drank a little too much pipe juice, trying to get off the desert."

"I did drink a little too much pipe juice." Shan got a crooked grin on his face, and the expression made him look like a kid stealing cookies from a jar. "But Cyla can confirm that Ista had entire boards of computer chips, including mother chips. There are very few of those down here, and every single one is accounted for. If we start questioning people, I get the feeling we're going to find out that no one pulled their mother chip for cleaning the day I was in Red Plain, so that's a lead. God Almighty, that's probably why she tried to have me killed, because Ben is not the sort to panic and order me killed when I don't know enough to even bother looking twice at those computer chips."

"We can't go to the council," Temar said firmly.

"They have all the resources to investigate this."

"Can you really tell me for sure that Lilian Freeland isn't involved? She and Ben Gratu have known each other for decades. And if they're willing to kill you, what will stop them from killing Div? I had to live with thinking that you died because I had some stupid plan to tip you off about Ben. I sent you out there searching for answers, and they tried to kill you." Temar could feel the memory of that cold guilt claw at him. "I thought they had killed you. How would you feel, finding Div at the bottom of the stairs with his neck broken because we went to him for help?" Temar knew he'd won, just from the expression on Shan's face. They'd both escaped one trap, but they could still feel the edges of the larger trap all around, and one wrong move and people would die.

"We still need help," Shan said firmly, but he didn't look happy about it. Maybe that meant he was finally understanding the reality Temar had already grasped—Ben Gratu was a man whose power reached further than any of them had ever suspected. "We need to go to Naite."

"Naite Polli?" Temar heard his own voice squeak with disbelief. Naite was a man who loved his rules above all, so he was the last on the list of names Temar would try.

"I know he's not involved. The stick he has up his—" Shan cut himself off. "I clearly need to stay away from pipe trap juice. It makes me uncharitable. However, my brother would cut off his own arm before he would be involved with murder, and that is not an exaggeration. Besides, as an unskilled worker, Naite wasn't valuable enough to bother trying to manipulate until recently, and he's only been on the council for one season. Besides, manipulating Naite is like trying to convince a boar to pull a plow. There's every reason to trust him, and more importantly, we won't be able to do this alone."

Temar chewed on his lip, uncomfortable with telling more people because every new person was a new threat, and he did not want to know how Ben would react to being threatened. Finally, he nodded. They'd tell Naite.

chapter
fourteen

THE KELLIGAN farm had long rows of verdant corn, rising from the ground, like wisps of grass in the shade of the darker amaranth, with their broad leaves. The cliff face offered very little shelter here, and there was a long strip of gravel where the rock met the fields. A few tiny pipe trap plants had thrown up pale leaves through the gravel and sand, but otherwise the strip was as barren as a moon. They had to run from one boulder to another as they tried to get closer to the farm where Naite was working… hopefully. Temar still thought this was a bad idea, but he didn't have a better one.

"I could—" Shan started to say.

"No." Temar crouched down so his nightshirt would cover more. He knew exactly what Shan was offering, but he would wait until they had a knife sharp enough for him to cut the rope himself. He didn't need any more pity out of Shan. And if Shan saw the belt marks on his back and ass, pity would fill those dark eyes.

Shan sighed, but he didn't say anything else. He leaned back against the boulder and pulled a pale pipe-trap leaf up. The plant was so young that it hadn't yet developed its underground trap or started producing poison, so only a long, thin root came up with it. Shan started twisting it into knots.

So far, no one was searching the valley, but Temar had to fight an urge to flee at top speed. Or, since he didn't have shoes, flee slowly by picking his way over the rocks. When the council arrested someone, they always took a person's shoes, and after a day of trying to cover the two miles between the cave where they'd spent the night and this far edge of the Kelligan farm, Temar understood why. The lack of shoes was a larger handicap than his bound hands.

Actually, he was regretting not taking Shan up on an offer to share his shoes, each wearing them for part of the day. However, once Temar had turned down the offer, he couldn't bring himself to tell Shan he'd changed his mind. Temar rocked forward onto his toes to take his weight off his left heel, with its deep bruise. Maybe his pride needed to take a backseat to his abused feet. "If Naite doesn't come out here—"

"Then he's not working this farm," Shan said firmly. "He walks the perimeter every night. It's a ritual with him, as important to him as communion."

Temar leaned against the warm boulder. His heel throbbed. Temar could not imagine why anyone would walk the perimeter of a farm unless he had a slave owner standing behind him, making him. After working next to Ben and seeing how much workers had to do on a farm running at full production—something Temar's farm had never done—Temar couldn't imagine anything other than collapsing in exhaustion when the work was over. An unskilled worker's life was hard enough without picking out more work to do on his own time, and even if Temar could figure out a way not to end up back in Ben's bed, this was going to be his life. He had no training, and he had committed the crime of water theft.

Shan made an unhappy noise. "I really hope we don't have to walk to the Sulli place. If we do, we're going to get you set up back at the cave, and then I'll run over there."

"Alone?" Temar got a firm hold on the fear that was suddenly rising. "No, if we need to go to the Sulli farm, we'll go together."

Shan turned around and looked at him. For several seconds, Shan was silent, and Temar could feel his frustration rising. Yeah, he was being unreasonable. He'd never make it that far, but he had the right to try.

It took some time, but Shan finally answered in a soft voice, "You don't even have shoes."

Temar flinched back and let his gaze drift over to a spire of white rock that rose from the ground. He hated fighting... hated it with a passion. However, since being in Ben's bed, he hated the idea of being told what to do. He hated the idea of going back to the cave and staying there alone. And he hated the idea of having to cross the wide valley floor to reach the Sulli farm. Actually, he hated a lot of things, which probably wasn't all that healthy. He refused to say anything. Long seconds dragged past in silence.

"If we cross at night, we can probably stay on the path, where you don't need shoes," Shan conceded. Temar nodded without answering. After that, the evening turned into a long, dusty wait.

A buteo cried sharply as it circled and then landed on its nest in the cliff face, far above them. Even after it landed, Temar heard its cries echoing against the rock, and he wondered if the bird was trying to find a mate or if it had come home to find sandrats had eaten the eggs. Temar was in such a dark mood that he could picture the broken shells, the carefully tended nest slick and yellowed from the yolk. Eventually the bird quieted, and the air cooled. The late winds blew sand over the wide mouth of the valley. The protective screen would catch any rare sand that managed to slip between the rock cliffs, so they were safe. However, the sandstorm blocked the dying rays of sun, so the night fell faster than Temar expected.

"We could steal some water and head over to the Sulli place tonight," Shan offered softy. They were the first words either of them had spoken in a long time. Temar shifted around to stretch a leg that had fallen asleep.

"Do you think it's dark enough?"

"Probably not for a while." The silence came again, settling into the cracks and crevasses until Temar squirmed with a need to do or say something—he just didn't know what. Shan sat by the rock, perfectly still. "I think someone's coming," Shan whispered.

Boredom snapped into pure fear so fast that Temar lost his ability to breathe for a precious half minute. Moving slowly, he edged closer to Shan. Now he wished he had his hands free. It was stupid to leave himself helpless instead of letting Shan see a few whip marks. The man could certainly imagine what Ben had been doing, and the whip was the least of the humiliations.

Shan shifted so his hands rested on the ground, and then he inched forward. For long minutes, Temar didn't dare breathe as they waited. The wind groaned as it passed over the top of the valley, and Shan slowly got to his knees and leaned forward.

"Stay here," he whispered. Pushing himself up, he moved to the side of the boulder where they'd been hiding. Temar tried to curl into the smallest possible space as Shan took a step away from the boulder.

"Naite?" he called. For a moment, there was only silence, and Temar was sure he was about to have a heart attack.

"Shan? Shan! Oh my God. What in the name of the gods and stars happened to you?"

Shan gave a dry and humorless laugh. "Had some trouble."

"So it seems. You look ready to fall over, and either you bathed in pipe juice or you're so drunk you're sweating the stuff."

"A bit of both. I walked off the desert, drinking water evaporated out of straight pipe juice, so I probably am sweating the stuff." That brought a long silence.

"Gods. You always loved the survival stories as a kid, but what the hell inspired you to try them out? What happened to your radio and your emergency rations? What happened to you?" Naite sounded friendly, and Temar took the chance of moving forward to the edge of the boulder, so he could see the two brothers.

Naite had both his hands on Shan's shoulders as he looked into his brother's face. Seeing them side-by-side, Temar was suddenly struck by how much weight Shan had lost. He'd never been anywhere near as large as his brother, but now he looked like an insubstantial shadow compared to Naite. He reminded Temar of the abstract glass he'd seen Dee'eta Sun make. The glass had a colored center that mimicked the shape of the larger piece in which it was trapped. She was so skilled that the inner center was a faultless replica with only half the width, perfectly centered in the whole. That's what Shan looked like. He was Naite with only half the width, and he looked ready to fall over.

"We're in a little trouble, Naite." Shan looked over his shoulder at the boulder. With a deep breath and a quick prayer that the stars show him a little luck for once, Temar stood.

"We?" Naite was asking as Temar stood. For a long second, Naite only stared. "Temar? Shan, what's going on?" He turned back to his brother, and this was the moment when they discovered whether or not Ben had corrupted Naite. Only now did Temar remember that it had been Naite who had turned down Cyla's request for a council hearing. He shuffled backward, well aware that if Naite wanted, he could physically overpower both of them.

"We need help," Shan said softly.

Again, there was a moment of silence, where Naite looked from Shan to Temar and then back to Shan. "You need to get the boy back to his master," he said firmly. Turning to Temar, he softened his voice so it had the same timbre as when he'd spoken to Temar in that shed where the council had first imprisoned him. Back then, the voice had been reassuring, but now, he could only feel cold, pure fear as Naite stepped toward him. "Temar, I understand the fear that comes with losing your control, I truly do. I'll even go back with you and talk to Ben with—"

"Look at him!" Shan snarled, grabbing his brother's arm and pulling him to a stop. "Just stop and look at him before you start preaching about the wonders of slavery. Look at him!"

Temar held his breath as the two brothers stared at each other in some contest of wills. He wanted to sink down and hide his legs, his bruises, the marks that proved how poorly he'd defended himself. He wanted to run before Shan could tell anyone else what had happened. He wanted to sink into the ground. Instead, he clenched his teeth and stood silent as Naite flicked on a flashlight and swung the beam over to him. The light traveled up his legs and hovered over the bruises. On his left leg, the bruise still had the shape of the hand that made it.

When he spoke, Naite's voice had an artificial calm to it. "Temar? How bad? How far did this go?"

"Do you need to ask?" Shan answered for him. "He wouldn't let me untie him because he's hiding the rest of the marks, so maybe you could lend him a knife so he can cut himself free." Naite clicked the light off and reached for his belt. When he walked forward, knife in hand and held out, handle first, his expression was as neutral as his voice. He didn't even glance down as Temar had to lift the bottom of his shirt to reach for the knife with hands half numb with being tied. He fumbled at the handle, not able to grip it right. It clattered to the ground, and Naite bent down to pick it up so fast that Temar didn't have a chance to get the nightshirt down in time to cover him.

Still crouching, Naite reached up with the knife and caught the rope with the blade, yanking at it so that Temar was pulled a step forward before the rope split. His hands were still tied, but they weren't tethered to his waist anymore. Wordlessly, Naite reached for his hands and slid the knife under one of the knots, slicing it before he turned his back.

Temar worked to shake the ropes loose, rubbing the newly freed ends against his stomach to unravel them as Naite walked back toward his brother.

"I'm going to see that man exiled."

"Naite—"

"I'm going to beat Ben Gratu until he begs for mercy, and then I'm going to see him exiled," Naite corrected himself, anger now coloring his words.

"Naite, wait a second." Shan put a hand in the middle of Naite's chest to stop him.

Naite pushed Shan's hand away. "I'm going to watch him. I'm going to go out there in a lifter and watch him as he lies on the sands and gets eaten alive by sandrats." He started back down the path, and Temar struggled to get his arms into the armholes of the shirt before he joined the conversation. Shan grabbed Naite's arm.

"Naite, stop. You can't do that." Naite dragged Shan for several yards before he stopped and slowly turned toward his brother.

"What?"

"You can't tell anyone what Ben did."

"You have two seconds to explain why you're defending this piece of pig shit, and then I'm going to make some unpleasant assumptions about you, brother."

Shan took a fast step back. "You can't think I would ever—"

"I wouldn't have thought you'd ever defend a man who did this," Naite gestured toward Temar.

"Now, as far as I'm concerned, defending a man who hurts someone is just as bad as being an abuser yourself, so no hiding behind your collar here, Shan. You explain why you want to keep this quiet, or I swear, you'll be meeting your God sooner than you expect."

Reaching out, Shan rested his hand on Naite's arm. From the way Naite slowly looked down at where they touched, he didn't exactly welcome the contact. "This is about more than what Ben did."

Naite crossed his arms and didn't look convinced.

"His friend has my sister," Temar spoke up for the first time.

"Cyla? She was sold to Ista Songwind. She's not even in Landing."

The disbelief cut at Temar until he wanted to simply be quiet and let Shan explain, but he wouldn't put Cyla in danger, and right now, Shan was not having a lot of luck convincing his brother of anything. "I heard Ben talking to someone on the phone, telling them to buy Cyla, and he said if I told anyone that he'd have someone kill her."

The first moon was up, and the winds had grown quiet, so the glow filtered down into the valley. Even in the dim light, the look of pure fury on Naite's face silenced him. The muscles on the sides of his neck corded, and his fists came up like he was going to hit someone, but instead he dropped his arms back down to his side.

"To hell with exile, I'm going to strangle him with my own hands. But, why?"

Temar ducked his head. "This is where it starts to sound a little crazy."

"It already sounds crazy, I just… I know those bruises too well, and for all his many faults, my idiot brother would never lie about something like this."

"Thank you for that vote of confidence," Shan said.

Naite only shrugged before he took a step toward Temar, focusing his attention there. "He might hallucinate, and from the amount of pipe juice he's been drinking, I don't doubt he's been talking to the pretty little elves following him around."

"Actually, it was you following me around. Even my hallucinations like to annoy me. However, that doesn't change the fact that this is bigger than the evil Ben has done to Temar."

Naite didn't turn to look at Shan or answer him, but he stopped. Temar watched the two brothers, and he could see Naite struggle with the need to do something. He could understand that, because every time he'd lain down for Ben, he'd felt the same thing. He'd known he should do something different, that he should have a better way to handle it, but he'd never been able to find any solution other than lying down and silently enduring. "Shan's right," Temar said softly. "It sounds crazy, but this is about more than what he did to me. What he did to me... it isn't anything compared to whatever is going on in the valley."

"It's enough to condemn him," Naite said firmly. "But I'm listening. Let's hear your crazy story."

chapter
fifteen

NAITE SAT on a boulder, his head in his hands, as Temar and Shan finished their story. "I still want to strangle him and let the sandrats have his body," he said, but his voice had a weariness to it that suggested he wasn't about to track Ben down at that exact moment.

"I have first dibs at strangling him," Shan said, and once again he was looking at Temar with guilt and despair. Temar didn't say anything, but he thought he should get the first chance at Ben. He thought of his hands around Ben's neck, but the fantasy quickly slid out of his control and turned into Ben's hands on him. He shook his head and forced himself to focus on the present… on the cooling night air and the dust under his butt as he sat on the ground… on the two brothers who sat near each other on the boulder.

"You're a priest. You're supposed to be turning the other cheek."

"I ran out of cheeks."

Naite snorted, but Temar had to smile at the joke. The smile chased away the last lingering wisps of the dark memory that had tried to catch him.

"You can only plow a field one row at a time. So, we need to get you two somewhere that you can heal up some, we need to get Cyla out of Songwind's custody, and we need to figure out what sort of games Ben is playing with water."

"Any ideas?" Shan asked. He finally looked away from Temar to really focus on his brother, and Temar shifted uncomfortably on the ground.

"Fuck, no. You're the grand planner."

"We could grab her." Shan didn't sound confident about that answer. As much as Temar wanted to grab Cyla, he didn't like the plan either. He'd been afraid to even tell Naite, so they didn't know who they could trust. If they grabbed her, who knew how many people would accuse them of kidnapping, or worse. Temar didn't plan to end up food for sandcats, not after everything he'd done to survive. They needed a reason to bring her back to Landing without letting anyone know that Shan and Temar were involved. If Ben smelled a plot, he could do terrible things before anyone stopped him.

"Does anyone know I'm missing?" Temar asked. He got a leg under him and tried to find the pebble that was incessantly poking his thigh.

Naite shrugged. "Don't know. If I asked around, I could find out. Most of the workers talk to me, even when the landowners think they don't."

Temar finally caught the pebble between his fingers, rolling it back and forth as he thought about the need to get Cyla out of danger. "If you thought I'd run away from Ben, what would you do?"

"Congratulate you and gut that son of a planetless whore."

Temar shook his head. "No, I mean before. If you still thought Ben was as good as Tom Sulli, what would you do?"

"There are other rumors," Shan said, before Naite could answer. "The rumor is that Erqu Gazer abused Temar. Sua Smith told me that they're all worried because Ben is having so much trouble keeping him from flying off into rages." Temar heard the guilt in Shan's voice, like he had done something wrong by believing her, even though Temar had thrown enough fits to convince anyone that he was mad.

"Temar? Rages?" Naite didn't even try to hide his disbelief as he looked over.

That made Temar blush, because he'd hated the public humiliations nearly as much as the private pain. "Ben ordered me to throw fits so he would have an excuse to tie me up and punish me," Temar admitted. He threw the pebble as far as he could into the field. "But if you'd heard all these rumors and then found out I'd run away, what would you do?"

Naite thought about that for a second. "I would want to find you, to help you before you did something too unforgivably stupid. People strike out when they're hurt, and they don't always strike out at the right person, so I'd argue for giving you a second chance before stripping your adult rights."

Temar was half surprised Naite didn't talk about exile, but then stripping a person of their rights was, in some ways, as terrible as exile. If he'd ended up in Ben's custody with no chance of freedom, he would have preferred exile.

"Wait," Shan said, "I see where Temar's going. Naite, last night we hid in that old crack behind the Kelligan farm. You remember that place?"

"Yeah. I still don't see where you two are going." Naite crossed his arms.

"If I were hiding, you would be about the only person who would know all my hiding spots in the valley," Shan said, his voice growing more confident with each word. "Our valley is the largest of the three valleys, and a full search could take weeks. Maybe months if someone really knew the territory."

"And I do," Temar added.

"But siblings know each other well enough to know each other's secrets." Relief made Shan's words tumble out, so that the normally articulate priest sounded young and breathless.

"We didn't," Naite simply said, his voice flat. Temar could see how that shut Shan down. After listening to Shan's drunken conversations with an invisible Naite, he could well imagine the secret the two brothers hadn't shared until after they were grown. He wondered what happened to Yan Polli. He had vague memories of the man from his childhood, but then he wasn't there anymore, and no one had explained.

"Cyla knows me that well," Temar said before the brothers could get off track. "When Dad was in a bad mood from the pipe juice, we'd hide on Ben's farm. There's a narrow path that leads to nowhere. You can sit in the shade in the afternoon and see this half of the valley from there. And there are a dozen other spots where she'd know to look. But she wouldn't want to help you."

Naite nodded. "Which would actually be better. If she's not cooperative, then I have good cause to keep her in my custody and try to convince her to help. Trust me, if she's with me, she'll be safe. I'll gut Ben Gratu myself before I'll let him touch her."

The look on Naite's face was murderously clear, even in the light of the double moons. Temar didn't realize how afraid he'd been until the fear was suddenly eased. Even though he hadn't really known Naite well before tonight, he did trust that Cyla would be safe with him. They would probably enjoy cursing each other out and trying to stare each other down. "But she can't know," Temar suddenly blurted. "She'll want to kill Ben, so you can't tell her about...."

"I know how she'd feel." Naite stood. "So, as soon as I catch a hint of a rumor, I'll go get Cyla, and that's one row that's plowed under. The second problem is getting you two fed and dressed in something that doesn't make you look like refugees straight off a shipwreck."

Shan got up. "I know we need to clean up. Right now, anyone could track me from the smell, but we have to be careful who we trust. I was thinking of trying to get into town and taking refuge in the church with Div."

Naite looked like he was going to follow, but he didn't. Shan got a couple of steps down the path before he noticed that Naite was still standing by the boulder with his arms crossed. "We'd have to cover a lot of territory. Without a sled, we'd be lucky to get there by morning." Naite's voice made it clear he didn't like the plan.

"It's not like we have a lot of choices," Shan said. "If Ben Gratu is involved, who can we trust? Normally, I'd call Lilian Freeland the most incorruptible woman on Livre, but she has power, and now that I know what Ben was doing behind closed doors, God forgive me, I'm wondering about the rest of the planet."

Instead of arguing that point, Naite nodded his agreement. "I've never been one for trusting people, so I'm not even going to try to defend Lilian. That woman will do whatever she wants, and if the rest of the world agrees or disagrees, I don't think she cares. I say we go to Tom Sulli."

"Naite," Shan objected loudly, but Naite held up his hand to stop him.

"I trust Tom. After I left our farm, I was… I had trouble adjusting." Naite made a face like he'd bit something sour. When Naite turned away from Shan and focused on Temar, his expression got softer. "At home, I learned to make trades that a man maybe shouldn't. But once I'd learned to make that particular bargain, it seemed natural. It seemed safe. I tempted Tom more than once, and if that man had evil in him, he had every chance to show it."

Temar held his breath because he understood exactly what Naite meant. Every time he lay down for Ben, it had felt more natural, until Temar almost wished he was back there now. He'd hated being in Ben's control, but he knew the rules there. He had a certain safety, as long as he could dance with the monster. But out here, things were more confusing and more dangerous. He wasn't dancing with the monster; he was prey for it.

"What do you mean, you 'tempted' him?" Shan asked. Temar glanced over, and Shan looked honestly confused.

"Figure it out," Naite suggested coldly. "So, Temar, do we try to make a run into town to reach Div, or do we trust Tom?"

The question curdled in Temar's stomach, because as much as he wanted to reclaim the control that had been taken from him, he didn't want it. He had trusted the wrong people and made the wrong choices, and he didn't want to make this decision. "Do you trust him?" Temar asked, his voice coming out so soft he wasn't sure they heard him.

Naite nodded. "With my life. More importantly, I trust him with your life."

"Shan?" Temar asked. He looked at the priest, hoping to find some sort of guidance.

Shaking his head, Shan returned to his brother's side. "If we get caught, I will never let you forget that I thought this was a bad idea, Naite," he said, but he passed them as he walked toward the Sulli farm.

"And if we don't get caught, you're going to give your God credit. You never do change." Naite's words didn't come out as condemning as Temar expected… they sounded almost fond. Sometimes he and Cyla would fight the same way. They had a game where they pretended the terraforming ships came with a wealth of water and new settlers, and they fought over what they would do with the money. Temar would purchase an internship with Dee'eta Sun and hire out workers to pull every pipe trap out of their land. Cyla would argue for selling the land and investing the money by loaning it out to the settlers until she could get enough profit to buy the whole damn valley. Naite's voice had that same exasperation that Cyla's had when she explained the advantage of interest and the credit system that ruled most of the universe.

However, Shan was quicker with the comeback than Temar normally was. "At least I don't think the world ends at the edge of the field." The jab didn't seem to bother Naite much.

"Easier to live in a field than a cloud."

The brothers continued their half fight in whispers and hand gestures that grew more and more animated as they walked the dusty path. Temar hadn't noticed how close Naite had come until the man's shoulder brushed against him. He lost a half step as fear curled around him. He looked up, expecting anger or lust, but Naite was looking at his brother with a sort of fond disgust. In fact, he was ignoring Temar so totally that he continued to walk, leaving Temar a bit behind, trotting to catch up. Shan was so caught up in the fight that he was too busy to even look at Temar with pity and guilt, and Temar only realized how much those emotions had weighed him down, once they were gone. He hurried up and reached Naite's side again, walking next to him as the brothers' fight grew more and more heated. It was strange listening to real anger seep into the words, even though they were still talking in whispers.

"Okay, peace, already," Naite whispered.

"That's right, call off the fight when you're on the verge of losing it." Shan's whisper sounded so genuinely aggravated that even Naite stopped and gave him a second look.

"I'm calling off the fight because we're coming up on the Sulli buildings. I don't think you want to get caught out here, but if you want to get caught and trust your God to fix it, go ahead." Naite stepped to the side and gestured up the path. Shan glared, but Naite shook his head and ignored the expression. Maybe, like Temar, he couldn't figure it out.

"You two need to hide while I go in and make sure the way is clear. If it isn't, I'll find some excuse to bring a hauler out, and we'll have to hide you and hope no one smells Shan. No offense, but as bad as you smell, Shan, you need to hide here." He gestured toward the end of a long fence with grapevines nearly burying it. "I'll take Temar in closer."

"What?" Shan took a step toward Naite, his fists clenched, and Temar backed up, really not understanding the relationship here.

Naite didn't look particularly threatened, but he was a good fifty pounds heavier than a healthy Shan, and Shan wasn't healthy right now. He was a stick-figure version of himself, and Temar wanted to grab his arm and pull him back before he did something to anger Naite too much. He wasn't sure if he was more afraid of Naite striking out or of him leaving. He and Shan couldn't do this alone. Ben had too many people, and he had hidden his tracks too well.

"If one of you is found, that won't be the end of the game. If Temar is caught, he needs to keep quiet, and Ben will assume he's still controlling the boy. It's going to take a lot for Ben to believe Temar would turn on him, isn't it?" Naite looked at him. For a second, Temar had to think about that. In the end, though, he could only nod. Ben might believe he panicked or that he tried to get away, but he would never believe Temar would plot against him. He certainly wouldn't feel threatened, not until he had proof.

"And if you're caught, no one is going to listen to anything you say as long as you smell like you've been swimming in pipe juice. Besides, from the story you told, you didn't actually know much before Temar filled in the blanks. Use your head for something other than praying, Shan. I'll take Temar in a little closer, since we need to get him inside quicker."

Shan opened his mouth like he was going to argue, but then he took a step backward without unclenching his fists.

"Come on, Temar. You can hide behind the compost." Naite moved toward the farm more carefully.

Temar looked at Shan for some sort of explanation, but Shan looked away and knelt down beside the grape arbor, in the shadow, so even the moonlight didn't reach him. That didn't leave Temar much choice, and he went trotting after Naite, still not understanding the currents around him. He never did understand people well. He didn't understand his sister's anger or his father's despair. He didn't even understand the kids at school, so his sudden inability to understand Shan shouldn't be a surprise, but it still upset him somehow. Ever since seeing Shan drunk, he felt like he had some sort of key to seeing what Shan really had inside. It was like Shan had gone from being an untouchable part of the church to a real man, with hopes and fears and this incredible sense of honor, and for one moment, Temar had the key to understanding him. Now someone had taken that key away.

Naite was moving fast, now that the buildings were coming into view. The Sulli place was much smaller than the Gratu farm. The main house was tall and narrow, like Ben's. The early buildings had corner struts of steel that allowed them to stand tall and square without buckling in the wind. However, the buildings added later used windwood, with sloping walls to shrug off the wind that snuck into the valley during storms. Temar didn't come out this way often, and he didn't know which buildings had workers and which had storage and which stood empty, waiting for harvest.

Naite stopped near a tall round tank that pointed up toward the sky, and Temar ran to his side, his heart pounding with fear. There were men and women nearby who would look at him with pity and hold him down and call for Ben to come get him. They would congratulate Ben on his patience and tell Temar to be grateful that he had such a good master. The thought made his stomach twist with a need to vomit out all the fear.

When he stopped, he stopped close enough that his leg pressed against Naite as they crouched.

"Okay, I'm going to go talk to Tom. Temar, you do... you understand why Shan came to me, right?" Naite's voice was normally clipped and fast, like he didn't have time to stop and talk to someone while work needed to get done. But now he sounded almost like Shan.

Temar nodded. "Shan said things. He was drunk."

"Shan still is drunk," Naite corrected him, the edge back in his voice, but then his next words were soft again. "I don't know how much he let slip when he was talking to the invisible fairies in his head."

"He said your father did the things that...." Temar stopped.

"That Ben did to you," Naite finished for him. "Yeah, he did. And that's why Shan knows that I will kill someone before I let that happen again. I'm not the boy who offered to warm Tom's bed for a promise that he wouldn't make me go back to my father."

Temar had been studying the pattern of the shadows on the dust, but he looked up at that.

"I won't let anyone turn me into that again, but I'm not going to feel bad about what I did back then either. It didn't make me weak—it made me a survivor. It's like being in one of those survival vids, where people in a disabled ship eat the dead to stay alive." Temar's stomach was really churning now, and he wished Naite hadn't brought up the topic at all, but Naite kept going. "But don't think that Shan doesn't have issues of his own. He's about as likely to have a self-enlightened moment as a sandcat."

"He's the priest," Temar objected. Shan had rescued him, and he felt some obligation to stand up for the man. Even before everything had gone so very wrong, Shan had always been kind, and he'd spoken with a slow calm that made Temar believe there was a bigger purpose to life... that God was looking out for him. True, recent events had shaken his confidence a bit.

"He is what he is," Naite answered without really answering. "If you're going to take out your piss and vinegar on someone, take it out on Tom. He can handle it better than Shan. Deal?"

Temar nodded, not entirely sure what he was agreeing to. Naite gave a deep sigh before he turned toward the house and strolled up, like it was perfectly normal for someone to come calling in the middle of the night. It was so late even lovers would have given up the privacy of the field, and the children would have fallen asleep. However, Naite walked right through the front door of the Sulli house, and all Temar could do was wait because, for now, it was all out of his control. He found that a relief.

chapter
sixteen

TEMAR DIDN'T have long to wait before Naite came back out, but he walked around to the side of the house. Temar ducked down lower, fear crawling through his belly. He hadn't always been afraid all the time, but now he couldn't control his own emotions. After a few seconds, Naite returned, pushing a wheelbarrow.

He walked over to a circle in the yard. It was a stone circle, no more than six or eight inches high, with a metal cover about two feet in diameter. Naite pulled the cover off and then dumped the contents of the wheelbarrow down into what was obviously some sort of well. After he put the cover back on, Naite pushed the wheelbarrow toward Temar.

He moved silently in the dark, and when he came around the corner, he stopped and flipped back a canvas cover attached to the metal frame of the wheelbarrow.

"Get in," Naite said.

"But—"

"It's not that unusual for me to help Tom out if things get busy around here. But a small, blond man is going to stand out. Just get in." Naite's voice grew gentler for a moment. "It's okay, Temar. We're only going as far as the house."

Temar looked at the wind-worn house and the large yard that separated his hiding place from the front door. With a nod, he crawled up into the wheelbarrow and curled himself into a tight ball. Naite flicked the canvas over his head, and then Temar felt the world tip and tilt as Naite pushed him toward the house.

The darkness, the silence, the sense of the world swaying, all combined to make the bile rise in Temar's throat, but before he could throw up, the wheelbarrow thumped down onto the ground, and Naite pulled back the canvas cover. "Go," he whispered, nodding toward an open door.

Temar swallowed as he looked at that black doorway against the gray night. Run into it. Run into the unknown. His heart pounded so fast that Temar could feel the pulse in his skin, feel the pressure building behind his eyes.

"Go. I'll go get Shan."

They needed to get Shan inside—he was in even more danger than Temar. Ben liked his games too much to give up a playtoy, but Shan… if Ben or Ista Songwind found out he was alive, they'd kill him. Temar gave one quick nod before he climbed out of the wheelbarrow and dashed for that door.

"Temar?" a voice whispered the moment he crossed the threshold. Temar nearly turned around and fled back out into the night. "I'm Tom. Naite told you about me, right?" A very small light turned on, and now the shape of a man sitting on the bottom step of the stairs was clear. He was a large man, and his gray hair shone in the dim light. Tom Sulli. Temar vaguely recognized him from the season-end festival.

"You held his slave papers… after his father hurt him," Temar answered. In the dim light, he saw Tom nod.

"I did. Naite says you need help." When Temar didn't answer, Tom continued. "Naite's going to bring Shan in the same way, but we may need some help with him. From the way Naite described him, he's good and drunk. The last thing we need is a drunk priest waking all the field hands."

"He had to drink pipe juice to walk out of the desert."

Tom leaned forward. "Naite said something about that. What the hell happened?"

"Tom?" a woman called from upstairs.

"Naite's here, Hannal. I'll be up in a bit," Tom answered.

There was a pause. "If you two want breakfast, let me know." There was a definite click as the door closed upstairs.

Temar frowned. "Naite still comes here?"

The clock ticked in the silence as Tom thought about his answer. "Some wounds, they don't heal fast, and they don't heal clean. I suppose most men would go to the priest, but that's not easy when the priest is your brother and you're angry at God." Tom pushed himself up to his feet. "There's a room through there. We'll probably need to burn the clothes, if they're as bad as Naite says. I'll get the incinerator going. You get some water run into the slosh stall," he said with a nod toward an open door that led to a bedroom. Tom had to pass close to Temar to get past, and Temar held his breath. "My father built this for my grandparents, so it has its own bathroom attached." Then Tom headed into the mechanics room to start the incinerator, leaving Temar to get the bathroom ready.

He quickly found the door to the bathroom on the other side of the first floor bedroom, and Temar filled the slosh bucket with warm water. When he'd been in Ben's house, Ben always claimed he didn't trust Temar with water. He'd make Temar stand with his hands flat against the chilly metal wall while Ben poured cups of water over him, soaping him down. The sight of the slosh stall made Temar shiver now. He wasn't naked, though. He wasn't powerless. True, he had very little power, compared to Ben Gratu, who had his mysterious friends and his plans and his schemes. However, he didn't have to fear a bathroom.

The tall stall with the stark, metal walls, designed to guide every drop of water into a reclamation drain, inspired fear… that made a wave of anger crash into Temar. He wasn't a helpless child. He wouldn't be afraid of a damned bathroom. He wasn't weak.

Forcing his legs to work despite the mingling of fear and anger, Temar moved into the bathroom.

"I'm fine," a voice quietly snapped.

"You're drunk," a second voice answered, so quiet that Temar couldn't identify the speaker, although a good guess would be Naite.

"I know that. You should have seen how drunk I was yesterday. Or the day before. Mary and Joseph, I don't even know how long I've been drunk. You were there. How long was it?"

Temar went through the bedroom to stand in the door while Naite tried to get Shan to cross the kitchen, one foot at a time.

"I wasn't there. You did this on your own."

Tom came to the entry to the mechanics room, his eyes going to the stairs. "Maybe we should get Hannal."

"The fewer people who know, the less the danger," Naite disagreed. "Hannal is a wonderful woman, but every thought she has goes across her face."

"And if she saw what Ben has done, she'd gut him with a meat knife," Tom agreed.

"Funny, I thought she'd use a dull knife, to make it last longer," Naite said. "Shan, just walk," he snapped, his voice quiet, even if the tone took on a sharper edge.

"Shan, you need to come this way," Temar said. Shan's steps had been uncoordinated, and he'd staggered most of the day, but in here, there were tables and walls and rugs to navigate. He wasn't doing all that well. Temar had noticed that his father's body always recovered slower than his mind. It meant his father's body rarely recovered at all, because by the time his father had sobered up enough to have a conversation, he stumbled out to get more pipe juice.

Shan looked up and made a bleary sort of eye contact before he moved toward Temar. "I'm really not that drunk. I can't get my feet to work," he apologized in a whisper. Shan and Naite struggled through the doorway to the bedroom, and Tom followed before closing the door behind him.

"You are that drunk, Shan. I've never seen anyone as drunk as you."

"You should have seen dad at the end. He was really drunk," Shan said in an exaggerated whisper. "When he lay down in the sand, he didn't even twitch."

"Shan," Naite said in a disgusted voice, "you weren't there. You don't know."

"I watched him do it. Before I left home. He'd wander up to the Cygnus gate to watch the sunset and sit on the rock out there."

"That's not the same." Naite shoved Shan at a wall and sort of wedged him into a corner formed by a dresser before he pulled at Shan's dirty shirt.

"It is," Shan protested. "I used to tell him he should lie down in the sand."

"I told him that all the time." Naite struggled to get Shan's arm out of the shirt.

"I'm a priest, Naite. I'm supposed to be morally better than that. But I basically told him to go kill himself, and I want to kill Ben Gratu with my own two hands." Shan kept gesturing with his hands, which made getting the shirt off harder.

"That's normal enough. So do I."

"Would someone like to explain why we're not killing Ben? Right now, I'd be fine with that plan," Tom interrupted. Temar's guts twisted in fear, and he backed up toward the far wall. There were too many people in the room, too much anger, and too many emotions that he couldn't understand.

"He's having Ista Songwind hold Cyla hostage," Naite said.

"Which I just about blew everything by going over to Red Plain," Shan said, his voice muffled as Naite pulled his shirt over his head.

"Holy stars, Shan. You look like a stick figure," Naite complained. Temar had to agree. Shan's ribs stuck out so much it looked like someone had carved the flesh out from between them.

"That's nothing. You should see my leg," Shan said with a shrug.

"I think I need to get the medicine kit. And I'm telling Hannal about the murder attempt and the desert journey the priest took."

"Tom," Naite growled. He turned around, and Shan caught Naite's arm, like he could really keep Naite back.

Holding up a hand, Tom continued. "I won't tell her about Temar, and a murder attempt is reason enough that she'll understand that we cannot tell anyone he's here, but she trained with a doctor for a year. She'll be able to check him better than either of us, Naite."

"What about me?" Temar asked. He suddenly found himself afraid to leave Shan. It was almost as if the fantasy rescue would vanish with Shan.

Tom frowned. "Would it bother you to hide in the closet?" he asked, nodding toward a tall closet chest that stood on the other side of the bed. It was large enough for Temar to stretch out and sleep on the bottom. The early settlers had owned more personal belongings than Temar could understand one person owning. When he'd been at Ben's, he would have enjoyed a chance to curl up in a small, private place like a closet.

"The slosh stall scared me. The closet would actually be cozy," Temar said, the words slipping out before he could think about how crazy they made him sound. He was tired, exhausted even. He hadn't slept much lately, and he hadn't slept at all for two nights now. All three men were silent, and Temar felt the heat rise to his face.

"If you can face your fears already, you're a stronger man than I was at your age," Naite said with a sympathetic look, and Temar wasn't sure how to take that.

Tom changed the topic back to practical matters. "You smell a bit like Shan here. If you're in the closet, Hannal might smell you, and you're certainly going to be stuck smelling yourself. Do you want to clean up?"

"You don't have to use the slosh stall," Naite added.

"It's the fastest way to clean up," Temar said. "I'll be quick so you can get Shan some help." Ignoring his own dry fear, Temar hurried into the bathroom and closed the door behind him. For a second, the echo of the closing door against the smooth metal of the slosh stall made Temar cold, as he thought of Ben's smile and his hands on Temar's skin. But Ben wasn't here.

Clenching his teeth, Temar stripped out of his dirty shirt, and for the first time, he realized that he did smell bad. It was just that Shan smelled so much worse, he hadn't noticed. The sharp stench of fear clung to him, along with his own musky sweat smell and enough of Shan's pipe-juice smell to tickle his nose.

He cleaned up as fast as he could. The water from the cup running over his smooth skin reminded him too much of those mornings when Ben would spend time in the stall, pouring water over Temar's welts and then running a rough thumb over the bruises. He'd enjoyed Temar's bruises the way another man might appreciate the beauty in a piece of glass. It was as if he'd demoted Temar from a human to an object, and that had been harder than the beatings, harder than the sex, and the sex was hard because Temar had had very few lovers before Ben… not that Ben had been a lover. Temar knew what Ben had done, even if his mind skittered away from the word. He didn't have time to panic, not now.

When Temar used the cup to rinse the last of the soap and dirt off his body, he realized he had only one nightshirt, which smelled as bad as Shan. Carefully inching the door open, he looked into the bedroom, hiding behind the door. Tom and Naite stood near the bed, and Shan's one bare leg was visible between them.

"Unholy stars, how the hell did you walk with that?"

"I was drunk."

"Clearly, you were very drunk," Naite said.

"I could have told you that. Wait. I did tell you that. Your memory is worse than mine, and I'm still half drunk."

"You're still completely drunk, and you're a shitty drunk, Shan," Naite disagreed. He shifted, and Temar had a view of Shan's leg. The whole side of it was torn open and weeping blood and pus. Temar's stomach revolted, and he gave a loud dry heave before he could slam the door shut and stagger to the toilet.

Temar's throat and mouth burned as he threw up yellow bile. How could he have missed the fact that Shan had a serious injury?

There was a soft knock on the door. "Temar?" It sounded like Tom.

"I don't have any clothes," Temar said, even though that didn't seem like a very big worry now. Shan could lose his leg with an injury like that.

"Crack the door open, and I can pass you some," Tom suggested. Temar hung over the toilet, wondering if his stomach would try to turn inside out again if he stood, but he risked it. The world spun a little, but Temar turned the handle and opened the door enough for Tom to hand in a brown shirt and gray pants. "The wound is a burn. They always look worse than they are, but Hannal will call in the doctor if she can't handle it."

"And then Ben will find him," Temar said as he pulled on the clothes. They were a little large, and the cut of the pants suggested they'd been made for a woman. The crotch rode up uncomfortably, but he felt better for having clean clothes on. However, he didn't feel better about calling a doctor and risking more people finding out that Shan was alive and Temar on the run. He couldn't see a way out of the trap Ben had built. Even if these men turned on Ben, he was nothing more than the leaf of a pipe trap plant. Unless they pulled out the root, the whole thing would grow back. The truth was that they didn't know where to find the root. Ista Songwind was part of it, but from the way Ben talked to her, she wasn't all that important.

"Ben won't find him or hurt him," Tom promised. "I made a promise to Naite once. I promised that he would always have a safe place here, and in ten years, I've never gone back on my word. I'm giving you that same promise now. You and Shan will always be safe in this house."

Temar pulled the door open and looked at Tom. Now that the lights were on, he could see him more clearly. Age lines around his eyes and mouth suggested he'd smiled a lot in his life, but he had a serious expression on his face now. Temar wanted to believe him. He did. But he'd trusted wrong too many times. Cyla had destroyed their family through stupidity and impatience. Ben had betrayed them. His father had failed to protect them.

"If you hide in the closet, I'll get Hannal. That burn needs to get tended." Tom stepped away from the bathroom door.

"I'll be fine, Temar. I burned it on the bike," Shan said, apparently not bothered by the huge, weeping burn on his leg. Temar's father once put a nail through his foot and hadn't even noticed it.

"The idiot will survive," Naite seconded. His hand rested on his brother's shoulder, and Temar realized he couldn't do anything to help. He either trusted Hannal enough to let her in on his secret, or he hid in the closet, but he couldn't do anything to help Shan.

Without a word, Temar headed for the closet. He wasn't ready to trust anyone else.

chapter
seventeen

TEMAR FINALLY fell asleep to the sound of Hannal fussing over Shan. The closet had slits at the bottom of the doors to let air move, and he watched legs and feet enter and leave as she treated Shan, but no doctor showed up before Temar finally drifted off. The closet was small, and his elbow was jammed into a corner with a box that smelled like feet, but he was more comfortable than he had been in weeks, and he couldn't put off sleep any longer.

When Temar woke, he thought for a moment that he was home—that he had fallen asleep on the floor. He didn't have any restraints on, and Ben always woke before him. Every day he woke to Ben's hands exploring, finding the edge of the most convenient bruise and pushing his thumb into it. The feeling of stillness and the quiet left him disoriented enough that he panicked before he finally realized where he was.

After realizing he was in Tom's closet, Temar sat with his knees pulled up to his chest as he tried to give his heart time to slow.

"Is that you?" Shan asked quietly. Temar leaned down to look out the ventilation shafts, but there weren't any legs in his field of view.

With infinite slowness, Temar pushed the closet door open and looked out into the room. Shan was clean and shaved and dressed in a dark green shirt that made his sunburn look even worse. "Are we alone?" he whispered, so softly he wasn't sure Shan heard him.

Shan nodded. "Hannal finally left me to rest. But then she keeps coming in and making me drink more water, so I can't sleep."

"Why?"

Shan shrugged. "Something about me looking yellow and her worrying about my liver. After all the pipe juice I drank on the desert, if I didn't die out there, I'm not going to drop dead in here."

Temar wasn't sure that was true, but he didn't argue. He stretched and came close to the bed, looking at Shan's legs under the cover of the sheet. "Is your leg…?"

"It's fine."

"It didn't look fine."

Shan flipped the sheet back so Temar could see the white bandage taped over his lower leg. "It is fine. It looked bad last night because it was so dirty, and the dead skin was all stuck to it. I burned it days ago."

"Then why did it look… moist?" Temar asked with a moue of disgust.

With a shrug, Shan put the sheet back. "I don't think it could heal right without me eating or drinking enough. It was a little crusty."

"And full of pus."

"It isn't that bad. Hannal didn't even threaten to call the doctor… at least not after Tom and Naite explained about the murder plot."

Temar sat on the edge of the bed and tried to wrap his thoughts around it all. The sun was up, so he must have slept at least eight hours. His stomach rumbled unhappily, and he eyed the plate of food next to Shan's bed. The man had nearly died, so taking his food seemed a little uncharitable, but Temar's stomach felt like it was ready to collapse in on itself.

"You have to be hungry. Grab something," Shan said, gesturing toward the tray. "Tom has snuck me some extra food, so we don't have to share."

Temar didn't argue. The tray had a bowl of nuts and another of fresh peas, bright green in the white bowl, and then fresh bread with some sort of fruit spread on it. He grabbed a piece of the bread.

"Did Naite go to get Cyla yet?" he asked. His neck muscles felt overstretched and sore, but other than that, Temar felt a lot better this morning. Shan looked at him with some amusement that Temar didn't understand.

"Naite heard from one of the workers over on the Gratu farm that you vanished. Ben tried to keep it quiet until full sunup, when his workers found him searching for you. Then Naite told everyone that siblings knew each other's hiding places before he headed over to Red Plain."

"Hopefully he'll get to Cyla before Ista can do anything to her," Temar said, his mouth full of bread.

"He got her and came back already," Shan said.

"But... how?" Temar looked at the clock, but it was only a little past noon, so Naite hadn't had the time to go and get back.

"You lost a whole day, Temar. Naite went to get her yesterday and got back late last night. Cyla is loudly accusing the men over at the Gratu farm, and even Ben himself, of driving you away. She's telling everyone that your artistic temperament couldn't handle slavery." Shan frowned. "You're a lot stronger than your sister gives you credit for."

Temar shrugged. "She only sees that glass is fragile, not that it can be incredibly strong when used right."

Shan frowned again. "I guess that's true. How are you feeling?"

Until Shan asked, Temar hadn't given much thought to how he was feeling. His ass had a distant itch that had replaced the normal overly stretched and hot feeling he'd learned to live with. His neck hurt, and a few of the bruises were still bothering him. Physically, he felt better than he had in a long time. However, he felt like he was trying to walk down a sand dune. One wrong move and the whole mountain of sand would land on his head and drown him.

"Afraid."

"You're doing better than I am, then. I'm terrified and confused," Shan confessed. "'You see my casting down, and are afraid,'" he said in that gentle voice he often used in church.

"Is that the Bible?"

Shan nodded. "The Book of Job. God decided to test a good man in order to prove a point to the devil. Div tells me that I should spend less time reading Job and more time reading Matthew."

Temar had no idea what that meant, but he was starting to see Shan as not only a flesh and blood man with a life apart from the church, but also as someone who clearly didn't see himself as a particularly good priest.

"I always thought you were a good priest," Temar blurted out.

"Um… thank you." Shan frowned. "While I always appreciate a compliment, is there a reason for this one?"

Temar stood up from the bed and moved to the wall. Someone had painted a picture of a lander, with its heavy, shielded bottom, rockets firing as it came down on the face of Livre. This room faced the rock, and it didn't have a window. So the painter had painted a frame around the scene, as though the person in the room was looking out onto those early landings. "When you were drunk, you were saying some things."

Shan groaned. "I imagine I said quite a lot."

"You insulted yourself a lot."

"Why does that not surprise me?" Shan sounded tired. Temar turned around to look at him. "I suppose you could say I've been having a crisis of conscience lately."

"About me?" Temar asked. He could put some of the pieces together. Shan's father had hurt Naite, and Shan hadn't understood that as a child, so he'd done his own share of trying to get his revenge on their father's favorite son. Given that background, Temar wasn't surprised Shan had assumed Temar's father had hurt him, that he had missed the signs. However, during all their walking, Shan kept talking to both Temar and some hallucination of Temar, and some things simply didn't make a lot of sense.

Shan's gaze dropped to the bed. "I'm trying to figure that out for myself, Temar. Sometimes people expect priests to be perfect, and we're people, with all the same flaws as the rest of the species." He slowly looked up.

"Like fear?"

"Like fear," Shan agreed.

"And lust?"

Shan froze and grew pale. "I wouldn't ever...." Shan stopped and took a deep breath before changing tactics. "I took a vow. I committed myself to the church, and if I'm struggling with that vow, I still won't break it."

Temar didn't know what Shan meant by that. "So, you're going to stay a priest?"

Shan closed his eyes. "I may question my faith, and I may choose to leave the priesthood, but I won't break a vow. You are safe with me. I would never touch you," Shan said in a contrite voice. "You don't have to be afraid of me."

Temar studied Shan. He'd never been afraid of Shan. Never. Okay, maybe a little at first. Or a lot. And when Shan moved fast, sometimes Temar's heart pounded fast because it panicked before Temar could stop and remind it that Shan would never hurt him. Drunk and suffering, Shan had still protected him. "I'm not afraid of you," Temar said.

When Shan looked up, it was clear that he didn't believe Temar at all.

"I know you're not like Ben. I know that," Temar said firmly. He needed to hear the words out loud. He needed to remind himself that not everyone would hurt him. His father had been a gentle man, even when drunk. The moment he thought that, Temar remembered a time when he'd been ten or twelve when he'd yelled at his father, and his father had exploded in rage. However, that had been the rare exception. Violence wasn't inevitable. Shan hadn't been violent. "Sometimes movement startles me... I remember Ben's hands on me, or I'll see something out of the corner of my eye, and I'll think it's Ben reaching for me," Temar admitted.

Shan swallowed, his Adam's apple bobbing as he fisted the sheets. Temar looked around the room, uncomfortable with Shan's sudden discomfort. It happened. He didn't want to give the memory more power than to just accept that it happened.

"When a blower has a piece explode in his hands," Temar started slowly, feeling his way through the words, "he has to learn to watch the glass more carefully, or he has to give up working glass. I'm more careful, Shan. I'm not going to stop working glass."

Temar made deliberate eye contact with Shan. Shan met his gaze and held it for several minutes.

"I'm glad," he finally said. "Whatever I said when I was drunk, I apologize. I may not have behaved well—"

"You did your best to protect me, even when you were so drunk you fell on the rhubarb," Temar interrupted.

Shan cringed a little. "Not my finest moment. And I suspect that I was verbally clumsy, so if I've said anything to make you worry about my commitment to the priesthood or my lust, I am sorry."

"I have to pee," Temar said before he turned and fled for the bathroom, not willing to have any more discussion on the point. You didn't cool the glass too quickly. Glass had to settle on its own time, or it would shatter. Behind him, Shan didn't say a word as Temar closed the bathroom door. Too late, Temar wondered if Hannal had heard any of that. If she had, Temar could only hope they could trust her. His stomach churned at the thought that this was getting too large—too many people knew, and any one of them could let something slip to Ben. Worse, they didn't know who else might be working with him.

Temar listened at the door before edging carefully out.

"Is Hannal around?"

Shan shook his head. "She's got two kids of her own under six and four more young ones from workers on the farm. She'll have her hands full until nightfall, when the workers get in from the field."

Blowing out a relieved breath, Temar came the rest of the way into the bedroom and grabbed the bowl of fresh peas. Ben's farm didn't have children, but most did. Retired unskilled workers, who couldn't handle the fields anymore, would settle on some farm with kids and live out a sort of retirement as they tended the ones too young to go to school yet and did small odd jobs they could still manage with swollen fingers. If Tom had that many families on the farm, he would have even more school-aged kids who would return from Landing when school ended.

"We're going to have trouble getting out of here without being seen."

"If we leave before three or four in the morning, yes, we are," Shan agreed.

Temar popped several fresh peas into his mouth. Peas tasted the way Temar imaged Earth must have smelled—green. They were an expensive crop and a luxury Temar rarely got to enjoy, so he took a second to savor them. "Do we stay here and wait for Naite to do something?" Temar wasn't sure what Naite could do. Ben had covered his tracks well. When Temar thought Landholder Young stole their water, it took him six months to collect enough data to even justify a full investigation. And Ben had burned that.

"When Naite dragged your sister over to your old farm to try to make her show him all your old hiding places, Naite threw a fit about the state of the land. As a council member, he demanded a full water audit of the entire line."

"And no one's suspicious?" Temar figured that Ben had to be a little worried at this point.

Shan shrugged. "Everyone thinks Naite's being a sandcat because his idiot brother got reckless with his bike and drove it off a cliff."

Temar blinked. "They what?"

"Someone found my bike at the bottom of a narrow canyon, southwest of Red Plain. Apparently I have a reputation for being careless with my driving, and everyone thinks I wrecked, trying to shed speed coming off a dune."

"So everyone thinks you're dead?"

"Yeah. And everyone is wrong about my driving. I could drive a sand bike by ten, and I haven't lost control of one since I was thirteen. I didn't even lose control when I had people shooting at me, so assuming that I would drive off a cliff is a little insulting."

Temar smiled. If Shan could complain about something that trivial, maybe things weren't all that bad. Shan grinned with him.

"You're not what I expected," Temar admitted.

"We can both say that. So, do you think Naite's audit will find evidence against Ben or his partners?"

Temar shook his head. He hoped it did, but he wouldn't hold his breath.

"Me, either. Unfortunately, you were asleep, and trying to get Naite to listen to me would take a miracle beyond my questionable talents, and God wasn't intervening."

"So, what do we do?"

Shan took a long time to think about that. "First we heal up and sleep, and in a couple of days, I say we head out to the one place that has data that can't be faked."

"Livre Communications Relay?" Temar asked. The relay building was the center of all the tech put down by the first settlers. Three valleys had to share the limited terraforming water, and the relay tracked all of it. If the inner planets hadn't decided to break their contract to terraform Livre, the relay would be the center of distributing terraforming water, microbes, seeds, and animals. As it was, the relay sat in the middle of the desert, at a point roughly between Hope Valley, Landing Valley, and Zhang Valley, watching as the three valleys and the towns slowly died. It might take a few more generations, but those instruments measured how the desert reclaimed more life with every season-end.

"Can't Naite call for the relay to audit the Landing water lines?"

Shan nodded. "Yes, but if Ben has stolen from everyone on his line, including himself, where is all that water?"

Temar closed his eyes as he realized what Shan was saying. Someone at the relay was part of this conspiracy with Ista and Ben. There were so many people involved in this that Temar had no idea how they'd managed to keep it secret or what they planned to do.

"This doesn't make sense," Temar said.

"I know," Shan agreed. "But right now we both need to sleep a little more and eat and drink a lot more before we can do anything about it."

That was true. Pushing the dark reality to one side, Temar ate his peas and studied the painting. The underside of the lander was hot, like glass out of the glory hole, and Temar wondered if the artist was one of those people who had been around to see those old landers coming through the atmosphere. If so, the painting had to be old.

chapter
eighteen

SHAN SAT at the main table and scratched his healing leg. The healing was worse than the burn. Of course, he'd been falling-down drunk for the worst of the burn. However, right now he was even more bothered by the fact that Temar had chosen to stay in the closet with a light and a book, but he couldn't ask the man to trust anyone else, not even Hannal. She would put her life between an innocent and any danger, but Temar had already committed himself to trusting both Naite and Tom without knowing them, and Shan figured there was a limit to how much any man could be asked to take on faith. As a priest, he shouldn't believe that, but he did.

He sat at the table while Hannal did the farm's accounting on a small computer, and Tom stirred the stew. Outside, children's voices shouted, and Shan could distantly hear the song of some worker. Computers and even books were getting rarer every generation, so the songs and ballads of the settlers, the inner planets and their wars, and even local celebrities like Lilian Freeland showed up in song.

"I think it's done. Do you think it's hot yet?" Tom asked as he stirred.

"If you want some, take some," Hannal said with an edge of frustration. Then again, Tom had asked about dinner three times now.

Tom sighed. "I'll wait until it's hot," he said, letting go of the spoon and coming back to the table where Shan and Naite sat. Hannal looked up at him with some amusement. "How is Cyla taking the disappearance of her brother?" Tom asked. Shan looked up so he could watch his brother's reactions. Naite kept secrets better than any man Shan knew, but he'd learned to read his brother a little better over the years. It didn't take a genius to see the distaste flash on his brother's face. Four days with Cyla, and Naite had pretty much decided he hated her. However, he wouldn't let that keep him from the plan.

"She's mouthy. I don't know how she survived Ista Songwind's temper with that mouth of hers."

"Sometimes people can strike out verbally when they don't have the freedom to walk away," Tom said mildly, but Shan saw the flash of shame on his brother's face. This man had owned Naite, and yet Naite sat at a table with him and his wife. Some things Shan would never understand.

"I know that. I just never thought I'd have to be on this side of the bad temper," Naite said. He sounded tired.

Hannal put her computer down. She was a formidable woman, with hair that had a mahogany glint that showed up in the sun and strong cheekbones. "No one would blame you for letting someone else handle this. I understand why you feel like you have to hide Shan until you can find out who attacked him, but you're trying to investigate two mysteries at once. You could let someone else handle the search for the Gazer boy."

"And the water waste on the Gazer land," Tom added.

Hannal nodded. "Most people think you're pushing too hard, especially since they think you lost your brother. They worry that you're pushing this instead of dealing with your grief." Hannal looked at Shan.

"You know I'm not," Naite snapped, and Hannal looked back at him.

"No, I think you're pushing this instead of handling your fear over nearly losing your brother. I think you're searching for the Gazer boy and chasing demons in the water line because you're angry that someone tried to hurt your family."

Naite clenched his teeth, and Tom got up and grabbed a bowl and filled it with stew, even if it wasn't hot yet. "I don't need advice on how to handle my business." Naite spit the words out.

"Yes, you do, but you're not likely to take it from me," Hannal said as she poked her computer's power button. She looked at Tom and then back to Naite. "So ask for the honest opinion of someone you do listen to, Naite. Ask Tom for his opinion on this. I'm going to eat with the farmhands." She picked up her computer and left the room, slamming the door a little harder than necessary.

Tom stood at the stove with his bowl of stew in one hand and his spoon in the other as he ate, and Naite scowled at no one in particular.

"I didn't say anything," Tom defended himself.

"I know you didn't," Naite said.

Shan looked from one to the other. "If you were going to say something, what would it be?" Shan asked Tom.

That earned him nasty glares from both men. Naite stood quickly, his chair sliding over the floor with a screech. "I'm not out of control."

"No, you aren't," Tom hurried to say. "You're angry. You have every right to be angry."

Naite turned and gave Tom a cold look. "You're doing it again."

"What?" Tom asked with exaggerated innocence before he shoved a big spoonful of stew into his mouth. He concentrated on chewing for a time, and Naite glared.

"Naite?" Shan asked, "What's going on?"

"Nothing."

Tom didn't answer, but he snorted.

"I'm not tipping my hand to Ben or the others," Naite snapped.

"No, because you're angry with everyone," Tom pointed out. "Not that I have anything to say about it."

"So you agree with Hannal? You think I should stop looking for Temar?" Naite demanded with a meaningful look toward the bedroom where Temar was hiding.

"No. I think this is going to take a lot longer than the four of us originally thought. I think we might need to consider bringing more people in, because you're tearing yourself apart, Naite," Tom said firmly.

"I'm fine."

"It's not you I'm worried about. It's the rest of the world."

Naite clenched his teeth. "Meaning?" In that one moment, Shan could see their father's fury in Naite's face. He'd brought this problem to his brother, and now his brother was suffering for it. Guilt gnawed on the edges of Shan's conscience.

"Meaning you're reaching a breaking point, and you and Cyla are probably aggravating each other to the point that any sane person would leave the planet before dealing with either of you," Tom said, calmly enough. If Shan had said anything near that sharp, Naite would have exploded. Instead, Naite sagged as all the fury vanished under weariness Shan had never seen in his brother.

"I'm fine," Naite repeated, and he didn't sound any more convincing now that his voice came out thick with exhaustion.

"No, you aren't. This bastard has hidden his tracks too well, Naite. It's time to bring in some mechanics, someone who can track the missing water."

Naite's eyes flicked over to the bedroom door. "So, we break our word to him? We tell more people his secret?"

"No, we talk to him about why we need to change the plan," Tom said calmly. He came over and sat down at the table carefully, the way a farmhand might approach a boar. Shan kept his mouth shut, because he suspected that anything he said would set Naite off.

"I've checked every water line, dragged Cyla from one side of the valley to another. I can't find anything. What makes you think someone else can?"

"Because none of us are mechanics. We don't have a clue about how someone would go about stealing water on this scale." Tom made a good point, except Shan did have a pretty good idea. He'd been over a year into his internship with Holmes before leaving for the church, so he had the general mechanics down, even if he knew more about a bike than a water system. Water theft, beyond a simple changing of the gears or levers controlling flow, would require the use of the terraforming pipes that connected the valleys, and that meant going through Livre Communications Relay. Shan had suggested that earlier and been verbally slapped down by Naite.

"If Temar wants to bring someone in, fine, but I'm not going to give up looking for the evidence. No one is smart enough to hide this kind of theft forever." Without another word, Naite headed for the door, his heavy footsteps just short of stomping. Shan held his breath until Naite slammed the door.

Tom kept eating his lukewarm stew, and Shan sat at the table, not sure what to think of that. His brother didn't usually have that little emotional control, at least not anymore. As a young man, Naite had had all kinds of anger issues, but those had vanished by the time Naite was an adult. However, Tom wasn't bothered as he ate his stew, so maybe he'd seen Naite's temper before. Shan had the feeling he'd seen it a whole lot.

"That was interesting," Shan said slowly.

Tom shrugged. "It usually is when those two spend too much time together."

"Naite doesn't like Hannal?" Shan frowned. Naite had flaws, including a certain habit of assuming he was always right, but he was fair in his judgments of people. If someone was competent and honest, Naite liked them.

Tom scratched his arm. "I don't think it's that they don't like each other. Years ago, when I was friends with Hannal, who had come out to work with a sick animal, I told her that I was attracted to Naite. I told her it scared me that I would never know how much he cared about me versus how much he needed me and my protection. I was the first man to defend him. I couldn't start a relationship with someone who needed me, so I chose to be his family instead."

"Naite can care about you and need you at the same time," Shan protested.

Tom smiled, but it was a sad expression. "Maybe, maybe not. I just know that the longer I spent with Hannal, the more I realized that we loved each other without this all-consuming need that pushed everything else out. I mean, Hannal doesn't really need me. She's a strong woman, and if I make a mistake and come home and complain about the stew too often, I don't have to worry about hurting her."

"And you worry about Naite? Do you really think he's that easily hurt?"

Tom thought about that. "From most people? No. But I think you or I could hurt him pretty easily if we really tried. I think he needs something from me that I can't risk screwing up."

"So you chose Hannal?"

"I chose not to hurt anyone," Tom said as he pushed his chair back. "I chose to be your brother's family instead of his lover, and I fell in love with someone else. We're all adults, and we all understand each other's feelings. That doesn't mean Naite wants to hear advice from Hannal. That's why she goes out of her way to avoid giving any, even though she's famous for mothering everyone else on the farm." Shan wasn't sure if Naite or Hannal were as accepting as Tom seemed to believe, but given his own doubts and fears, perhaps he wasn't the one to give anyone advice on love. "I think you priests are right about celibacy. It's not easy to have more than one relationship with someone, and when a relationship is as important as the one Naite and I share, it's not worth risking."

"Because he sees you as a father figure?"

"Because he needs someone to love him all the time," Tom countered. "Without the mess of being in love."

When Shan made his miraculous return from the dead, he figured he'd have to send Div out to this farm to counsel all of them. "He knows you care about him. He knows you always will care about him."

"Because I never take my frustration out on him, like I sometimes do on Hannal. That's the unpleasant side of marriage, Shan. Anyway, I'd better go talk to Naite. I think he'll be more willing to listen if...."

"If I'm not around?" Shan guessed. Temar might struggle to see Shan as anything other than a priest, but Naite could only see Shan as a mean-tempered little boy who didn't understand why his father didn't love him.

Tom looked at him for a time. "He loves you," he said quietly.

Shan nodded. "And I love him. That doesn't mean I have to like everything he does."

That made Tom laugh. "No, you don't. The kids are asleep, but if they wake up, lock yourself in the bedroom, and they'll wander out to find one of us."

"I'll take some stew in to Temar and eat in there." Shan got up and headed for the stove. "If you need anything...."

"I've handled your brother's temper for a long time. I might not own him, but I know how to get him to listen," Tom said kindly. After finishing his last couple of bites of stew, he dropped the bowl in the sink and headed out the door.

Shan was filling bowls when Temar appeared at the open door, his eyes going up to the stairs. The kids didn't come down after dark. The older ones had homework, and the younger ones were asleep. However, Shan didn't want to risk one of them seeing Temar. He nodded back toward the room, and Temar faded back into the shadow while Shan quickly filled two bowls and headed into the bedroom.

When Shan crossed the threshold, Temar appeared and took one of the bowls. "We're going to have to do something, aren't we?" he asked.

They were, but Shan sighed, considering whether he wanted to tell Temar the truth. Of all of them, Temar was the one most at risk. Shan had seen his father's obsession with Naite, and he suspected Ben had the same obsession with Temar. Men like that enjoyed control and humiliation, and when they found a victim, they wouldn't give up easily. At least Shan's father hadn't. He hadn't stopped trying to get his sons back until a neighbor found him with his entire back ripped open and all his internal organs stolen by a nest of sandrats, as he lay in the sand.

"If Naite can't find anything, we can still bring charges based on what he did to you."

"Which won't stop whatever he's part of." Temar sat on the edge of the bed and started eating the stew. "What do you think he's doing? I keep thinking about it, but it doesn't make sense. If he used all that water, someone would get suspicious. George Young would bring charges against him in two seconds, if he thought Ben's crops got more water than his."

"Yeah, he would," Shan agreed as he sat on the woven grass chair.

"So, this isn't limited to Ben, it's about whatever he's trying to do. If Naite isn't finding anything, it's time for us to do something. We're both healed. Mostly." Temar gave Shan's leg a long look, and Shan had to ignore the way the healing burn suddenly itched. It had been a nasty burn, and he was going to have a hellacious scar, but it wasn't a serious threat anymore. If it hadn't killed Shan out on the desert, it wouldn't slow him down now.

What was slowing him down was the thought of putting Temar at risk. Shan had been part of the group to condemn Temar to slavery. It had been his own failure to convince the others of the potential harm that had led to Temar's abuse. The whip marks had faded, but Temar would still startle at random times. He still insisted he was more comfortable sleeping in the bottom of a closet, and Shan didn't even want to think about that. Shan had even offered to abandon the bed and take a turn sleeping on the floor, but Temar insisted he wanted one more door between him and any intruder, and Shan suspected that he worried about Ben breaking in here. Temar wasn't weak, but he hadn't healed.

Shan thought about Naite's flash of anger and his sudden weariness. For the first time in his life, Shan wondered if his brother had ever truly healed. Had he condemned Temar to a life of struggling with this because he couldn't convince the others to only fine Cyla and Temar?

How could he justify putting Temar in even more danger now?

Shan focused on his stew as silence settled over the room. He would have to get out there and check the mechanics at the relay, but he couldn't put Temar in the middle of that. If Ben or his coconspirators caught Shan again, he wouldn't bet on the Lord to save him a second time. Shan really did believe God had guided him to the valley, turning him at the last second so that Shan would see the beacon.

True, he'd never expected God to take the form of a pipe-induced hallucination, but Shan found that more believable than the idea of a man walking the desert alone without any water or shelter. The Lord wasn't likely to give him a second miracle.

"Do you have any theories?" Temar asked again.

Shan shrugged and put his empty bowl on top of the dresser. "Motherboards and water make sense if you're going to open a new valley."

Sucking in a fast breath, Temar asked, "Red Plain Valley?"

"Maybe," Shan admitted.

"Okay, how do we test that theory?" Temar asked.

For a second, Shan stared at the man. Every time Shan expected to shock Temar or for him to curl up in terror, Temar kept going. Every time Shan thought Temar had put the abuse behind him, the man flinched back from a casual touch or slept on the floor of the closet.

"If he's trying to use the terraforming equipment, he has to run that through the relay."

"So, we head to the relay?" Temar asked, not even hesitating before offering himself up for danger. Shan wanted to order Temar to stay behind, to stay safe. He wanted to relieve his guilt by putting his own body between Temar and any threat. However, he had a streak of cowardice in him, because he found himself nodding in agreement rather than explaining all the reasons why Temar should stay behind.

Temar smiled, and Shan figured they'd have at least one more night here, and then he'd have to find a way to make it clear that Temar should stay behind. Shan wouldn't do any more damage to a young man who had already suffered too much.

chapter
nineteen

TEMAR LEFT the mouth of the narrow cave. It was high on the side of the valley, exactly where Tom had told them to look, but Temar couldn't escape the feeling that Tom and Shan were hiding something. He'd accuse Naite of the same, only he hadn't come back after last night, when Temar had heard him talking with Shan and Tom. He still had trouble thinking of Naite as being someone so fragile that Tom worried about hurting him.

On the other hand, Temar knew how often he felt like a fragile glass tube, about to explode from the pressure of memories. It was almost worse now that all the physical symptoms had healed. Before he'd been able to run his hand over a hot bruise and hold onto the anger. Now he struggled to divide fears from memories, to decide which shadow was a memory trying to creep in and which was a windwood tree swaying in the breeze.

He felt even more off balance after spending four days sharing a room and becoming increasingly aware of Shan as a man. Temar lay in his closet with his hands between his legs, debating how to handle his cock's increasing interest. Maybe he was feeling withdrawal after having sex three times a day. Maybe he was frustrated because he couldn't touch himself with a priest on the other side of the closet door.

He was even more annoyed with the feeling that Shan wasn't telling him the entire truth. Since last night, he'd grown quiet. Shan had told him to keep watch, but Temar made a decision. Turning his back on the narrow crack that led to an old, crumbling trail that led up to the top of the valley, Temar followed Shan into the deepest part of the long, narrow cave.

Shan had taken a light into the cave, and the sunlight quickly faded as Temar headed deeper in. If not for Shan's light shining ahead of him, he would have turned back. However, he followed, deep into the cave, past old crates that had markings Temar didn't recognize. This stuff might even be from one of the drop ships, and Temar wondered if Ben was the only one keeping secrets. If Tom had hidden these supplies away, either he trusted them not to tell the council, or they weren't terribly important.

Since Shan was on the council, Temar had to assume the second was true. The floor sloped up and curved slightly, and Temar found himself in a slightly wider chamber. Shan and his light were in the middle.

Shan crouched next to a sand bike, the side panel lying next to him on the ground. Temar watched as Shan ran his long fingers over the belts of the old sand cycle. Age and the desert sand had blasted off the paint, and Temar didn't know all that much about bikes, but it looked like an old one, maybe even from the early drop ships.

Shan's eyes were closed as his fingers traced the gears and belts exposed on the side. He looked peaceful, and Temar hesitated to interrupt. Ever since Shan had shown up, he'd looked drawn and harried. That, added to Temar's own strange feelings, combined to make their conversations increasingly uncomfortable. Before all this, Shan and the church had been part of an island of calm. It was as if Temar didn't see Shan at all… he'd been a prop that stood at the front of the church and spoke in a low voice that rolled through Temar, washing away disappointments and fear that crashed into him the second he stepped out of the church.

Now, though, Shan was a real man. Shan had his own history, a brother he fought with, a father who'd killed himself with pipe juice. And maybe what had happened, maybe his time in Ben's bed had changed something, but Temar couldn't help but notice Shan's shoulders and his large hands. He wondered what they would feel like.

Would Shan be hesitant? Would he be confident? Would he explore with his hands? Temar was pretty sure of two things: he was sexually off balance, and he was going to hell for having these thoughts about a priest. Temar shook his head and struggled to focus on the current mystery—why Shan was stroking the sand bike.

"Problem?" Temar asked. Shan sucked in a breath and turned so fast that he had to put out a hand to keep from falling over.

"Actually, no. She's in good shape," Shan answered with a smile, but Temar could feel the awkwardness in the cavern. Shan wanted privacy, and maybe Temar had grown a little paranoid, but that made him nervous. Instead of retreating, which was his first instinct, Temar went with his second impulse, to get nosey.

He took a step into the dim cavern. "I didn't know there was a bike in here."

"Tom told me about it."

"Tom." Temar clenched his teeth at the idea of more secrets.

"He didn't know if it would handle a desert trip, but she's more reliable than any planet-built machine."

Temar crossed his arms, and he spotted an answering flash of worry in Shan's face. "I didn't know you were that good with machines, good enough to know if that is reliable enough for a desert trip."

Standing all the way up, Shan brushed off his hands and then wiped them against his jeans. "I always thought I would be a mechanic. Maybe I should have stuck with sand bikes." Shan looked up at him, and for a time, the silence grew heavy between them. "I wish I was half the priest Div was in his prime. I can't help but think he would have noticed something, that he could have fixed something," Shan said. "I thought the Lord called me to the church to devote my life to it, but now I'm wondering if he just didn't want me safe for a time."

"What did you need to be safe from?" The words came out bitter. However, from everything Temar had heard and overheard, Naite had been their father's victim, not Shan.

Shan looked up, his dark eyes wide with some emotion Temar didn't understand. Now that Temar thought about it, Shan had been in the house after Naite had been sent to Tom. Maybe there was more there than Shan had told anyone. The raw pain was there in his eyes. It bothered Temar—the idea that Shan's own father had…. Temar's mind skittered away from the word that tried to form in his mind.

"I guess…." Shan let out a breath. "I guess I finally figured out what my father was really like." Shan put the screwdriver on the ground and sat right in the dirt of the cavern floor. "I guess I finally figured out why Naite was out causing trouble, trying to get anyone to pull him out of there. I guess I figured out that I'd spent a lifetime trying to hurt Naite because I was jealous, and I'd been part of the problem. I hurt him, and I needed to be safe from my own self-hate." Shan stopped, but not before Temar heard the hatred in his voice. Then Shan shrugged, like none of it was important. "Besides, the church was the next best way to get out of the house."

"So he never…?"

Shan shook his head. "No. He never touched me." Shan rubbed his hand over his face. "Some days I wish…." He stopped again.

"Wish what?" Temar studied Shan, seeing not the priest or even the man, but imagining the lanky boy Shan must have been. For the first time, Temar realized there was more than one way to be hurt. Would Cyla feel this pain? When she realized her plan had turned Temar into the perfect victim, would her eyes be as haunted? Temar didn't want that. He didn't want to tell the council what Ben had done. He'd rather the man be exiled for water theft.

Shan looked up for a second before closing his eyes and shaking his head. "Never mind."

Anger flashed through Temar. Shan was no better than he was. They both carried their scars and their guilt. "Do you think that I can't handle hearing the truth?" Temar demanded. "Do you know Ben's favorite game? Do you?" Temar advanced into the cave, his hands fisted at his sides. "He liked to make me choose. He loved it. He loved hearing me ask to be hurt, so do you really think you have to change the subject, as though I were some sort of child?"

Temar stood over Shan, staring down as the silence settled around them, dust motes dancing in the air. Temar breathed fast, embarrassment pushing aside the worst of the fury. He didn't want people knowing that, and yet here he was talking about it.

"I think you suffered more than you should have," Shan said softly. "I'm sorry."

"Sorry doesn't really change anything." Temar turned his back, and for one instant, he felt cold fear, as though Shan might tackle him from behind. Hurrying, Temar got to the mouth of the cavern and turned, but Shan was still on the ground. His emotions raged, and Temar took several deep breaths, smelling the coppery dust of the cave as he struggled to calm the storm inside of him.

"You're right. 'Sorry' doesn't change anything," Shan agreed after a long pause.

Temar's emotions cooled, like glass pulled from the furnace. And maybe he was shedding heat too fast, because he could almost hear his emotions crackle as they cooled and threatened to shatter. If he didn't get a handle on these emotions, Shan would never let him go on this trip, and this was too important. If he didn't get evidence against Ben.... Temar refused to even consider what that failure would feel like.

"I'm not weak," Temar said in a calmer voice, carefully controlling his emotions. "You don't have to protect me like I'm some child who doesn't know what happens out there in the real world."

Shan leaned back, his mouth pulled into a tight pucker, and now Temar felt bone weary. He might not be a child, but he wasn't acting like a rational adult, either. He didn't know what he was. Crazy, maybe.

"I wish sometimes my father would have hurt me... hurt me more, anyway," Shan said, the words coming out so fast that Temar thought, at first, that he must have misheard. However, Shan had this look of self-loathing on his face that matched the words. Temar wondered if he had some company in his insanity.

"I didn't know what our father was doing to Naite," Shan went on. "I didn't understand, and I hated that Naite was the favorite." Shan spit the last word out as though it was a curse. "I hated it. I wanted to be the favorite, and I used to do my best to torture Naite when we were kids. I thought if I could show our father I was better or smarter that he'd pay more attention to me. And then Naite left, and our father starting trying to...." Shan swallowed, his Adam's apple bobbing.

"I didn't understand," Shan repeated, this time softer. "And when I did, I felt horrible that Naite had to carry this alone, that I'd acted like a sandrat." Shan spit the words out.

"Would it make it any better if he'd hurt you too?"

"I don't know." Shan spun the screwdriver between his fingers. "At least then I would have known. I wouldn't have been part of the problem. I'm the priest, and until yesterday, I couldn't even see how much pain Naite carries. Maybe if our father had—" He stopped and swallowed.

"You can't think Naite blames you." Temar kept his voice soft, because right now, he wasn't the only piece of hot glass struggling to shed heat without cracking.

Shan thought about that. "I don't think so, but it's not like we get along."

From Temar's point of view, the brothers got along pretty damn well. Naite hadn't hesitated to help them. True, they fought, but their arguments never got hateful. They never made the sort of insults that would cut a person to the bone.

"I wouldn't want Cyla hurt, not even if it meant she was nicer about all this," Temar said. "And let's be honest, Cyla is not going to be all that reasonable about this."

"Maybe she shouldn't be," Shan pointed out.

Temar nodded. There was plenty of reason for getting upset about the situation. The problem was that Temar really didn't need his sister coming in and stirring everything up, including his own feelings. "I don't need her acting like I can't take care of myself, and Naite doesn't need you to feel guilty." Temar thought maybe he'd offended Shan because the man looked at him. Shan's hand had been traveling over the dusty bike, but now it stopped, the fingers resting against the rusted fender.

"Maybe you should go into the priesthood."

"No." Temar quickly answered. "I'd rather work with my hands." He felt a flash of desire as he thought about working glass, watching it grow on the end of his blowpipe. But the joy faded. Even if people believed him about Ben, Dee'eta Sun wouldn't want to train him. She'd probably feel so guilty about sentencing him to serve Ben that she wouldn't be able to look him in the face. Shan was having trouble with that. And other glassblowers needed the income from apprentice fees to keep their shops going. They could not afford to train someone for free.

"Temar?" Shan's voice was soft, almost apologetic.

"When are we leaving?" Temar kept his voice sharp. He didn't need apologies, and when Shan kept offering them, it stirred Temar's emotions too much.

Shan physically jerked back at the tone, his gaze skittering away. "It might be best if you stayed here. There's food, and the cave hasn't been used for years. It's safe."

That was the tone Cyla always used before doing something outrageously stupid. "Here?"

"Here," Shan said firmly.

"Oh no. This is my fight. If you're going, I'm going."

"I don't need you to come along."

That stung. Part of Temar wanted to curl away from those sharp words, and the flash of guilt on Shan's face suggested that Shan hadn't meant to be quite so harsh. However, Temar wasn't a child. He didn't back away from a little discomfort. Or even a lot of discomfort. He would like to figure out which of his feelings were real, and there was a tiny voice at the back of his mind that said he could do that more easily if he had some distance from Shan, but they didn't have time for that.

"You need someone to watch your back while you do this finding out, and if I don't go, you won't have anyone."

"I won't get caught."

Temar snorted. "The last time I heard that, it was Cyla saying it about going into Landowner Young's field. Or maybe it was Ben.

Ben's pretty damn sure he's never going to get caught. Both got caught." Temar frowned as he realized that wasn't quite true. "Cyla got caught, and Ben is more in the process of getting caught, but no one can be that confident. You need someone to watch your back."

Shan left the bike, taking two steps toward Temar. "If they catch you…." He stopped, but the truth hung in the air between them. Ben would kill Temar. No question. He'd kill Cyla too, only Temar trusted Naite to keep her safe.

"And they'll kill you," Temar answered. He watched as Shan's fingers twitched open and closed.

"I can tell them some story. I don't know who shot at me, but I walked off the desert."

"All the way to the relay?"

That made Shan flinch. The story had so many holes that it wouldn't even carry stones, much less sand. And the truth was much finer than sand, as the saying went. "It would make them think twice. They don't know that I have any information."

There was this strange inflection on the word "information" that made the hair on the back of Temar's neck stand up. It was like feeling the air from the kiln wash over him. "What do you know?" he asked.

Concern flickered on Shan's face. "About the water Ben's diverting." He said that too fast. Temar took a step forward and studied Shan's face.

"Are priests supposed to lie?"

Shan almost smiled. "I thought we already established that I'm not the best priest."

"What aren't you telling me?"

Turning his back, Shan rested his fingers against the bike again. The silence grew heavy between them, and Temar's discomfort intensified. Two months ago, he would have retreated, but he had a whole new definition of and tolerance for discomfort these days.

"Ista Songwind had circuits," Shan admitted. From the way he said it, slow and soft, he hadn't wanted to offer up that bit of information, but Temar couldn't figure out why Songwind shouldn't have circuits. She specialized in cleaning and restoring them. If she had a motherboard circuit, that would fit with the idea they thought to make a grab for more land, but they'd talked about that possibility. No, there wasn't enough land. However, without more water, trying to terraform more land would be idiotic. Even if they did steal enough water to get the land going, all the other valleys would find a way to make them pay for a theft of that scale.

"What haven't you told me?"

Shan's hand, which had gone back to stroking the sand bike, now curled into a fist. "The big master circuit boards that are used for valley doors...."

Temar waited for more of an explanation. Eventually Shan turned around and leaned back on the bike. "There was more than one or two. There aren't more than a dozen of those on the whole world, and they're all carefully protected. At least, that's what Holmes told me when I apprenticed with him, and he was a master mechanic who would have known. But she had a dozen of them, and she had your sister cleaning them. An apprentice. A new apprentice."

"But why have a new apprentice—?"

Shan cut him off. "An apprentice so new that she wouldn't know what she was looking at or ask too many questions. I thought maybe some sand devil had forced Red Plains to pull all their circuits, but Tom said the weather's been quiet. So where did all those circuits come from? Why do they need so many? She had more there than Landing's Valley, and that's the largest growing valley on Livre. I don't understand it, but none of this is adding up."

"We already knew most of this. Even if you think you're wrong about the valley, we have to check at the relay. Why should I stay here?" Temar didn't understand what had changed.

Shan looked at him with honest pain in his expression. "If they find you, they'll kill you."

"They'll kill you just as quickly. They already have tried to kill you!" Temar protested. He remembered the cold guilt when he thought Shan was dead because Temar had sent him off on some chase. He remembered that guilt, and he wouldn't live with it again. "I will go with you."

"It'll be—"

"Don't," Temar interrupted. "Don't tell me what I can and can't do. Don't take away my choice, here." Temar swallowed. He hadn't meant to say that much—reveal that much.

Shan looked at him, a dozen expressions flitting across his strong features, and Temar couldn't understand any of them.

"If you get yourself killed, my soul is going to implode from the weight of the guilt," Shan warned seriously.

Temar grinned. "I don't plan to. I'm the cautious one, so I fully intend to watch your back from a very safe position."

"If this conspiracy is as far spread as I suspect, I'm not sure where that safe position might be." Shan didn't even try to hide his worry. However, Temar had grown up worrying about his father, his farm, his sister's growing recklessness, and his own increasingly dismal future. Worrying was an old friend. As long as he didn't get left behind like some child, he could handle whatever got thrown at them.

"The only danger I can't handle right now is the danger that you're going to leave me here to worry and feel useless. Shan, I really can't handle that. Everything we do is one more step toward making Ben Gratu pay for everything he did to me. I need that," Temar said firmly. Shan studied his face, and Temar felt the emotions shift between them.

"I'm a priest. I should counsel you against seeking revenge."

"You don't even believe that," Temar said. Shan didn't disagree. He did spend a lot of time studying Temar, and Temar bridled under the tacit judgment.

"I'd welcome the help," Shan finally said. Reaching out, he patted Temar on the shoulder, just as he probably had a dozen times before when Temar visited the church. This time, Temar jerked away, and Shan froze, his face a mask of horror.

He could handle it as long as no one touched him, Temar mentally added. "So, when do we leave?"

"As soon as we get supplies together?" Shan asked, looking to Temar for approval. Temar knew Shan was probably doing that simply to avoid making Temar feel helpless again, rather than out of any uncertainty. He still appreciated the gesture.

"Sounds good."

chapter
twenty

THE SAND bike started slipping down the dune face, and Temar's breath caught in his throat as he clung to Shan. The man leaned back, his weight added to Temar's on the back of the cycle, and Temar had a flash of panic as he felt trapped, pinned by Shan's weight.

Then the bike shifted, and Shan moved forward, gunning the engine so that it whined, and then they both lurched forward. Temar barely avoided decorating the back of Shan's neck with vomit. Finally they headed down a long trough between two of the slow-moving dunes, and Temar's stomach unknotted at the long, straight path ahead of them. Before this, Temar hadn't really understood how Shan could have survived, riding a sand bike through a canyon while people shot at him. However, Shan controlled the bike with a confidence that allowed him to make impossible turns.

Shan leaned forward, and because Temar held on, he was pulled down so that he was almost lying on Shan's back as they sped across the white sands. Temar had watched Shan pace the front of the church many times, but he'd never felt the power. He'd never allowed himself to really indulge in thoughts of Shan as a sexual being. However, pressed up close while Shan's strong body shifted with the bike, Temar could think of little else.

Temar's sexual experiences were limited to two boys from school that he'd played with. Each time, they'd pretended to understand their own bodies and each other's bodies, even though the lie was comically transparent. They'd fumbled, pulled too hard, put knees in awkward places. They'd gotten as far as fingers up the backside before pulling back, each sure that nothing bigger than a finger would ever get up that hole. Back then, sex had been exciting and confusing and fumbling. Now that Temar had seen Shan controlling a sand bike, he figured Shan wasn't someone who'd ever fumbled.

The way Shan moved was closer to Ben. What Ben had done to him wasn't sex. Temar couldn't think of it that way. It'd been payment… fear… it'd been survival. But Ben's body moved with a confidence and surety that reminded Temar of Shan's movements. They understood themselves and their world, and they moved into it with strength. Before being slaved to him, Temar always thought Ben had a quiet strength, but now he could see that described Shan, not Ben. Ben liked to show off his power, but he kept that preference behind closed doors. Even behind closed doors, even drunk, Shan didn't abuse his strength.

Before riding on the bike, Temar hadn't known Shan had such strong arms under the robes. He'd lost weight from his time in the desert, but his muscles gathered under his skin as he moved with the sand bike, holding its weight as they skittered down the side of a dune or slid down a dune face.

Temar leaned into that body and closed his eyes as his mouth went dry. The feel of another's heat pressing into him was too familiar. The sound of another's heart beating frightened him. But he'd never wrapped his arms around Ben. This was Shan. The bike tilted as they climbed the side of a dune, sand crumbling under them and cascading down to the bottom of the valley. But Shan leaned into the dune, his knee creating a gash in the sand mountain as they climbed.

"Almost there," Shan shouted. Temar didn't know if he meant that they were almost to the top of the dune or almost to the relay. His stomach rolled, either way. One meant enemies ready to kill them. The other meant having to go sailing down a dune face on an out-of-control bike. Temar figured he'd spend more time freaking out about being this close to another human being if he wasn't busy being terrified in general. If Shan was right, this conspiracy went way beyond stealing water from his father. Circuit boards and water were two of the most vital resources on Livre, and hoarding either was an offense that could get a person exiled.

They crested the dune, and the Livre Communications Relay was laid out in front of them, a long, silver snake set into a stone canyon so narrow that a decent-sized house would touch each side.

"Won't they see us?" Temar shouted over the wind. He would be afraid of someone in the valley hearing his shout, only the bike engine rumbled, and a storm was making dust devils swirl into the air. The wind hit the rocky canyon on either side of the relay's small canyon and whistled loudly.

"That's the original landing site," Shan shouted over his shoulder. "No wind-safe glass. They used solid ship sheeting. They won't hear or see anything."

Temar didn't answer. He pressed closely to Shan's back and held on as Shan fishtailed the bike down a steep slope toward where the canyon petered out to sand. Large crags of rock rose up from the sand, like icebergs Temar had seen on old vids from Earth. Shan pointed the bike right at the field of rock, and Temar sucked in a breath and hung on more tightly. They were going to end up splatted on the side of a crag, their broken bodies food for sandrats.

The bike turned so sharply that it threw up a curtain of sand, and then they slid to the side before Shan leaned back, and the bike lunged forward, right between two of the largest rocks. A small cry slipped out before Temar could stop it, and the bike's engine powered down with a low, rumbling hum.

"You okay?" Shan asked as they threaded through the rocks at a much slower speed.

"Not really, no. I do think I peed myself," Temar said, and he was only 80 percent sure that was a joke.

"These things don't have effective brakes. I can lose some speed fishtailing it, but if I try to actually slow the wheel rotation, I'm going to lose all control."

"It felt like you did lose control," Temar pointed out. He had to order his arms to loosen up before he squeezed the life out of Shan.

Looking over his shoulder, Shan grinned. "I haven't wrecked a bike since I was a kid."

"I thought you drove your last one over a cliff."

"Someone shot at me. That's not the same." Shan guided the bike into the shadow of a long, flat rock taller than a house and powered the engine down. The machine shuddered and then fell silent. "I should check the fuel lines. Old bikes like this get temperamental."

"Tell me it isn't going to break and leave us stranded out here."

Shan patted the part of the bike where the handles went into the frame. "This old girl is built to last. She'll be around long after us."

"Hopefully you're trying to compliment the bike and not suggest that our life expectancy is growing shorter by the minute."

Shan gave him another of those worried looks.

"Just a joke," Temar said with the best smile he could muster. It didn't convince Shan.

"You could stay here with the bike."

"If you get killed in there, my chances of riding out are about the same as your chances of trying to blow a serviceable bowl the first time you pick up a blow pipe."

A frown crossed Shan's face. "We did glassblowing in school, and I was never particularly talented at it, so I suspect that's not good."

"No, it's not. And if I try to ride that sand bike anywhere, you're going to be picking pieces of my hair and bones out of sandrat nests. So we go together, and we come back together."

Shifting his weight, Shan swung a leg over the front of the bike and slid off. Temar had to put out his feet to keep from tipping over with the bike, but Shan used his foot to extend the long sand stabilizers so Temar could climb off. "You surprise me, Temar Gazer."

Temar wasn't sure how to take that. "Why?"

"You're a strong man."

"And that surprises you?" Now Temar really wasn't sure how to take that.

"Maybe a little," Shan said with a shrug. He had to come around to Temar's side to extend the sand stabilizers on that side. "I knew you were a good man. I knew you'd survived a lot with your father. I knew you were an attractive one, and God forgive me, I've struggled to remember my vows more than once. It hadn't occurred to me that you couldn't drive yourself out of here if I ran into trouble, or that you were the kind of man who would come anyway."

"Which is why you'd better not get killed," Temar pointed out.

"I'll do my best."

"Yeah, well remember, if you don't, you have to live with the guilt of it up in that heaven of yours."

"Trust me, I know that." Shan suspected he would carry his guilt with him to the next life if he failed Temar.

Temar hadn't intended to poke at Shan's guilt button again. He opened his mouth to explain that the last thing he wanted was to cause more guilt, but Shan was already moving away from the bike and toward the edge of the rock. Not sure what he could say to alleviate the guilt he'd unintentionally inspired, Temar followed behind. Near the edge of the rock, Shan held up a hand, and Temar stopped, his heart already rising in his throat. The last time he'd been this scared, Cyla had gotten them both arrested, and look how well that had turned out.

"It looks quiet."

"Is it supposed to look like that?"

Shan nodded. "It usually is. When I first started my apprenticeship for mechanics, I came out here a couple of times. It's one family that controls the communications relay. There aren't that many people out here."

"Is it just me, or is that a pretty bad plan? I mean, one family running the communications relay? I love my family, but if it was my family left in charge of the communications relay, there would not be a lot of communicating going on," Temar pointed out.

Over his shoulder, Shan gave him a crooked grin. "The family's required to keep it open for inspection by any member of any council from any of the valleys or cities. They run the equipment, but this valley isn't big enough for any sort of food production or terraforming."

"Are they the ones who get the quotas, the crop quotas at the end of every season?" Temar had never wondered about the quotas much. Their farm had barely produced food for the three of them, which exempted them from quotas... at least Temar thought it had. Ben suggested that his father would have lost the land a long time ago if anyone had pressed a complaint with the council.

Shan nodded. "For the most part. Doctors have access to some of the quota stores for patients who can't work anymore. Families can apply for it if they have some sort of temporary hardship. But a lot of the quota does go to them. They're out here taking care of equipment, hoping that the rest of the universe will—"

"Live up to their end of the deal?" Temar asked. Everyone who grew up on Livre knew it was a slowly dying planet, because the inner worlds hadn't finished the terraforming.

"They'll call eventually. The government will need something from us, and they'll call. If we don't have our communications relay open, I don't know what would happen."

"Do they even know we're here anymore?"

That answer required Shan to think some. "I don't know," he admitted finally. "I know the relay sends out its required reports. I know that the family who mans this place is listening for any sort of signal. I also know that the relay keeps track of all of the original infrastructure designed by the terraforming crews. The water reclamation systems, the irrigation systems, communication systems—they have blueprints and tracking systems for all of it."

"So what do we hope to find?"

"Hopefully something that I'll recognize when I see it." When Shan said that, Temar gave him a worried look. Maybe Shan could read his expression, because he moved slowly, putting a hand on Temar's shoulder. "I'm not your sister. I'm going to recognize motherboards if they have them sitting around. And I won't break anything."

Temar nodded as he looked toward the long building. "Do you think they're in on it?"

Shan gave a small sigh and took some time before answering. "I don't know. As a priest, I'm supposed to assume the best of people. I'm supposed to offer absolution and forgiveness. I'm supposed to be Div." Shan paused long enough to emphasize that "supposed to" didn't mean anything when it came to what happened in reality. Pulling his sand veil off, he rubbed his hand over his mouth. "Right now I'm a lot more suspicious than he ever dreamed of being. The relay should have tracked every single motherboard coming off the ships. If they had extra motherboards, they should have offered them for medical diagnosis or for the schools. We stopped training students on any of the higher maths because we didn't have the computing power to show the models. One motherboard could run a computer network that was able to do jump ship simulations or teach multidimensional calculus."

"Personally, my vote would be for the doctors to get the circuit boards. But I can see what you mean. These things are important."

"They are as important as water. And we don't have enough of either."

"And these people were supposed to be tracking them and making sure everyone shared, right?"

Shan nodded. "That was the plan. It's why they're independent from any of the valleys or towns—they're the neutral arbiters of the resources."

"So the question is, are they getting tricked, or are they part of the problem?"

Shan got a thoughtful look on his face. "I think it's time someone asked exactly that question." Ducking low, Shan ran for the next rock. His long legs covered the ground quickly, so Temar had to scramble to keep up. His heart pounded painfully fast as he slid into place behind the rock Shan had chosen.

"I thought you said they wouldn't see us?" Temar hissed.

"Probably, they won't. Probably." Shan made a little huffing sound. "I don't know about your family, but in mine, sometimes we got on each other's nerves. The last thing I want is to get caught by some little brother, out for a walk because he needs some space."

Temar imagined what it would mean to live in one building with your family… no valley to walk, no town to visit, no church to hide in when the family overwhelmed you. That was his definition of hell. If this were his home, he'd be walking the outside wall all the time. "Thank you for that cheery thought."

"You're a lot more sarcastic than I expected." Shan's observation surprised Temar.

The fact was that when he was home, he wasn't all that sarcastic. His sister had claimed that territory. Now, though, the feelings bubbled up until he wanted to say something cutting, something sharp. He wanted to throw Shan off balance. It was like he was a glass bubble that was a little warped. That happened when the heat wasn't even. If he were a piece of glass, he'd know what to do. He had to be reheated, he had to be rolled along the marver. The wide, smooth metal of a marver let a glassblower roll a hot ball of glass up and down until the ball smoothed and the sides cooled enough that you could blow the glass without making the sides too thin. Maybe he needed to be reheated. Maybe he needed his surface smoothed out.

Shan looked at him. "I didn't mean that as an insult. I'm known to be rather sarcastic myself."

"I thought you were the kind of priest who sat home and read the Bible and talked to people and wrote sermons. I didn't think you were the sort of priest who got sarcastic and rode sand bikes through the desert as people shot at you."

"I'm talented that way." Shan grinned. "Are you ready?"

"No. However, if these people are stealing water, we should go anyway."

Shan rested his hand on Temar's arm. At first, Temar's skin crawled at the touch, but he rode through that feeling, smiling at Shan. They could do this. He could do this.

Without another word, Shan turned and raced toward the building, darting from shadow to shadow. The building had the odd, square lines of those early buildings, the ones the first settlers had built before they learned to create walls that shrugged off the winds or leaned into rock. So as they got closer, the wind from the gathering storm circled and slapped at them. Tiny wind devils rose from the canyon floor and swept along the bottom until they hit the station and scattered.

The wall had rivets in straight lines, every seven or eight feet, and a low doorway in the center of each section.

"Which one do we go in?"

"I'm not sure," Shan admitted.

Temar's chest tightened.

Shan reached for one of the handles and turned it slowly. "When I open it, duck around the rock," he whispered, nodding toward the nearest good-sized rock. "If someone's in here, hopefully they'll think the wind pulled it open."

Temar leaned closer. "You're terrible at planning."

"Do you have a better plan?"

Temar opened his mouth to protest that he could come up with one. This felt too much like Cyla's plan—too much like rushing in without enough information. However, they didn't have time to come up with another plan, not now. They were here. Temar played with the idea of demanding that Shan drive them back to Tom's cave hideaway so they could come up with a better plan. Shan looked at him, waiting.

"Don't die," Temar said firmly. Then he turned and retreated to the rock Shan had chosen.

chapter
twenty-one

FEAR MADE Temar's heart pound painfully fast as he put a knee in the dust and watched as Shan pulled the door open and then ran for another rock. The metal door banged against the wall, each time making the metal of the entire wall ring like an out-of-tune bell. Temar flinched with every hit, waiting for people to rush out the door and find them. Fear made him crouch lower, but he fisted his hands and waited. Cyla was safe with Naite, and if Temar was going to get caught, he'd fight. He'd fight until they had to kill him before he'd go back to Ben. Ghost hands ran over Temar's back, making him shiver. He wasn't under Ben's hands, and he wouldn't ever be in that position again.

From behind his rock, Shan slowly stood, a wind devil making his black hair dance. Shan inched forward, his body coiled and ready for a fight. Temar crouched in the dust and fought against two equal fears, the fear that Shan would be caught and the fear that he was going to crouch in the dust like a worthless lump of clay the whole time. Shan got up close to the door and peered around the edge. Immediately, his body language relaxed. He moved into the building, and Temar slowly stood to follow.

The only place in Landing that looked anything like this was the council building. The walls stood square against the floor, and every corner was as even as if a ruler had been used. Despite the wind outside, when Temar pulled the door closed behind them, the winds vanished. "The walls are so solid," Temar said as he laid a hand against the metal.

"Solid enough to hold out space," Shan agreed. "If we leave the door open, they'll think the wind pulled it open."

That was probably true. No one left a door open, not when a storm threatened and the house was so clean. Metal tables as smooth as any marver were bolted to the wall, and chairs with thick padding sat in front of them. "It's like another world," Temar said in a soft voice thick with reverence. From the way Shan looked around, he felt the same.

"The first time I came here, I was afraid to touch anything. But this is the way the planet was supposed to be… the people who first came here thought their grandchildren would live in homes like this one."

"They were wrong," Temar said.

"Yes, they were." Shan went over and put his ear to yet another metal door that led farther into the building. He stood for some time, but Temar figured if anyone was in the house at all, they would have come when the outer door banged against the wall. Even now, the wind slammed it around, so that the metal reverberated with every hit. Sand swirled through the air, ruining the perfect lines formed by the metal construction.

"Sounds clear. Be ready to run," Shan said as he moved his hand to the doorknob and started slowly turning. Temar was so afraid that he wasn't sure he could run, but he braced himself on one of the tables and waited. Shan pulled the door open, and again his body sagged with relief. He headed through the door, and Temar followed.

"We're on the wrong side," Shan whispered. "This side has the private quarters."

Temar looked around and saw two separate vid screens, like schools used, bolted to the wall, and more padded chairs. Several books stood on a shelf, which was unusual enough, but a half-dozen pad computers had been left in the room—one on the table, a couple on a shelf by the vid screen, and one on the padded couch. This was the wealthiest house Temar had ever seen, and that included Ben's big house.

"We need to get to the workshop areas, so we need a door into the west half," Shan said. Temar nodded, but he was too busy looking around to pay much attention to doors. A hand brushed across his shoulder, and Temar jumped back, sucking in a fast breath.

"Sorry," Shan whispered, his hands held up in supplication. "I didn't mean to startle you. We need to focus here, okay?" He looked so intense that for a second Temar had the impression that Shan was peering straight into him and seeing all the wondrous and childish awe he was feeling. It was a house, nothing more. Temar nodded.

Shan kept looking at him for several seconds before he nodded and headed down the long room to the door on the other end. Temar stayed back by the door to the outside while Shan slowly opened this one, checking before he headed into the next room. When he followed, Temar discovered a long, clean mechanical room with machines Temar couldn't even guess at. The familiar incinerator and recycler stood on one wall, but a dozen other machines were a total mystery to him. However, obviously none were important, because Shan moved to the next door. This room had that west-facing door, and Shan pressed his ear to the metal, listening for some time before he pushed it open.

Again, his body language eased as he pulled the door open and went into a room that looked like a vid of one of the ship control rooms. Machines lined every wall, and Shan's eyes went wide as he looked around. Temar followed, and this time he rested his hand on Shan's arm to focus him.

"Am I the only one who expected someone to challenge us before now?" Temar whispered.

Shan's expression turned grim. "I did think I'd be either bluffing or throwing a few punches by now," Shan admitted. "I don't understand why no one is here."

"Because they're somewhere else?"

"Brilliant," Shan said, but the grin made up for the dry tone. "This computer runs the tracking program for water usage," Shan said as he started it. Slipping into one of the chairs, he focused totally on the screens as they reported out figures. Since Shan had found his computer, Temar moved to check the two other doors, one north and one south. The north one had what looked like a storage room, with deep shelves on either side of a narrow aisle. The south door led to another mechanical room, this time with various machines in parts all over shelves and on one long table that ran the length of the room. There were even more machines and tools that Temar didn't recognize.

"Shan," he said as he held the door open for Shan to see.

Shan glanced over. "When I interned with Holmes, he came over here to work on all sorts of equipment. If a local mechanic can't get it fixed, they'll send it here. They have training vids here too, although I didn't know they had vid units in the living quarters." Shan's fingers typed as his voice trailed off.

Temar walked through and poked at a couple of the stranger machines before he returned to Shan and his computer. There were actually about six computers in the room—big things that bolted to the wall with keyboards that slid out. He wondered if they were part of the original ship that had brought people to Livre. It was strange to see these artifacts of a world that had ceased to exist before his grandparents were born. The inner worlds had begun to default on the deliveries within a few generations, and then when war broke out, they'd abandoned Livre altogether. But this place looked as if people from another planet might land any time. The windwood furniture and elaborate glassware of a wealthy Livre home was missing. The walls weren't painted with some mural, and there weren't any thick, wind-resistant glass panels that made the world bend and warp when you looked out them.

"Damn it," Shan swore.

Temar turned and waited for some sort of explanation, but Shan pushed himself away from the keyboard, his chair rolling over the metal floor.

"Nothing. There's nothing," Shan snapped. Temar's eyes darted to the door, as he half expected someone to hear and come running, but if there was anyone home, they didn't want to confront a couple of intruders.

"Maybe Ben's tampered with the gauges on the line itself," Temar suggested. That's what he and Cyla had assumed when they thought Landowner Young had stolen their water.

Shan shook his head. "Too easy to catch that. Worse, you couldn't steal from everyone on a line, because the computers here would recognize that the water going into the line and the water use on it weren't consistent."

"And it doesn't show that?" Temar guessed.

"No. It shows that everything is working fine. It shows that the line Ben and Young and your father share is registering fully functional. I don't understand this." Shan ran his fingers through his black hair, so that when he finished, it stuck up at odd angles.

"So, where's the water?"

"I don't know." Shan practically leaped up, his whole body jerking with repressed emotion as he threw himself at the door and braced himself against the sides. Temar found himself retreating from the strong emotion, not sure how to handle the flashes of fury in Shan's expression. Shan, however, kept right on talking. "The numbers all show equal distribution of water. The computer says that everything is fine. But we know it's not. But computers can't lie." Shan leaned forward until he could rest his forehead against the closed door. "I don't understand any of this. It doesn't make sense."

"Has Ben changed something, broken something?" Temar forced himself to ask the question, even though Shan's anger frightened him.

For a second, Shan continued to stand there against the door. Slowly he turned around. "Could he have broken the computer?" Shan looked toward Temar.

Temar could only stare with wide eyes. He didn't know enough about computers to even turn one on consistently.

"Computers take the information that they're given, and then they have little tiny machines inside of them to compare the numbers and store the numbers."

"Like gears?"

"I wish I knew. I'm great with bikes, and I'm even passable with water lines, I don't know anything about computers. Well, I know how to run them. However, I don't know how to fix them or how to spot it if someone else has broken them."

"So there's no way for us to tell what they've done? Ben can steal all that water, and there's no record?"

"You'd think his partners would know him well enough not to trust him, wouldn't you?"

"What do you mean?"

Shan leaned back against the wall. "We thought Ben was this warm, affable man. We never saw any evidence that would suggest he could steal water from an entire valley. But his partners know that he lies. They know he can smile at someone's face and pat them on the back and give them encouragement, and the whole time he's stealing from them. They know he's a two-faced hypocritical—" Shan stopped. "I'm not feeling very priestly."

"So, would they keep records somewhere else?"

"Water use records would be huge. You have to track all the water coming in, the water going out, the weather, the evaporation rates, the dew hitting the underside of the water catchers…. That takes a computer." Shan straightened up slowly, his eyes scanning the room. "And they have a lot of computers here," he said in an odd tone of voice. "Temar, turn them on. Turn them all on."

"But…." Temar looked, but only two of the computers had keyboards that allowed access. Short of a button that said "on," he didn't know how to work one of these machines. "How?"

"Using this." Shan pulled a small black thing out of the front of one of the two computers that had a keyboard control sitting in front of it. "This tells the keyboard to control this computer. I always assumed these other computers were inoperable, but try to push the control thing in the front and power them up."

Following Shan's lead and half afraid he was going to damage one of the most valuable assets on the planet—again—Temar pulled the little button out of the front of the second computer. For a second, it resisted, but then it slid out so fast that Temar stumbled back before looking at the tiny thing in his hand. Moving carefully, Temar slid the silver end into the next computer and hit the power button on the keyboard.

"You have to push it all the way in, like a plug," Shan said. Before Temar could ask him what that meant, Shan put his hand over

Temar's and pushed, so they both felt the thing click in place. But then Shan hesitated, his hand covering Temar's, and Temar felt the heat gather in his skin. Time paused. For one moment, Temar felt the strong touch, and he wasn't afraid. The computer beeped, and Shan jerked his hand back. "Sorry," he offered quickly before he turned to his own work.

Feeling flustered, Temar powered the computer up, and lines of numbers that didn't mean anything scrolled across the screen. Once he knew the system was turning on, he pulled out the black plug and moved to the next machine, repeating the process until Temar had turned on three computers, and Shan had another four running, so that the entire panel of nine computers clicked and beeped away in the room.

"What does all this mean?" Temar asked as the computer screens started showing different figures and numbers.

"I'm not sure. I think this is weather tracking."

"They know the weather?" Temar leaned closer to study the long line of the eastern mountains and small red dots for White Hills and Landing and Red Plain and Gambles and Blue Hope. A series of dots with ever-changing numbers moved toward the red dot in the middle that had "LCR" next to it. "Wind speeds?" Temar guessed as he watched the cloud of numbers creep toward LCR.

"It makes sense. I know the settlers could anticipate storms. Some of the old manuals recommend moving all equipment inside and securing it at least thirty minutes before any storm activity."

Temar snorted. "Any storm that gives you thirty minutes' warning is moving slower than creepweed."

"Exactly. But if they had this, they knew it was coming."

"We still have this, but no one's using it." Temar wondered if there was something nefarious behind that, or if the failure of the communication satellite thirty years ago made the information useless to the towns. "And if that is coming at us, we're going to be trapped in here," Temar warned as he pointed at the screen. It wasn't a monster coming at them, but on Livre, even the moderately large storms could kill you if you weren't in a valley or building, or at the very least, under something really heavy.

"And the Suettes are going to be trapped, wherever they are."

Temar gave Shan a confused look.

"The Suette family runs the relay," Shan explained. "This one is more interesting. I can't figure out what that is." Shan moved to another computer and pointed to a red "x" just south of LCR. There wasn't anything out there but desert.

"Did the drop ships have another landing site?"

"Not that I know of, but then I wasn't the greatest student of history. I always had my head in a manual for fixing a sand bike," Shan confessed.

"So it could be something old?" Temar reached out to touch the screen, and he yanked his hand back when the whole display changed the minute he touched it. "Gods and stars. It's one of those touchable ones."

Shan whistled. "I feel like I'm in a vid, with all this technology."

"I feel like someone is about to jump out and hit us on the head for seeing all this," Temar said with a little less enthusiasm.

"They'll have to hit me first."

"That doesn't make me feel any better," Temar pointed out, but Shan was already poking the screen, his face lit with pleasure as he used the new toy. The red "x" vanished, replaced with the heading "Livre Emergency Evacuation" and a plan that looked like a very odd floor plan, with circles inside of circles.

"Shan?"

"I have no idea." Shan touched the screen again and again, the data changing so fast that Temar couldn't make sense of one bit before Shan had changed to another. Finally the whole screen blinked, and then the stylized figures gave way to a real picture. Temar saw several people walking around a tall rocket, the sort used to push off a planet.

"Vid?" Temar asked as he leaned in closer. In school, vids of the rockets and the ships were boring, but after poking around this house and seeing how these settlers might have lived, Temar was a little more interested.

"No." Shan's voice was utterly flat. Temar turned and gave him an odd look. Shan pointed to the screen. "That's Jorok Suette." Temar frowned as he looked at a tiny man kneeling next to a tall rocket.

"But… that's impossible."

"Livre Evacuation Plan." Shan spit the words out, but Temar still didn't understand. Shan moved closer, his hip bumping Temar, and Temar backed away, still not sure what was going on. Shan poked at the computer screen so hard Temar was afraid he'd break it.

"Is that now? Is that a real rocket? A working rocket?"

Shan's jaw bulged in a gesture that Temar had seen on Naite, but never Shan before. "It is. It's part of an evacuation plan. I need a storage reader, something to record this," Shan snapped.

Temar looked around for one, but there were so many devices, he wasn't sure he'd spot one in all this technology. "Shan, what are they doing?"

Shan braced his hands on either side of the screen, and for a second, Temar really thought Shan was angry enough to hit something. He retreated to the far wall and used his search for a storage reader to head into the next room. A rocket. An evacuation rocket. Adults on Livre tended to be pretty honest with their children. Any schoolchild who could do math knew the whole planet was dying, and even the work of farmers like George Young, who specialized in low-water crops, could only slow that down. However, no one had ever mentioned a rocket.

Finally, Temar spotted a small computer recorder, and he grabbed it before heading back in and offering it up. "Shan, how many people can fit in that rocket?"

Shan stared at the computer screen, his jaw bulging and his hands curled into fists. He poked at the computer with vicious, short jabs of his fingers. It took him several seconds to get an answer out. "Two hundred and seven, including crew."

Temar sucked in a breath. Two hundred. There were more than two hundred in the Valley alone, not counting Landing or any of the other towns or valleys.

"They'll never get everyone in there."

"They aren't even going to try, Temar."

"You mean…." Temar stopped, his stomach souring as reality hit him like a sandstorm. Ben and his friends were going to leave. They were going to take that rocket and leave everyone else to slowly die, generation by generation. "The water?" Temar asked, his voice weak and his head throbbing heavily.

"They've poached over twelve million gallons for their rocket launch."

Temar stumbled back until he hit the wall, and then he slid down. Twelve million gallons. That was… that was an infinite wealth of water. That was so much he couldn't conceive of it. That would be enough to feed the farms for an entire season, without even recycling. Temar had no idea how that much water would change the water-use projections. How many more generations could the valleys survive with that much water?

"Why? Why steal so much?" The words came out as a whisper, even though Temar wanted to scream.

Shan turned his back on the computer, and he looked old, older than Temar had ever seen him. "The equipment at the launch pad separates the hydrogen and oxygen, to use them as fuel."

"They're using our water to launch their ship?" Temar couldn't breathe. When Ben had threatened to kill him, the horror of it was enough to make some part of Temar want to curl up and die, but Shan was describing a plan to kill an entire planet.

"It's worse," Shan said. He crouched down, but then he fell back against the wall under the computer, as if his legs couldn't hold him up anymore. "When a rocket launches, the sound waves from the engines warp things, bend them."

Temar frowned, not sure how that was worse.

"They stop the waves by dumping hundreds of thousands of gallons out onto the ground as the rocket launches—to break up the sound waves."

Temar's stomach rolled. He barely had time to lean to the side before he started throwing up. The sour stench made his stomach roll even more, and dry heaving racked his body. A hand rubbed comforting circles on his back. "It's okay. We'll stop them. It's okay, Temar. I promise we'll stop them. I promise before God that we'll stop them." Shan kept up a steady litany of promises as Temar's body heaved and rolled. He envisioned a generation of children, of Hannal and Tom's kids, of the kids he'd gone to school with and the ones who would race down Landing's main road after church... he imagined them all dying of thirst while Ben dumped thousands of gallons onto the dry ground. Temar kept heaving until his stomach hurt and Shan's soft vows had fallen silent.

chapter
twenty-two

TEMAR FOLDED his sand scarf and wrapped it around his head twice before fastening it. "Are you sure we should go out in this?" Temar asked as he eyed the door to the outside.

"No, but I know that it looks like they're close to launching. Ista Songwind's circuits were the last part, and from what I can tell, they're doing some panicking. Some of them think your disappearance and my supposed death are going to push the councils to investigate too deeply."

"So if we don't stop them, all that water will be—" Temar stopped, his stomach rolling again. He didn't want to throw up anymore, especially since his stomach was empty.

"If they launch, the most the good Lord can do is make their sorry rocket crash."

"Which doesn't bring back all that water."

Shan sighed. "No, it doesn't. And it looks like they've started converting water to fuel, and we don't have time to go for help."

"So, it's just you and me?" Temar asked.

Shan gave him a sympathetic look. "I'd suggest you stay here, but I'm afraid you might hit me." He smiled to show that he was trying to joke, even if the attempt was pathetic.

"I would," Temar agreed. Twenty-four hours ago, he'd been haunted by the memory of what Ben had done to him, but now the image of children dying of thirst had replaced that fear. He couldn't change the past, but he could prevent Ben from creating that future.

"The place isn't more than thirty minutes' ride away."

"And how do we keep from getting lost in this storm?"

"With this." Shan held his arm up to show Temar a piece of metal strapped around it. It had a tiny computer screen, smaller than anything Temar had ever seen. "I saw Holmes use one once."

"Shan, do you think…." Temar stopped. He didn't want to start questioning every person he'd met. He didn't want to wonder which of his friends and neighbors would let an entire planet die just to save themselves. He really didn't want to make Shan question people like Holmes, who'd been so important to him.

"I have the list on the storage reader, but I couldn't look," Shan said, answering Temar's question even though Temar hadn't asked it out loud. "Cover your eyes or you're going to go blind by the other end of this." Shan changed the subject and pulled goggles over his head before tying off his sand scarf. Temar pulled his own goggles on and settled them on his face before adding another loop of scarf over the top of his head to protect his forehead. Bad storms were enough to etch glass, so Temar suspected any bit of exposed skin would be raw before they got to the launch site, even if it was close.

Shan headed out, and Temar followed, not bothering to secure the door behind him. If the pristine living quarters were ruined, Temar didn't care. By next week, the Suette family and Ben and every other evil person on this planet were either going to be in space or in exile. Their chairs didn't matter much. A little part of Temar quailed at the waste, but a bigger part felt the need to damage something, and the chairs were a good target.

Temar had to hold onto Shan's belt to keep from losing him in the thick sand that blew down the valley, blasting them. Even with the goggles, Temar's eyes started to itch, so he closed them and followed wherever Shan led. When they stopped, he knew they'd reached the bike, but it seemed to take Shan a long time to get the machine going. Temar stood with his hand braced on the back of the sand bike, wondering if there was any way to get help. It had taken them three hours to get here from Landing, and that was without the storm. Shan was probably right that they didn't have time to waste on getting help, but Temar wasn't one to rush into things. He'd obviously missed out on inheriting whatever gene allowed Shan and Cyla to rush in and trust that they'd come out the other end. Temar wasn't that certain. However, he would rather go down trying to stop these people than sit in the safety of the relay buildings as a group of selfish men and women condemned an entire world to death.

The wind was sharp enough to feel like prickles against his skin by the time the roar of the bike rose over the sound of the wind, crashing down the narrow valley. Temar cracked his eyes open, and through the fog of dust, he saw Shan throw his leg over the sand bike. Temar followed, pressing himself tightly against Shan's back, and then they were off.

Temar wasn't sure how Shan could even see through the storm, but he guided the bike over one shifting sand dune after another. Each time they came to the crest, the wind tore at them, and the bike shuddered under Temar, but Shan guided them down into the trough between dunes, where sand devils rose in violent swirls.

Soon the sand thinned, and the sand bike bounced as the wide tires found purchase on solid rock. When Shan pulled the bike so sharply to the side that they nearly went over, Temar's eyes came open in time to see the foggy outline of a crag rise up from the floor of a shallow valley. "Shan?" Temar yelled over the wind and the motor.

"Soon. This is the mouth of the valley," Shan yelled back, the wind whipping his words away almost before Temar could hear them. He drove slower now, and Temar tried to blink away the sting in his eyes from the fine particles of sand that had worked their way under his goggles.

The valley stayed narrow, even narrower than the one where the Livre Communication Relay sat. However, the floor of the valley quickly dropped far below the level of the sand dunes, with rock walls on either side. Small valleys like this sometimes had dunes crash over the top, burying them, and Temar eyed the top of the rocky walls as the air started to clear.

"How deep is this?" Temar asked. He hadn't known there was anything west of the relay, but this felt… wrong. It was too deep, and the walls didn't have the worn edges of the Landing Valley.

"Deep," Shan shouted back. "Is it just me, or does this look almost like it's been cut?"

Now that Shan said it, Temar saw the evidence. The slope of the valley floor was too sharp—the walls were too straight. It reminded Temar of the relay station and all the unnatural angles. "Did the settlers have machines that could have done this?" Temar asked.

Shan shifted the bike into another gear, and the roar turned into a rumble as they slowed. "I don't think so, but explorers and military units were on Livre before it was opened for settlement. I know one of the planets tried to set up mining here, but the cost of importing everything the miners demanded was more than the optic glass exports were worth. I guess settlers and a terraforming setup were cheaper in the long run."

With that, Shan guided the bike into a corner formed by the straight wall and a fallen chunk of rock with two square edges. "We should walk from here." Shan stared straight ahead, his sand scarf and goggles obscuring his expression.

"Why?" Temar asked.

Shan looked over his shoulder, but the gray dust covering Shan hid his emotions. "You can stay here," Shan said. From his jacket, he pulled out a long bar that Temar hadn't seen him put in there. Reality hit him. Guards. These people would have put guards on the place if they were nervous. Shan was talking about fighting their own people.

Taking a deep breath, Temar squared his shoulders. "I'm going with you." For a second, Shan looked at him, but then he nodded and swung his leg off the bike. Since he was shorter, Temar had to scramble a little to get off, but when he did, he grabbed for Shan's arm. "You're a priest. You shouldn't have to…." Temar looked down at the pipe. The simple fact was that Shan was taller and heavier, even if he had lost a lot of weight recently. Temar wouldn't have the same strength behind his hits, but he figured he should be the one swinging the pipe, since Shan was a priest. Temar had a knife he could use, but he really did hope to avoid doing too much damage.

Shan pulled his goggles off and wiped a hand over his eyes. "I'll ask God to forgive me later," Shan said, his voice trembling with emotion. "But I won't stand by and watch children I've baptized condemned because of men like Ben Gratu. That isn't moral." Shan's voice was cold on the last part, and Temar felt a tremor of fear. Then

Shan pulled his hand away from his eyes, and Temar saw the pain in them.

"I'll be there with you," Temar promised, and the look Shan gave him was almost grateful.

"Just don't stand so close I accidentally hit you with this. It's been a long time since I played stickball or tried to hit anyone." Shan's attempt at humor sounded strained and painful, but Temar smiled anyway.

"That's fair. And Shan?"

"Yes?"

Temar closed his mouth, not sure what to say, but he had to say something about how much Shan had meant to him... how much Shan had helped him. Despite the vagueness of Temar's clue, Shan had followed it. Because Temar had kept Ben's secret, Shan had nearly died, and he never blamed Temar. When Temar felt dirtied by Ben's touch, the fact that Shan still felt desire made him almost believe.... Temar struggled to put a word to it. He almost felt whole. It made Temar think maybe people could see him and not focus only on those bruises. For the longest time, Temar felt like he didn't exist, like the hand-shaped bruises on his thighs were real, and he was the shadow that wore them. But Shan had seen those marks... he'd seen the belt marks on the backs of his legs, and he still saw Temar. He still wanted Temar, even when Temar flinched from a simple touch.

"Thank you," Temar said, the words catching in his throat.

Shan looked confused. "For what?"

Temar chewed on his lower lip, his thoughts too chaotic to explain how much it all meant to him. Shan dropped his gaze to the ground between them for a moment before reaching out to slowly touch Temar on the shoulder. "Hey, we're in this together, right? After all, it was a hallucination of you that got me through the desert."

Temar smiled and gave a nod. He didn't have anything to do with that. As much as Temar sometimes doubted the existence of God, he suspected God had more to do with Shan's hallucinations than he did. However, he was glad his image had helped Shan. Overhead, streaks of gray and tan stained the sky as the wind ripped the sand across the face of Livre.

"So, let's take care of this," Shan said, his face suddenly grim.

Temar unwound his sand scarf and wrapped it around his right hand before he made a fist. He didn't have to answer because Shan was moving down the valley, staying close to the side and taking advantage of where the sunlight didn't actually reach the ground. It hit the sand cloud overhead and illuminated every grain of sand, so that the sky glowed like overheated glass. However that meant that the sunlight couldn't shine down, so they were in a strange twilight.

Running in silence, Temar fought an urge to cough. Ahead he could see a black square that had the same perfect lines as the relay or the council house in Landing. There was a metal building up ahead. Shan stopped behind a rock and crouched down, and Temar found his own hiding spot several yards behind Shan.

Shan held up a hand and pointed, and Temar nodded, even though Shan didn't bother to turn and look at the gesture. Slowly, Shan moved closer, but Temar waited, watching the valley. He couldn't see anyone, and his guts were tangled in one big knot.

Without a sound, Shan darted out from behind his rock, his weapon raised. Temar couldn't see anyone in the deep shadow, but there was a pained cry as someone went down. Crouching low, Temar raced forward, terrified that Shan needed him and he wasn't there to help. When he got close, Shan stared down at a body lying in the dust.

"Shan?" The stillness frightened Temar.

"I know him," Shan said, his eyes still on the person lying on the ground. The man's limbs were thrown out at awkward angles, but he was breathing. "I know him," Shan repeated, softer this time. Temar couldn't find any words to say. Before he could blurt out something inappropriate, Shan shook himself free of the paralysis and looked toward the door. "If they have a patrol, they're going to know we're here now."

"So, we go in?"

Shan looked over. "Or we give up and run like hell." His tone made it clear that he wouldn't blame Temar if he picked option two.

"We go in," Temar said, heading for the door. Part of him said they'd be better off running and coming back with a plan and a whole lot of help, but with the storm, neither was possible. Shan caught his arm, and Temar couldn't help that moment of fear that made him flinch away. Shan let his hand drop.

"Let me go first. I look like about half the planet, Temar. I'm downright average as long as no one looks at the nose too long. They see me first, and they're going to hesitate as they wonder who I am. They see you, and they're going to know exactly who you are. You should stay behind me."

"I can fight," Temar said. Ever since he'd lain under Ben, biting his lip to keep from screaming, he'd felt the anger, like an itch under his skin, and he wanted a fight.

Nodding, Shan agreed. "I know you can, but we may need those few extra seconds."

Temar clenched his teeth, but he didn't protest when Shan moved in front of him, pipe still in hand. The door was closed, but at Shan's push, the heavy metal slid back, and cooler air from a deep cave drifted up, bathing them. Temar breathed in the scent of metal. He exchanged a concerned look with Shan, but then Shan was moving into the dark.

The first room was pitch black, but a glow at the far end led them toward a hall that took a ninety-degree turn and was illuminated with lights set into the wall about every six inches. The whole floor sloped down into the bowels of the artificial cave. Temar couldn't help but think that this was an incredible waste of resources. "What is this place?" he whispered, but his words echoed along the bare walls.

Shan gave a helpless shrug and kept moving. Temar heard footsteps long before he saw anyone, and Shan started pulling at doors until he found one unlocked. He yanked the door open, holding it for Temar to duck inside before following. Shan stood with his hand on the door as the footsteps passed them in the hall.

In a voice little more than a breath, Shan said, "We have to assume they'll find Devin."

"Who?"

Shan gave Temar an odd look. "The man I hit."

"Oh."

With a deep breath, Shan opened the door and headed back into the hall. Temar felt an odd calm, as if his soul had just gotten so tired of being scared that it had gone numb. He tried to swallow, but his throat was so dry that the sides stuck together, and he had to fight down another urge to cough as he followed Shan out into the hall. Shan was trotting now, moving so fast that Temar had to break into a jog to keep up.

Voices echoed ahead of him, and Temar could feel his head getting light and overstuffed at the same time. It took him a little longer than it should have to realize he'd stopped breathing, but then his body wasn't really talking to his mind at this point. He could feel his muscles tremble, but he couldn't quite feel the emotion that generated that excess energy. He should be afraid. He should be terrified. And it really should have occurred to Temar that the two of them were heading into the mountain with no real plan. Next time someone tried to set up a giant water conspiracy, Temar was going to insist on being the one to make the plans, because Cyla and Shan both lacked any kind of skill at the matter.

Shan stopped and pointed straight down. Temar frowned as he looked at the stone floor. While he felt more than a little awe at the tool that could cut so smoothly, he didn't think this was the time for sightseeing. He gave Shan a confused look. Silently and slowly, Shan tugged at Temar's shirt, pulling him forward until Temar spotted the grate set into that smooth, stone floor under Shan's feet. Below them, pipes rumbled, and steam sluggishly swirled through the air. Steam. Temar figured he was about the only person on all of Livre to see both steam and mud on this water-starved world. The mud had horrified him, the sheer waste of water made him ill, but this was worse. The steam that slowly rose from the machinery below them had been intentionally stolen.

Kneeling down, Shan wrapped his fingers around the grate and pulled, small grunts the only sign of how much effort he was putting into it. Nothing moved. Temar got down on the ground, the stone floor nearly crushing his kneecaps as he tried to help.

Shan's face was set in a mask of frustration as he pulled a tool out of a pocket and started working the bolts on the side. His arm flew as he worked the bolt, little clicking sounds as the tool loosened it with every crank. Standing up, Temar looked nervously down one way and then the other. If the person who passed found the guard, he or she would come running back through here or call lots and lots of people to run up through here, but either way, they'd be caught.

When Shan finally got the last bolt out and dropped it into his pocket, he breathed in hungry gasps and knelt with both hands braced against the floor. Temar pulled at the grate, straining when the heavy metal resisted before scraping against the stone sides of the hole. However, it finally did lift, and Temar braced his knee against it to hold it up.

Leaning so close that Temar could smell the musk of his sweat, Shan whispered, "Wait here." Temar opened his mouth to object, but Shan lay on his stomach, and his top half vanished into the hole. He was the mechanic. If someone had to break something, he was the reasonable choice for doing the breaking. However, Temar's arm hair rose as he held the grate open, and Shan vanished into the machines. Temar didn't hear thuds or screaming, so he assumed Shan had found a way down into the mechanical room that didn't involve falling twenty feet to the floor below.

Before he could consider following, a woman appeared in the hall that led out to the surface. Temar knelt on one knee, his other leg bracing the grate as he stared at her, something locking both of them in place. Her eyes were wide, and she vaguely looked familiar… from the church, maybe. Her mouth came open, and he lurched forward, the grate clattering into place with a huge racket, like a hundred pieces of glass hitting the ground all at once. The metal almost bounced on the stone, and the resulting rattle echoed forever.

Temar launched himself at the woman, tackling her with a shoulder in the stomach, and her yell cut off suddenly. It was almost a chirp of a scream—cut short before it could reach full volume. However, Temar figured that by dropping the grate, he'd already made enough noise to get the entire group's attention. So their only hope of saving the water was for Temar to keep their attention until Shan could finish.

Struggling back to his feet, Temar tried to run for the exit, figuring he'd make enough noise to pull them out after him. However, the woman on the ground caught his leg and wrapped her whole body around it. Temar might have felt bad about kicking a stranger before he'd found out about the water, before he'd found his own anger and hate in Ben's bed. Now he kicked with his free leg. She gave a pained squawk, but she held on through two more of Temar's hardest kicks until he finally wrenched his leg away from her and stumbled back.

Footsteps pounded down the hall, and Temar turned and ran for the exit, pausing at the place where the hall took its ninety-degree turn out into the open air of Livre. He needed them to see him. He needed to pull the attackers away from Shan. The first man to come racing from farther in the mountain slid to a stop near the woman Temar had kicked. She was curled on her side, her arms cradling her stomach, and Temar watched from sixty or seventy yards down the hall. It wasn't a great head start, but if they came after him, they were going to have a hell of a time catching up with him on foot. He could outrun them until Shan had saved the water.

Two more people appeared—a man with sunset-colored hair and a tall woman with a hawk's face. They both ran for Temar, and Temar prepared to dash away on his mission, but a voice called them all to a halt.

"Leave him!" Temar's guts felt like water—like they were sloshing around inside his skin as he recognized Ben's voice. "He wouldn't be here alone. Dusty, check the fuel lines. Juke, get to command."

Everyone stayed frozen as Ben came strolling out of the hidden base as casually as if he was crossing Landing's town center to go to church. "The boy's not going to walk in here alone. I know him. Dusty, Juke, check everything. We only have one chance at this." Ben stopped several feet short of the woman Temar had kicked. "Tyson, get Karan up to the ship and see if the doc can't give her something for the pain and get her settled into a medbed."

Ben gave a sad little laugh and shook his head before he looked right at Temar, and time stopped. If Temar's internal organs had turned to water before, they were now sloshing around inside until Temar wanted to vomit. There was seventy yards between them, but Temar could feel Ben's hands on him, and he had to carefully control his body to keep it from shaking apart into pieces.

"My little sandrat wouldn't be here if he didn't have a sandcat out there hunting the dunes for him, would you?" he asked in that sweet tone that always meant Temar would suffer.

"You're a thief," Temar spit out.

"I'm taking what my grandparents were promised… a terraformed planet or a ticket off." Ben spread his arms out, and as if he were a magician, time seemed to pick up where it left off. The man with the sunset hair and his partner turned and raced back into the base, and the man who had stopped to help the woman Temar had kicked lifted her into his arms with a grunt and started after them. That left Temar and Ben and a length of hallway that grew shorter by the second.

Frustration made Temar's hands curl into fists. All he had to do was distract the thieves until Shan could figure out how to break their valves and save the water. He couldn't even do that right. "You're stealing from everyone on the planet. You're a murderer." Temar spit the words out.

Ben gave an amused snort. "You tell the inner planets that. Their feud is killing the planet. I'm just getting off while the getting is good. So, who did you bring with you, Temar? It wouldn't have been a council attack party. Trust me, I would have heard the rumors if you'd gone to any of the councils. Ever since Ista panicked, I've wondered whether that priest who worried so much about you actually died out in that desert. That was sloppy work. I would have made sure to put a bullet in his head and then watch the sandcats drag his body parts out into the dunes if I wanted him dead." Ben sounded oddly amused by his own words, but then he always had been. Temar's breath came in little gasps. They were both so very dead, and Ben was still going to get his way.

"Shan?" Ben shouted. "Shan, are you lurking around here somewhere?"

Temar held his breath. He'd shout for Shan to stay hidden, only that would pretty much confirm that Shan was alive and hopefully breaking the machinery that turned their stolen water into fuel.

"No comment on that, boy? Maybe you learned to keep your mouth closed." Ben gave another chuckle as he walked over to the grate, which had landed with one corner stuck up in the air as another corner fell down into the hole. "So, who's down there?"

Temar stood in silence, fighting his fear with so much of his heart that he didn't have time to bother with Ben. He was too busy fighting his own fear and his irrational urge to beg for Ben not to hurt him. That hadn't worked well last time, and Temar suspected it wouldn't work any better now. He had to clamp his mouth shut to avoid saying the words anyway.

Footsteps came running, and Temar flinched, even though the person came up behind Ben, far enough away that they didn't pose any immediate threat. At the gesture, Ben gave Temar a knowing smile that made his guts roll and churn.

"What's going on? Do we have a problem?" The newcomer was a man with a narrow face.

"I guess that depends on whether we caught our intruders coming or going."

The man frowned at Temar. "Isn't that—"

"He's going to tell us who came with him."

"But—"

"So, young sandrat," Ben said, his smile faltering as he considered Temar, and Temar could feel the danger, like sand shifting under his feet. "Who did come with you? Shan? Some school friend? Or are you actually alone?"

Temar's feet grew so heavy he could only watch Ben and this new man.

"Did he get down there?" the new man asked.

Ben thought on that for a few long seconds. "We have to assume he did. Get the Suettes down there to check all the pipes and lines. If something's wrong, we need to know before we have a disaster."

"That will slow us down by hours, maybe days."

"Which is better than having the launch fail," Ben pointed out. "The storm is going to keep anyone at bay, and if the Suettes get down there now, we can get off planet by tomorrow. There'll be plenty of time for us all to catch up on sleep when we're on the ship."

The second man looked unsure, but after a bit, he nodded and headed back down into the sunken base. Ben pursed his lips. "And now we need to talk."

Temar watched, feeling like a sandrat caught in a pipe trap. Something moved behind him, and he tried to spin around, but arms caught his shoulder. Someone almost threw him against the wall, and

Temar tried to kick out, but his legs were weak from having stood so long with his knees locked. He couldn't get in a good kick, and before he could do anything, strong arms caught him around his elbows, trapping them against his body.

"I got him!" a man called, and heavy footsteps suggested that Ben was coming. Temar's body finally caught up with his mind, flooding him with fear that made his heart pound so hard he could feel the pressure behind his eyes.

"Excellent. Is everyone okay up there?"

"Devin's hurt pretty bad."

Temar felt a familiar hand wrap around his wrist, and then Ben yanked him away from the man who had jumped Temar from behind.

"Get him down to medical."

"Why do you care? You're killing how many people on Livre? Why do you care if you let one more die?" Temar demanded. His fear made his throat constrict, but he wouldn't live in fear of Ben's fists anymore. At worst, Ben would kill him, and unless Shan could stop their rocket, Ben was going to pretty much kill everyone Temar had ever loved by leaving them to die on a water-starved world.

"Such a black-and-white world you see," Ben said, with the sort of fondness parents used when discussing their children's mistakes, but Temar wasn't a child. He yanked at his arm, trying to free it. The wrist popped painfully, but Ben essentially dragged Temar back toward the grate while the other man headed back out the other end of the tunnel. "Shan, I have our little friend in hand." Ben's free hand came down on Temar's ass with such force that Temar yelped before he could stop himself. "Did you hear that?" Ben called. "If you don't come out, I'm going to amuse myself by doing a lot more damage to him."

"There's no one down there," Temar complained loudly. Hopefully he was loud enough for Shan to hear and understand that he had to get his job done—he had to sabotage the rocket.

"That's fine. That means that I can take all the time I want hurting you," Ben said in a voice only slightly lower. Temar's knees started shaking.

"Enough." Shan's voice came from somewhere below them, echoing against the concrete. "What kind of man hurts someone half his size?"

Ben looked down through the grate. Part of Temar wanted to do the same. He wanted to look down, but his eyes were locked on Ben. He felt as if the world would start spinning if he looked away from Ben for even one second.

"Find someone to surrender to or climb on up," Ben said in a friendly voice, "but every second you aren't standing right here, I have Temar to amuse me." When Ben looked up and met Temar's eyes, Temar's stomach lurched and rolled so badly he nearly threw up all over Ben, and he was pretty sure that wouldn't end well at all.

chapter
twenty-three

SHAN FOUGHT against an urge to shake his arms free of his two guards, but he didn't have a lot of power here, and if these people would kill a planet full of people to save themselves, Shan figured he didn't have much of a chance with them. That sense of helplessness was worse because he didn't know these two. They'd been in the mechanical room where Shan had surrendered, standing dangerously close to the valves that Shan had closed and then snapped off. He didn't know how long that would slow the group down, but at this rate, Shan figured God would have to take a more direct approach if he wanted to save Livre. Shan had managed to fail rather spectacularly. He'd failed his planet, and he'd failed Temar.

The two guards led him up a flight of stairs, but instead of heading up the corridor that angled slightly up and out, they led him farther into the complex. They passed Reddy Chilan. Shan had performed his marriage, but the man didn't even blink at the sight of Shan under guard. The guards finally came to an open door, and one went in ahead while the other stood behind Shan, holding Shan's upper arms so hard that Shan could feel the bruises forming.

Without arguing, Shan went into the room and found Ben sitting behind a desk, his left arm wrapped around Temar's waist, forcing Temar to stand next to him, their bodies touching. Shan felt ill.

"Well, if it isn't the priest." Ben's smile left Shan with an urge to punch him in the nose. It'd been a long time since Shan had fought, and back then he generally fought with and lost to Naite, but for Ben and his unctuous smile, Shan could make an exception.

"Temar, are you alright?" Shan asked as his two guards took up positions on either side of him.

Temar gave a quick nod, but he looked a rather alarming shade of white. The worst part was that Shan couldn't do anything to protect him. Ben had the power here, and all Shan could do was try to distract the sadist. Never before had Shan felt hate, not like this.

"How could you, Ben?" he demanded. "How could any of you?" Shan turned and looked at his two guards. Neither looked impressed with Shan's moral objections.

"Do you really think the better answer is to stay on this lump of sand until we all die?" Ben demanded. However, his arm loosened, allowing Temar the smallest fraction of an inch between them. Shan counted that as a victory.

Narrowing his eyes, Shan glared at the man. "Unfortunately, you aren't in any danger of dropping dead, any time soon."

Ben leaned back in his chair. "I want children. I want a family. I want to watch grandchildren and great grandchildren running around a farm. I want to have something that survives after me. Do you really think any of that is possible on Livre?"

"If you want that, find a woman to give you children instead of stealing from others' children."

For a second, Ben shook his head with this expression, like he was trying to be patient with a particularly stupid child. "Don't you get it? Don't you see what you're doing? You're bringing children into this world to die. You're pigs bred for slaughter, and this is the pen." Ben gestured toward the room, and that freed Temar. Instead of running, Temar inched backward, so he was about six inches away from Ben, and then he stopped. Shan's mouth went dry as he realized Temar was too afraid to move away. He was too afraid to run. Shan was going to hell for dragging Temar back into his worst nightmare.

"This is our home," Shan said from between clenched teeth.

"Our dying home. I won't die like a pig, slaughtered because of some war up there that I can't control."

Shaking his head, Shan realized that's what really had Ben upset. He couldn't control the inner planets and their distant war, and he couldn't handle that. Sometimes Shan chafed under Div's constant belief that God would fix whatever needed fixing. Sometimes Shan felt a seed of resentment at the idea of turning everything over to faith. However, he never felt Ben's need to control everything. "That's what this is really about… control," Shan said, his voice thick with disgust. "You're so in love with your control that you can't give it up. You have to control your farm and your farmhands and Temar and now, the whole world. You'd destroy the world just to control it."

Ben's smile was a little tighter, but he kept smiling. "I'm being logical."

"You're being immoral."

"Gods save us from priests." Ben threw both his hands up in the air, as though disgusted. "What's the morality of letting yourself die? Isn't that like suicide? I thought you church folk were against suicide. And you know, that's exactly what it means to stay on this rock."

Shan vehemently shook his head, denying the charge. "We're finding new ways to breed drought-tolerant crops every year."

"We're learning how to die slower," Ben interrupted.

"You're speeding things along by stealing water from the entire planet." Shan spit out the words, and he could feel the taller of the two guards shift nervously. Water theft carried with it such a terrible stigma on Livre that the guard twitched, clearly bothered by the charge. Shan made a mental note to work on turning the guard to their side as soon as they were away from Ben. Shan had no doubt Ben would cut out Shan's tongue before allowing him to talk a guard into thinking about the moral consequences of his behavior.

"The rest of you might lose ten or fifteen years from this. That's all," Ben said dismissively. "If we can't get help to come back to Livre, then your children instead of your grandchildren will die and end up food for sandcats. That is, unless they kill each other over water first. I won't be part of that."

"You're talking about things that may never happen. The war—"

"The war doesn't matter," Ben said, cutting him off. "They're going to leave us here to die. I won't have my children be pawns in their game."

"And when you get up there? What will you be then? A poor farmer from a poorer world?" Shan's cold words finally wiped the smile off Ben's face. For one shining moment, the mask slipped, and the monster within the man looked out through those cold eyes. Then the same old smug expression slipped back into place.

"I'll be the one who survived long enough to stand in a court and press a legal suit for breach of contract. I'll force those inner planets to face what they've done."

"And then what?" Shan pressed. "Send rescue? Force them to finish the terraforming? Are you really trying to pretend that you're the hero here?"

The tall guard spoke up. "It's a better plan than sitting here and dying with our world. At least some of us will live. At least there's a small chance we can get the established worlds to come back."

Sadly, Shan could tell from his earnest expression that he meant that. He was an idiot, but he was a devoutly earnest idiot.

"This isn't about rescue," Shan said. He focused on the guard even though Ben's chair slid across the floor as he stood. "This is about Ben's need for power… his need for money."

"Don't pretend to know me, priest. You sit in your church and wait for God. I'm taking action." Ben was standing now, leaning over his desk with both hands flat against the top. Shan glanced behind Ben to where Temar was a pale shadow of himself. Shan felt hate like a small beast clawing at his guts, as if he was a pipe plant and hate was a sandrat caught inside to run and run in circles. But instead of dying, the hate was seeping into his soul. His hands clenched into fists.

"I know what you did to Temar." Even though Shan's voice came out a whisper, the room went silent. The tall guard stilled his restless shifting, and Ben's face froze.

It took several seconds for Ben to shake himself free. "He enjoyed it. Hell, he begged for my touch."

A shiver took Shan. "You sick bastard."

"Call me what you will, but I'll survive. Temar would have survived too, if he'd stayed with me. I never would have left him to die. I actually care about him, not like you or the others. I never left him out in the world to get himself in trouble."

Up until now, Temar had remained frighteningly silent, but now he spoke up, his voice much more steady than Shan had expected. "I would rather be dead than live with you."

Ben whirled around. "Boy, you know that's not true." From his tone, he actually believed his own words. He sounded shocked.

Temar nodded, his face losing even more color. "Yes, it is."

"Temar." Ben's voice was sharp, an unambiguous warning. "You know I was always fond of you. I promised to protect you, and I did." The tone was so sincere that Shan had to wonder whether Ben had simply stopped engaging with reality at some point. More, he wondered how no one on Livre had ever noticed the monster living in their midst. The town had largely ostracized Shan's father. They might not have known exactly what Yan Polli had done, but they all recognized the moral rot at his center. But Ben… he smiled at all the right times, and even now he maintained such perfect innocence that Shan had trouble reconciling him with the monster who had raped Temar and who now stole water that would be life or death, no matter what lies he told himself to justify his own selfishness.

Temar brought his hands up, so that his elbows were bent, as if preparing for a fight. Slight tremors traveled through his hands. "What you did… that wasn't protection," Temar said, his voice even more firm, though the rest of his body screamed out his fear.

"Oh? The others would have killed you. I protected you, fed you, loved—"

"Raped me," Temar cut him off. At that, the rest of his blood left his face, and he was so pale that Shan felt himself grow more alarmed.

"You traded your affection for security, and I did more to protect you than your father ever did." Ben reached out, and Temar flinched and brought an arm up to block the touch. Temar lurched backward, and Shan instinctively moved forward, only to have the guards on either side catch his arms and hold him tight. With no help, Temar's break for freedom didn't last long. Ben moved fast for a large man, and he caught the arm Temar had used to block his first touch. Yanking on the arm, Ben pulled Temar close. Despite the small, animalistic cry, Temar couldn't resist. He did, however, get in one good punch to Ben's side. Ben gave a startled oomph and then wrapped his other arm around

Temar, hugging him so close that Temar could only struggle, silent despite the frantic squirming.

"Hush, boy. The priest certainly hasn't improved your temper, but think about this—if you come with us, you live. You live in a world where water and computers and life are guaranteed." The struggle continued for several minutes, and Shan tried to pull his arms free, but the guards held him tightly while Temar was left to fight alone. Eventually, Temar stilled.

"And if I don't, you'll kill me with Shan?" Temar demanded, breathless from his desperate effort.

Ben laughed. "I don't plan to kill the priest. If he wants to stay on his planet, he can. We'll be long gone, and any revenge he or his council may dream about will be far out of their reach."

"So, you plan to let us go?" Shan asked, confused. That didn't sound likely, coming from Ben.

Sure enough, Ben shook his head. "Since I doubt you'll tell us exactly what you did to the equipment, we'll have to do a full check of all systems, which may take some time. You'll stay here until we're ready for liftoff. We even have a room with a nice view of the launch pad. You can see the rocket lift off." Ben smiled, and in that instant Shan realized what he was really saying… they'd have a nice view of thousands of gallons of water rushing down to break the sound waves that would rise from the bottom of the pad. The waste made Shan's stomach churn. Ben's arms wrapped tightly around Temar didn't help the sense of overwhelming nausea that threatened.

"Take them to the viewing deck on four and lock them in." Ben gave the order and slowly loosened his arms around Temar, his gaze locked on the younger man. With the two of them standing next to each other, Shan couldn't help but notice how much younger and physically smaller Temar was. His blond hair stuck up every which way, the result of being held close to Ben's chest as he struggled, and his eyes were so light brown they were almost the color of amber glass. Ben was barrel-chested and a good eight inches taller and fifteen years older. The thought of Ben forcing Temar horrified Shan so much acid burned the bottom of his throat. Temar had strength Shan couldn't even fathom, but physically he couldn't compete with Ben.

Ben's smile turned almost fatherly. "You can still come with us, Temar. The others won't like it, but you know I will always put you before them." The tone was so avuncular that Shan wondered if Ben could even understand the damage he'd done.

"I'd rather die," Temar said, spitting the words out as he stood with Ben's hands still on him, his back stiff.

Ben narrowed his eyes, but he didn't comment as he took a step back and let Temar go. "Take them both to the viewing deck," he ordered, all emotion gone from his voice. One of the guards caught Shan's arm and tugged him toward the door. It was the shorter guard, and Shan was grateful that the one who still had a seed of morality left in him took hold of Temar. They were two and two now, so maybe they could fight their way free. Shan tried to make eye contact with Temar, to somehow communicate the need to fight back. However, Temar had his eyes closed as Shan's guard pulled him out of the room.

As they walked down the carved stone corridor, they passed more people he knew. He'd see a woman who he'd taken confession from or a man he'd counseled, and their eyes would go large before their gaze would skitter off in some other direction.

The guards took them to a door and opened it. The shorter one gave Shan a good solid shove, making him stumble forward into a room large enough for a family to live in it. Whatever this place was, it had been built for a significant number of people. One of the walls was thick glass, and through it, Shan could see long lines of artificial lights illuminate a tall cylindrical rocket—the type used to jump off planet.

He sucked in a breath and turned in time to see the taller guard push the door closed. "This is wrong!" Shan called out as he lost his one chance to work on someone who had retained a small shred of integrity. A heavy click answered. Grabbing the door handle, Shan tested the door, but the lock could stop anything short of heavy machinery. Shan certainly wasn't going to move it by hand.

Defeat dragged at him, making Shan want to lie down and sleep until the worst of this was over. Instead, he paced the room. Two walls were metal, one stone, and the last the impact glass that separated them from the rocket. When the group took off, he and Temar would have a good view.

"Did you know Ben's great-great-grandfather mined here before the terraforming started? He told me when we were waiting for you." Temar sounded as bone weary as Shan did.

"Which is how he knew about this place."

"He said our grandparents voted not to use the rocket because not everyone would fit in. They voted to wait for the war to end."

"And sixty years later, the established worlds are still fighting." Shan walked over and leaned against the heavy glass as he studied the rocket. It might be old, but frontier equipment lasted for generations. It had to. On rough, half-terraformed worlds, people couldn't afford to throw away a piece of worn-out technology. On the other hand, this rocket was so old that there was a chance it might fail and send all the traitors burning to death in the atmosphere. As a priest, Shan should have prayed for God to spare people from such destruction, even if it was well deserved, but he couldn't bring himself to pray at all.

Behind him, Temar said in a voice that was little more than a whisper, "I'm sorry."

"You don't have anything to apologize for," Shan said firmly. He didn't need Temar blaming himself, because Shan's own conscience couldn't handle any more guilt. This had been his plan.

"I got caught."

"I made the plan."

"And I should have run and kept on running when someone first spotted me."

Turning around, Shan frowned. "I am not blaming you, because this is entirely Ben's fault, but why didn't you run?"

With a sigh, Temar sank down onto one of the metal benches bolted to the wall. "I was trying to give you more time. I didn't do very well."

Shan moved closer, sitting down next to him. "You gave me enough time to do some damage. We did our best, and I guess now that we've done what we could, we have to trust the Lord."

"And if I don't have any faith that God will send help?" Temar gave Shan a look that begged him for easy answers and reassurances, but Shan didn't have it in him to lie to this man, who had done so much to try and fight the evil.

"I don't know. Honestly, Div was always better at faith than I was. I trust God, but I like to fix things myself."

"Are we back to how you're a bad priest?" Temar almost sounded like he was joking, but he'd closed his eyes and leaned his head back against the wall, so it was hard for Shan to tell.

"Yes."

For a time, they sat next to each other in silence. There weren't any more words. They'd done their best, and they'd failed. Shan wondered how long it would take for them to find the valves he'd broken and check the rest of the lines. There wasn't a toilet in the room, and Shan's desert-born instincts made him loath to pee on the floor, where the water would go to waste.

"I'm sorry you had to hit that man," Temar finally offered in the silence. "You're a priest. I should have done that."

"You did your part distracting them," Shan said. "And I don't feel bad about hitting Devin." That was a slight exaggeration, because Shan could still feel the way the warm pipe thudded against Devin's head. Shan couldn't regret trying to save people, but he wished he could have done it without hitting someone. At the same time, he'd do it again. "The Bible says we should break the arm of the wicked man and call the evildoer to account for his wickedness that would not otherwise be found out. I think the Lord understands."

Temar opened his eyes. "Really? I thought the Bible was more about forgiveness."

"It says that in Psalms, but Div says I always remember the least appropriate quotes," Shan admitted with a smile.

"I would have said that Livre didn't have evildoers. Actually," Temar added after a second, "I think I would have said that my father, with his drunken neglect, was as bad as people got on Livre."

"People always bring selfishness and evil to every world they settle," Shan said as he thought back to his own father. He wondered if Yan Polli had that same unshakable belief in himself that Ben possessed. Had his own father believed that abuse was love? Shan's memories came distorted though the lens of a desperately unhappy childhood, so he couldn't know. Maybe Naite did, but that was one subject Shan intended to never discuss with his brother. After that, they both fell silent.

Time crawled by. A mechanical thump and whine made the room rumble, and for a second, Shan thought the rocket was launching. Temar sucked in a breath, so he probably thought the same. However, the only thing that happened was a door in the roof of the rocket rooms slid to one side, and the sky, still gray with settling dust, appeared.

They still didn't speak, and Shan finally had to pee in the corner. The sour smell of it made the room stink. Temar followed not long after that, and they sat in silence, watching the rocket as the sun came out and bathed it in light, so it looked like some historical vid.

chapter
twenty-four

SOMETHING WAS going on. Shan moved closer to the door and pressed his ear to the metal. In the corridor, someone shouted, but the thick metal distorted the words.

"What's going on?" Temar asked.

"I have no idea."

"Shan?" Temar's voice was tight with emotion, and Shan looked over his shoulder. "If they take off, are they going to bother letting us out of here?"

The same thought had occurred to Shan. If Ben's group took off without unlocking the door, he and Temar would slowly die of thirst. After nearly dying that way once, Shan had already decided that he'd rather find another way to die. Thirst drove a man insane. Shan could feel the tightness in his lips where the new skin was only now covering the splits that had formed during his long walk off the desert. "I don't know," he finally admitted.

Temar turned his back and stared out toward the rocket. In the hall, someone else shouted, and this time the sound was followed by something striking the door with enough force that the metal rang out and the vibrations rattled Shan's head. "Whoa," he said, stepping away from the door and rubbing the spot over his ear.

"What was that?"

"Something really heavy," Shan answered. "Something's going on."

Temar moved to Shan's side, and they exchanged a confused look.

 Lyn Gala

"Take the right, and I'll take left. If someone comes through the door, maybe we can take them."

Temar gave Shan a look that made it clear he didn't think the plan would work, but he moved to the right of the door. For a second time, the whole door shook as something hit it from the other side, and Shan frowned. If Ben's group were just blocking the door, burying him and Temar alive rather than risk that they'd escape, it didn't make sense to hit the door twice. But if they were going to come in, unlocking the door would be step one.

Voices shouted, and Shan's whole body tightened, ready to fight. Temar had his fists drawn up, but they couldn't do anything until the door came open. About the same time Shan thought that, the lock clicked, and the knob started to turn. Temar would be behind the door, so Shan stepped forward, determined to distract whoever came in the room until Temar could get them from behind.

Temar rolled forward onto his toes, looking like a bird about to swoop down, but then Shan focused on the slowly opening door. A hand appeared, pushing at the door.

"Shan, you in here?"

Shan's mouth fell open, even though it took his brain three more seconds to actually process the idea that Naite's voice was attached to the person pushing the door open. "Shan?" Naite called again as he pushed the door the rest of the way open. He stood in the doorway, his wide shoulders blocking it. "Are you okay?" Naite gave him a strange look before glancing over at Temar.

"Did you find them?" someone asked from behind.

"Yeah, but Shan looks like a couple of brain cells got knocked loose."

"What are you doing here?" Shan demanded, the insult finally making him believe that this was Naite and not another hallucination.

"What? I should have left you to handle this on your own?" Naite demanded, crossing his arms. "Maybe you should start by thanking me for hauling your ass out of this mess."

"Thank you," Temar said quickly, before Shan could come up with a response of his own. "We definitely needed the help."

Naite snorted. "This time, no thanking God. I'm the one who showed up," Naite said, poking a finger toward Shan.

"I never said you weren't. And I can thank both of you at the same time," Shan defended himself. "But Naite, seriously, how did you get here?"

"I just followed your trail of pathstones," he said casually. "Aila, did you get the rocket secured?"

A woman answered. "Songwind tried to override the computer controls, but let's see her override the big damn chunk of steel we dropped on the door."

"Any clue how many rats are in that pipe plant?"

"Nope," Aila answered.

Shan stepped forward. "You… did you stop the rocket?"

"That was the easy part," Naite admitted. "It may take a skilled worker to put this tech together, but even unskilled workers like us can take the crap apart." Naite gave a predatory smile. "I think the rocket's going to just sit there for a while. I hope they have food and water in there, because I don't plan to open that door until we have a whole lot more people here. When you decide to step into a sandrat nest, you step in a big one, don't you?" Naite walked into the room, his eyes going to the glass wall. The woman he'd been speaking to stepped forward and gave Shan and Temar a smile. She was a heavily muscled woman with short hair and dark skin that suggested she worked outside in the sun most of the time.

"The others have about a dozen of these idiots, including Ben Gratu, trapped in one of the offices," she offered.

"Great," Naite said sarcastically. "We're going to have to send someone back to Landing for more help."

"Maybe we should send someone over to Blue Hope. I'm pretty sure most of the unskilled laborers from Landing are already here," she pointed out.

"What in the name of God have you been doing?" Shan demanded.

Naite smiled. "Tom told me you'd run off to the relay to see where the water was going, so I followed. And since we knew that at least some of the landowners and skilled workers were involved, I decided to invite a few unskilled workers along for the ride. If there was a conspiracy, I knew that no one trusted us enough to let us in on the schemes."

"That's no joke," the woman said. "Besides, anyone who tried to get an unskilled worker to fall for this idiotic plan would have gotten a foot right up their ass."

Temar had been standing with his arms hanging at his sides, utterly still. He finally found his voice, though. "You have Ben? You're holding him?"

Naite looked at Temar with an expression that Shan couldn't understand, and for one second, he felt the same jealousy he'd felt as a child, when their father had chosen Naite. He didn't understand the emotion passing between them, but Shan still felt irrationally annoyed at being left out. Now that he was an adult, he could recognize his emotions were both illogical and ridiculous, but he still felt those wisps of jealousy clinging to him.

"You don't need to deal with that. The council will," Naite said firmly. Temar nodded, his Adam's apple bobbing as he swallowed.

Ignoring the fear that he was doing the wrong thing, Shan walked over and put his hand on Temar's shoulder. Temar looked up at him and gave him a small smile. "I'll be okay," Temar said.

"You will," Shan promised, and he believed that.

"All the councils are going to have to come. We have people from all five towns."

"What a mess," Shan said softly. This would rip their society apart. This many people turning against friends and neighbors and apprentices… leaving them to die. It was inconceivable.

"It would have been a bigger mess if you hadn't left a sign for us to follow," Naite pointed out. "If they'd taken off, it would have done more damage to our morale than our water systems, and I doubt either would have recovered."

Shan frowned. "Sign?" he asked. "What sign?"

Naite looked at them with a confused expression. "The computers. You left them on, with a big old map leading right to this place." Shan didn't remember that at all.

"That was an accident. We just didn't bother turning them off," Temar said.

"You...." Naite looked from Shan to Temar, his mouth coming open. "You didn't leave that on purpose? But.... What exactly was your grand plan?" Naite shouted.

"To stop Ben," Shan said coldly.

"Good job with that. I'm sure you were about to spring your big trap, right?" Naite moved toward Shan. "I mean, I know you aren't stupid enough to come after Ben with no plan at all before getting locked in a little room. That would be pathetic."

"We didn't have time to get help, not with them getting ready to leave."

"Yeah, and getting yourself killed is going to do a whole lot of good. And what the hell were you thinking, bringing Temar?" The vein at the side of Naite's neck throbbed.

"He didn't bring me! I chose to come," Temar said, stepping forward and shoving at Naite with both hands. Temar's gesture shocked Shan out of his anger toward his brother's attitude. Even Naite seemed a little surprised as he stepped away from Temar's attack. "And he slowed the launch down by sabotaging the machines."

"And what was his plan after that? To pray?" Naite demanded, and now his angry glare took in both Shan and Temar.

"No hitting a priest, Naite. It's bad luck," Aila said, but she stayed near the door.

"I'm hitting my idiot brother, whose brains clearly got cooked out on the desert."

"And I did what I thought was right. Should I point out that it worked?"

"Because I showed up," Naite about yelled. "And now you're telling me that was dumb luck rather than any actual plan on your part. I mean, when I found the computers, I cursed you to the stars for having irresponsible plans, but now you're telling me you didn't have any plan at all. Are you a moron?"

"The Lord works in mysterious ways," Shan offered smugly, even though a little voice in the back of his head agreed that it was stupid to assume no one would follow. Tom and Naite both knew about the water theft and Shan's suspicions, and neither of them were the type to sit back and wait for someone else to fix problems. Shan should have left a note or waited for them to come, but on the other hand, if they had waited, Ben and the water might have gotten off the planet.

Naite threw both his hands up. "God? If you don't stop counting on God to haul your ass out of trouble, you're going to end up dead." Turning his back, Naite headed for the door. "Temar, you can do better than that idiot; I'll tell you that."

Aila fell back, letting Naite pass. She had a smirk on her face, but then her eyes slid over the glass wall where the rocket stood with sunlight falling down over it, and the smile faltered. Raw pain flashed, and then she turned her back on the rocket and the people who thought so little of her life that they'd steal her water. Shan found himself wondering if she had children. It would be the parents who had the hardest time with this, since it was the children who would have to survive when the water ran out.

Shan shook his head, but then he froze as Naite's last words sank into his awareness. "What do you mean by that?" Shan yelled after his brother. Naite was gone, though, and Aila offered a quick nod of respect and followed him. The shouts from the corridor had vanished, and Shan could hear muffled voices—whispers that echoed as they followed the stone walls down the halls. Shan looked at Temar, and for a moment, he teetered on the verge of asking Temar that same question. However, fear and his own confusion kept his mouth closed so long that Temar started heading for the door.

"They took so much water. If we put it back in the system, how many more years do you think we can buy?" he asked as he stopped by the open door.

"I don't know," Shan admitted. If he had a computer, he might be able to figure out a few crude numbers, but irrigation and water systems had never been his specialty. "I do know that our systems are already a lot more efficient than the settlers ever expected. Men like George Young have developed some incredibly efficient crops."

A soft sigh slipped out of Temar.

Shan moved to his side, and Temar gave a little shudder, but then he actually shifted back toward Shan, so that their shoulders brushed.

"What are you thinking?" Shan asked when he couldn't understand Temar's expression.

Light brown eyes looked up at him, and Temar opened his mouth and closed it silently. He chewed on his lower lip for a second before he tried again. "I thought George was a monster, and I liked Ben."

Shan took a deep breath. He'd thought the same. He'd also thought his brother had stolen their father's love and that Yan Polli had given Naite all his attention out of love. "We don't even really know each other," he confessed.

Temar looked at him with a deep sadness reflected in his eyes. "That's a lonely way to live. I prefer to think that we have to work to get to know each other. After all, I did get to know Ben." Temar hesitated. "And you did eventually get to know both your father and your brother."

Shan sucked in a fast breath, shocked that Temar had touched so close to his thoughts. "Maybe you're right. Maybe we just need time to know each other as people," Shan admitted. He didn't add that he thought it was equally hard to get to know himself. "We should volunteer to ride over to Blue Hope. Or I could go alone," Shan added. Naite was here, and apparently he'd brought a whole lot of friends, so Temar was safe enough.

"No, we can go together." Temar smiled at him and rested his hand on Shan's arm. "It's not going to be easy to explain any of this."

"No," Shan agreed. "It's not."

"Then, we do it together," Temar said in the same tone he'd used to insist he was coming on this adventure. "Only…." Temar closed his mouth.

"What?" Shan asked.

Temar looked up, almost apologetically. "I would never say this to Naite, but he is right about your plans. If you have any more ideas about running off and saving the world, do you think that maybe you can be the person not planning the rescue?"

"You're insulting my plan?" Shan was shocked.

"Yes," Temar said firmly. "I respect that you trust God, but that was a little too much trust in God."

"It worked," Shan pointed out. Now that the danger was over, his legs felt like water, and he could admit the plan hadn't been exactly well thought out, but it had worked.

"And next time we have to save the world, we'll come up with another plan that works, only this one will rely a little less on God and dumb luck. You know," Temar said slowly, "I wasn't sure about the existence of God. When Ben had me, I thought that no God would ever let that happen. But after seeing how He rescued us from this mess, I'm almost ready to believe. I think that means you're a pretty good priest, if you managed to convert a doubter."

"The Lord works in mysterious ways," Shan agreed. He let his hand rest on Temar's shoulder as they headed out into the corridor. They'd need to get more help, and then each council would have to deal with their own citizens. Livre was in for a hard time, but at least the truth was out, and the evil was visible. Shan wondered if the man who'd raped the woman in Blue Hope had been part of the conspiracy. Once you started thinking your needs were more important than anyone else's, it wasn't a big leap to that sort of abuse.

"We'll all be fine," Temar promised him. They passed a room with a half dozen workers standing near an inner door to another room.

"I should be reassuring you."

Temar shook his head. "I don't need reassurance. I've had time to figure out that I'm strong enough to survive this. The rest of the world… they'll need a little more help."

Shan hadn't thought about it that way, but it was true. They'd all been betrayed and abused. They were silent then, until they reached the surface. The storm had passed, and the sky was a brilliant red, the stray pieces of fine dust lingering in the air after the sand settled. And each piece of dust reflected the sun, so that the world caught on fire. It was beautiful.

"Am I evil for being just a little relieved that Ben will be condemned for what he's done to Livre and not what he's done to me?" Temar asked as they both stared up at the sky and arranged their sand scarves.

"Don't you want him to pay for what he did to you?" Shan asked, not understanding the conversation. It didn't help his mood that Naite would have understood in a moment.

"I want him to pay," Temar said. "I just don't want to spend my life wondering if my anger sent him out to be food for sandcats. I don't want to be that angry."

"Then you're a better man than I am, because I am angry," Shan confessed. If Ben were in front of him right now, Shan thought he could gut the man and watch his blood spill out onto the rocks.

When Temar looked at him, Shan couldn't see the emotion beneath the scarf that hid his face. "I never said I wasn't angry. I said I didn't want to be angry."

The words sank in slowly. The saying went that the truth was finer than sand, that it slipped into uncomfortable places, unbidden. This truth did exactly that. Temar was strong, but he wasn't healed. It was a truth Shan needed to respect. "That's a place to start healing."

Temar nodded and then headed out toward the sand bike. Shan followed.

chapter
twenty-five

SHAN SAT down on the carved windwood bench outside of Landing's council house. Temar looked up in surprise. "I didn't expect you out here."

Shan shrugged. "Div's in there making judgments. If they think he'll be more merciful, they've never seen a man angry at the thought of all the babies he's baptized dying." If Shan had doubted his right to feel angry about the conspiracy, Div had dispelled that thought. Actually, talking to Div again had made a lot of things come clear. "Where's Cyla?" She'd been outside the council, thin-lipped with anger and pacing the whole time. No one would tell her what exactly had happened to Temar, but she'd understood enough to turn from vitriolic to this quiet sort of furious that worried Shan even more.

"Hannal took her back to Tom's for a good meal."

"And she went?" That surprised Shan. The way she looked at every one of the conspirators who came out of the council or the barn, he'd been sure she was waiting for a chance to gut one with a dull knife.

Temar shrugged. "I'm not sure if it was an invitation or a military strike. Hannal sort of invaded, scooped Cyla up with a hand around her shoulders and shoved her into a hauler while Cyla was still objecting."

Shan could imagine the scene. Tom tended to have a thing for strong partners, that was for sure. "Did you testify yet?" Shan asked. He couldn't imagine how difficult that must have been.

Temar nodded.

"Are you okay?"

Temar took some time to answer. "I can talk about it, or I can remember the feelings, but it's like I can't do both at the same time. If I talk about what Ben did, how he...." Temar stopped and shrugged. "If I talk about it and think about how I felt at the same time, it's like adding too much heat to the glass. I feel like parts of me are going to slide off. Do you know what I mean?"

Shan thought about his horror on the one night his father had crept into his room, his large hands finding Shan's leg and feeling up the length before Shan had kicked him in the stomach. If it hadn't been for the pipe juice, Shan might have been in the same position as Temar and Naite. "Yeah, I do. Sometimes I feel like it's unfair that I escaped the fire out of dumb luck."

"I thought you put faith in God, not luck."

Shan gave a small laugh, without any humor. "I wish I could change things."

"I can't think about that. It happened. I'm moving on," Temar said firmly. "It wasn't the end of the world, and on those days that I feel like it was, I remind myself that I'm alive and I have water to drink if I need it and friends I can talk to. It's more than Ben has right now. And I think I'm a little vindictive, because I really like that he spent the night tied up, with his shoes taken from him."

"That's justice," Shan said. The door to the council house opened, and Shan stiffened, expecting to see guards escorting Ben out. He was the first of Landing's accused to go before the council, and most of the town had managed to find some reason to come to town. Shopkeepers stood in front of their shops. Chalta was fixing a sand bike in the middle of the road, and Houghten had set up an informal ballad circle, singing to children in his soft, low voice. Shan couldn't hear the words, but he noticed all the eyes came to the council house in time to see Naite step out with a thunderous expression on his face.

"Naite?" Shan asked. His brother walked over and sat on the end of the bench nearest Shan.

"They kicked me out," Naite said with a shrug. "Apparently, I don't have the proper emotional distance from the situation to judge fairly." The sarcasm was thick enough to cut and serve for dinner.

"What did you say?"

"I suggested that we tie the bastard up and drop him on a sandrat nest," Naite said, in a tone that suggested he wasn't sorry he'd said it.

Shan rolled his eyes. "And they thought you were too emotional? Unbelievable."

"That's what happens when someone is exiled. I don't know why you're so fond of turning the other cheek. I mean, the Bible is fine, but sometimes a little rope and a nest of sandrats is better." Naite glared at the people gathered along the street, and most of them went back to pretending they weren't waiting on the council's decision. Most expected exile. Very few had argued for the mercy of slavery or the stripping of adult rights, at least not for Ben. A few of the others had their supporters willing to beg for mercy. Several people in town had vocally demanded more bloody and personal forms of justice, but Shan doubted the council would give in to a call for bloody vengeance.

"And I'm clearly a very poor priest, because part of me agrees," Shan admitted. Naite looked over, not bothering to hide his surprise.

Temar reached over and actually patted Shan on the leg. "You're allowed to hate him. We can hate him together."

"Priests are supposed to be better than that."

Naite snorted his disgust at that answer. "Priests are human, and humans are mean, selfish creatures."

"Just some of them," Temar said. Naite didn't correct him. For a time, the three of them sat on the bench, and like the rest of the town, pretended they weren't waiting on the verdict. Shan caught one or two words of Houghten's ballad and frowned. It almost sounded like the man had sung Shan's name. "What do you think they're going to do?" Temar finally asked in the relative silence.

"They'll exile him," Naite quickly answered.

Shan sighed deeply. "And for the first time in my life, I don't even want to go in there and argue for leniency."

"Good" was Naite's sharp answer.

Temar shook his head. "Now that he's locked up, there's a little part of me that feels sorry for him. I can't ever forgive him for what he did, but…." Words failed Temar and he fell silent.

"It'll pass," Naite said confidently.

"It's just… he was so sure that he was right. I don't know how anyone could get so twisted around that they can't see right from wrong like that. I mean, sometimes I think he really did believe he was protecting me. He really did believe that, in using that ship, he was saving a part of Livre, not condemning an entire planet to death." Temar shook his head. "It doesn't make any sense."

"Temar." Shan stopped. The anger he understood, but when Temar vacillated between anger and this awkward forgiveness, Shan wasn't sure what to say.

"He probably did," Naite said before Shan could collect his thoughts. "People like that… they don't connect well with reality. However, I still say the best thing is to toss them out into the sand and hope they aren't as stubbornly attached to life as my brother. The more interesting question is what the council is going to do about their own mistakes."

"Their mistakes?" Temar sounded genuinely confused, but Shan understood the moment Naite said it. Before Temar's case had ever come to light, they'd talked as a council about how unhappy they were with the council out of Blue Hope. A young woman in slavery had been raped. Yes, the council had exiled the man who'd abused the girl, but they hadn't taken any blame for allowing the man to purchase her contract. A council made decisions, and right or wrong, they had to be accountable for those decisions.

"We voted to allow Ben Gratu to buy you," Shan said softly. He didn't have the money many of the others did, so he wasn't sure what compensation he'd be asked to pay, but he'd pay it. It would never be enough to give Temar back what had been taken from him with such force, but he'd do what he could.

"You're the only one in the clear, as far as I'm concerned," Naite disagreed. "You were very loud and annoying in your arguments against slavery. Hell, you warned us that something like Blue Hope would happen again, and we all thought you were just being a prissy little pain in the ass." Naite paused for a second. "Or maybe I was the only one who thought you were being prissy, but the rest of them agreed to go along with the slavery. So any payment that's due Temar, you won't be paying it."

"No one should pay except Ben Gratu," Temar said firmly. "If you'd asked me, I would have named Ben as my first choice in owners. You can't be blamed for a mistake."

"Like mistakenly dumping two tanks of water onto a field?" Shan asked. Temar closed his mouth on whatever argument he was about to make. "And I was part of the council, so I won't challenge any punishment they assign. We all share in this."

Temar was still shaking his head, but he looked confused.

Naite slowly smiled. "Look at it this way, you'll probably end up owning a lot more land than your father did. You'll definitely get Ben Gratu's land, after what he did, and since George Young still hasn't burned off those damn pipe trap plants, you can take him to the council and demand work days from him." His smile grew wider. "That would be a sight to see."

Shan sighed. "It doesn't fix any of this. It doesn't change the fact that the council is going to have to exile not one person but forty-three." That loss of life tugged at Shan's soul. By stopping the rocket, they'd saved so many lives. The councils hadn't released the new water figures, but the planet would last for years, maybe decades longer with so much water, especially since the water-use predictions everyone had been using had included the stolen water, siphoned off year by year over almost twenty years. Their water technology was better than any of the skilled workers had calculated. However, by saving the planet, Shan had his part in condemning forty-three people.

Naite rolled his eyes. "Forty-three men and women from Landing agreed to abandon the rest of us to die. I don't feel guilty, and once they let me back in there after Ben's judgment, I plan to vote for exile on every one."

"Every one of them?" Shan felt a wave of horror.

"Unless they can come up with a very good excuse, yes. Every one. We have an obligation to apply the law fairly, and water theft of this seriousness can't be treated lightly."

"What about any that you decide to show mercy on?" Shan asked. Other than exile and fining, Livre had only one punishment.

"We need to monitor more closely, but I'm still not against slavery, Shan."

"By God, you are stubborn."

"You both are," Temar interrupted.

"That we are," Naite agreed. "And we need to make changes, but there isn't a better solution. And I'm saying that as someone who has both survived a long slavery sentence and is facing another."

"You... what?" Shan asked, his stomach souring at Naite's casual attitude toward slavery after all these horrors.

"Why would you be slaved out?" Temar sat up, his face alarmed.

Naite snorted. "I'm likely to be slaved out to you, Temar. I don't have any training, and I definitely don't have money for fines, so I'll be working your farm for a time. It's fair enough. Ben ran a tight ship, but a lot of unskilled laborers avoided the place because he did have a real prejudice against kids on his farm. Kids or retired folks. Most unskilled workers want to make connections on farms where they know they'll be welcomed when they're too old to work. If I'm there to get the workers back in shape, you'll get it running smooth faster."

"But... a slave?" Temar made a moue of disgust, and Shan didn't blame him. He felt the same way.

"It's that or hand over half my pay for the rest of my life, and trust me, I'd rather be slaved out for a time and have it done and over with." Naite got a thoughtful look on his face. "I wonder if I can serve on the council if I'm slaved out. Huh." He looked more curious than alarmed at the idea he might lose his position.

Temar was still shaking his head. "I don't want you as a slave."

"Then I'll slave out to someone else, and you'll get the slave fee," Naite said. "I'd rather you ask the council to avoid selling me to George Young. I'd earn extra years for telling him exactly what I think of him. The man might be brilliant at breeding plants, but he's a sandrat about most else."

Temar scooted to the edge of the bench. "But I don't want you slaved out at all."

Naite looked at Shan, but Shan wasn't saving his idiot brother from this. He'd been clear that he didn't like slavery, and that was even before all this mess. "If I don't repay you for my part in this, I'll live with that guilt. It'd be kinder to let me work it off."

"But you don't owe me anything," Temar protested.

Naite didn't answer right away. He looked up at the sky. "I know what Ben did. My father used to do the same, and I hated it. But even though I knew better than most what was out there, I made a poor judgment call. I trusted Ben when even my idiot brother knew that something was wrong. I didn't check to make sure you were safe, and because of that, you suffered. You suffered things that I understand all too well. You suffered when I would have seen the signs if I'd just paid more attention. One trip out to the Gratu farm and I would have known to take you in hand until I figured out the truth, and as a council member, that was my job." Naite looked at Temar. "I understand better than anyone else on that council how much we owe you, and for my part, putting Ben Gratu's farm in order is the least of what I can do to repay you. I am sorry."

The mood turned somber, and Temar had gone so pale that Shan itched to reach out and offer some comfort, but this wasn't a topic he really understood. He could imagine what had been done to Naite and Temar. He could even feel badly about it, but he couldn't understand what it meant to live through that. He was trapped outside, wanting to help them both and not knowing how.

"I don't blame you," Temar said quietly.

"Good to know. When your master blames you, it can get uncomfortable. However, your forgiveness doesn't change the fact that I do carry some of the blame here. Not all or even most, but some. We'll all have to decide how to pay for that." Naite frowned. "Except for my idiot brother, who actually did see this coming. I'm never going to live that down, am I?"

Shan shook his head. "I don't plan to ever mention it again."

"That'd be a surprise." Naite pushed himself up off the bench. "I'm going to go get some food and find someone to annoy until Lilian lets me back in." Naite strolled off, and for a time, silence fell over them.

"So, they're condemning him now?" Temar asked quietly.

"Yes."

"Why aren't you in there? Aren't you council?"

"I was. I'm not now," Shan said. It suddenly occurred to him, if the council decided to impose a punishment on all standing members when Temar had been punished, he might be looking at slavery himself. His stomach rolled at the thought. It was an evil. He still believed that.

"Why? Did they kick you off?" Temar looked angry enough to go challenge the entire council, and Shan smiled. Temar wasn't a boy, that's for sure. He'd gone through life moving in the shadows, but when he decided to step forward, he was a force. Shan could imagine him being on the council someday. Perhaps some day very soon if the rest of the council felt as guilty as he did. Lilian had been making noises about retiring every season-end, and Bari… Bari Ruiz was such a gentle man that Shan couldn't imagine how he'd handled the news.

"What's going on?" Temar demanded in a louder voice.

"You don't need to go defend my rights. I quit the priesthood. I can't represent the church if I'm not a member of the clergy," Shan said. Temar's mouth fell open as he stared at Shan. Shan raised his eyebrows. "You can't be that surprised. It's not like I was acting like a priest."

"But… you aren't…." Temar closed his mouth so quickly that his teeth clicked.

Shan smiled. Div certainly hadn't been surprised, and neither had Naite, so it was nice that he'd managed to shock someone. "I thought I might see if I could apprentice out to a mechanic. I'm almost done with my training, so I think I can get someone to take me on."

"Not a priest?" Temar's voice sounded distant, like shock had robbed him of the volume.

"I didn't belong in the church anymore. God helped me off one path, and now I'm on another," Shan explained. Div had simply smiled when Shan had explained how he felt and then added that Shan needed to listen to his heart and God more often because God had been saying that for a couple of years. Well, Shan never had been a fast learner, not unless you were talking about sand bikes. Moving slowly, he let his fingertips rest against Temar's knee. Temar looked down to where they touched and then up at Shan's face.

"On another? Another path?" Temar's voice sounded unnaturally high.

Shan nodded. Hopefully it was a compliment that Temar couldn't find words. Either that or Shan was pushing far too fast.

Temar took a deep breath and then let it out slowly. "I think I like this path, but maybe…." He stopped and bit his upper lip as he frowned. Shan's stomach dropped as he realized Temar was unhappy.

Shan pulled his hand back. "I'm sorry. I don't—"

"Why?" Temar cut him off.

"I left because my path isn't with the church."

"Because of me?" Temar's voice still had that squeaky tone to it.

"No," Shan quickly said. "Maybe you made me look at myself, but I'm not leaving the church because of you, Temar. Not because of you and not for you."

"But you feel this thing between us?" This time Temar's voice actually sounded like Temar.

"If you're not interested, it's still time for me to move onto my real path. I'm still staying out of the priesthood and trying to find work as a mechanic." Shan cringed as he realized he'd backed Temar into a corner with this little announcement. Maybe he should get work near Naite, so his brother could insult him when he acted like a verbally incompetent moron.

"You're an idiot," Temar said with some amusement in his voice.

"I could have told you that," Shan said with a shrug. "But I don't want you to think I expect something from you. I don't. I did what I needed to do, and Div himself told me that I should have left the priesthood years ago, when I found myself spending more time fixing the roof than reading the Bible. He told me he would have kicked me out himself, only the roof really needed fixing." Shan smiled. He hadn't believed Div for a moment, but the comfortable insults made him believe Div still loved him, even though he chose to leave the priesthood.

Temar caught Shan's hand, curling his long fingers around it. "I hope that maybe we can share a path. I just hope that you're patient, because I'm still struggling to find my way."

Shan's stomach unknotted so fast that Shan let all his air out in one huge breath, relief forcing the air out. "Oh thank God. I thought I'd driven you away before I'd even asked you out on a first date."

"Considering that I've seen you so drunk on pipe juice that you couldn't walk, I don't think I can be scared away that easily," Temar said. "I do want this. Maybe when you rescued me I was confused about what I felt, but in the week since we got back to town, I've missed you. I miss your sense of humor, and I miss having someone to talk to. I just don't know how long it's going to take me to get my head together. Some days I feel like the boy who stood at the back of your church and listened to your sermons, and other days I feel unaccountably old."

Shan smiled. "I've waited nine years, Temar. In nine years I haven't touched another person with desire. I think I can wait as long as you need."

"It definitely won't be nine years," Temar said with a snort. "I'm not that screwed up."

"Well, I would hope not." The second the words were out of his mouth, Shan realized that was not the best phrasing.

Temar looked at him with a confused expression, and Shan cringed.

"Have I mentioned that I'm better with bikes than words?"

Temar smiled. "You might have, once or twice." Then Temar leaned closer, his eyes falling half closed. Shan remembered this, even if he was years out of practice. He moved closer and tilted his head so their lips met. The heat gathered between them as they kissed gently, lips brushing past one another.

Temar's free hand curled around the back of Shan's neck, pulling him closer even as Temar opened his mouth more. Their tongues slipped against each other, sending tingles up through his neck, and Shan felt the heat gather in his whole body. He reached up and let his hand rest against Temar's shoulder, his breath coming in fast gasps. When Temar hesitated, his grip on the back of Shan's neck easing, Shan pulled back and smiled.

The kiss was promise enough. Shan looked up at the sky and gave a silent prayer of thanks as Temar's fingers tightened around his hand. They'd find a way through this together. Now that Shan had learned to listen to his heart, he could practically hear God whisper that promise.

*Keep reading for an
excerpt of*

Desert World: Book Two

Desert World Rebirth

By Lyn Gala

New ambassadors Temar Gazer and Shan Polli stopped one disaster on Livre, but the battle isn't over. Temar is still struggling to work through the abuse he suffered. Livre, too, stands at a crossroads: it could ally with the breakaway planets—risking strange and dangerous beliefs—or the older alliance, which offers human rights protections but seeks to control the planet's resources. With everyone keeping secrets, it's impossible to know who to trust. Shan and Temar do their best to navigate cultures they don't understand and avoid the dangers lurking around every corner. It's a delicate balance, but they manage… until a disaster takes Shan away from Temar.

It's up to Temar to rescue Shan and guide their planet through the crisis safely, and he isn't sure he's ready. Just because he and Shan have chosen each other doesn't mean their love is strong enough to survive when the stirring sands around them change.

Coming soon to
http://www.dsppublications.com

chapter
one

SHAN heard the door chime and nearly jumped out of his skin. Three months living in the relay station set deep in the Livre desert, and he still wasn't used to some of the technology. Door chimes, for one. Another difference would be the sheer amount of space he lived in. In the church, he had privacy, time to search his thoughts. However, there he was always aware of Div shuffling somewhere in the house or softly praying, his Latin drifting through the air. Livre houses were generally small, built to stand up against the desert wind. Here, silence reigned. The early settlers had built the station before the inner worlds had largely abandoned Livre to survive—or die—on its own.

Shan walked through the storage room to one of the five living spaces. Through the thick window, he could see a shadowed form moving in the bright Livre sunshine. Maybe he'd been living alone too long, because his mind went to Ista and to all the men and women who had tried to kill him… to the wealthy and beloved landowner Ben, who had shown his true colors when he raped Temar. Shan could forgive the murder attempt more easily than Ben's willingness to rape. But considering Ben, Ista, and most of their coconspirators were dead, fearing that they'd turn up here suggested that he *had* been alone a little too long.

Pushing aside irrational fears, Shan opened the door and smiled as he saw Temar standing in the light, his sand veil hanging around his neck.

"Temar!" Stepping forward, he caught Temar in a quick hug. "I thought you were off working your glass this week." Temar often stopped by, running the long dunes to visit once or twice a week, but he'd already warned Shan that he wouldn't be able to visit this week.

A flash of pain crossed Temar's face, and he dropped his head so his shaggy blond hair hid his features.

"Temar?" Shan asked, his voice quieting.

Temar gave a shrug.

"Do you want to come in?" Shan took a step back to give Temar some room. He didn't want to push him, not after what Ben had done. So even if Shan's cock sometimes ached with need, and if he sometimes lay in bed stroking himself while thinking of Temar, Shan wouldn't physically crowd the man. He'd give Temar space to heal on his own.

With a small nod, Temar came into the station, passing through the room with the metal and plastic chairs and tables with the perfect lines and symmetrical bolts that Shan still found a little alien. When he and Temar had left the door open to pursue Ben, not even the wind and sand of the desert storm had left a mark on the sterile room. Shan was used to the curves of windwood, the uneven gaps formed by the twisted branches, and the way a truly great craftsman could make a piece curve with the human body. Every craftsman had his own style. Roget Ally from Landing created chairs and tables with small branches that intertwined so perfectly that the wood appeared to wrap around each other, as though in love. In comparison, these perfectly uniform chairs brought down by the drop ships that first carried settlers to Livre had no life.

Temar headed through the storage room, into the computer control room, and then through a door into the one living space Shan actually used. He dropped down onto the couch and pulled his sand veil off, fingering the edges.

"What happened?" Shan asked, settling into a chair near enough that he could reach out to offer a comforting hand if needed.

For some time, Temar seemed to struggle with his feelings. Most times, Temar wasn't an emotional man. The shyness clung to him, muffled his reactions, but right now, Shan could see the pain etched deep into his features. "Dee'eta hates me," Temar finally confessed in a miserable voice.

Shan doubted Dee'eta Sun's feelings were as simple as hate. "Why do you say that?"

Leaning back, Temar stared up at the perfectly flat metal ceiling. "She can barely look at me. Three weeks into my apprenticeship, and my glass-master can't even look me in the eye when showing me how to use the paddles to shape the piece. It's the most uncomfortable place I've ever been." Temar tilted his head and looked Shan right in the eye. "Ever," he repeated. Given that Temar had once been trapped in Ben's bed, a victim of both rape and a criminal justice system that had failed him, that was saying something.

Shan had been on the council that had sentenced Temar to a term of slavery after his vandalism had caused more damage than he could ever repay. Of course, he'd been following his sister's attempts to play detective when it had happened. It hadn't been fair, but Cyla had gone to an owner who trained her to work and Temar had gone to Ben, who had raped him and blackmailed him into not reporting it to the council. At least Shan could hold onto the fact that he had argued against slavery. Vehemently argued. Dee'eta didn't have that luxury. She had to look at Temar and know she'd played her part in sending him into that hell. "This can't be easy for either of you," Shan said, not entirely sure how to broach the subject of Dee'eta's guilt when it had been Temar who had suffered the most.

"No, not really," Temar said, his voice defeated. "I spent my entire childhood dreaming of an apprenticeship with her, and now that I have my dream, it's not…." Temar sighed. "It's not any good, Shan."

"Is that why you left?"

"I screwed up. I cooled the punty too much, and when Dee'eta tried to transfer the glass, it slipped off and broke."

"That happens with apprentices," Shan reassured him. "When I apprenticed for Div, the very first sermon I gave I mixed up John and Paul and said something very stupid about the Book of Matthew.

Luckily, I was so scared that I was preaching in a monotone that had put everyone to sleep by then."

Temar looked at Shan seriously. "Did he yell at you?"

Shan smiled. "In a way, I suppose he did. With Div, yelling was done in this really soft, disappointed voice that made you want to crawl into a hole and pull the sand in over you." He missed Div. Leaving the priesthood had been the right choice, no question. And when the councils had offered him a chance to finish his long-abandoned mechanics' apprenticeship by studying the relay station systems and reading a hundred years' worth of technical manuals, he'd jumped at the chance.

He still missed Div, though. He missed talking to him over breakfast and that odd look Div gave him when Shan had done something desperately foolish. That was how a father should act—not that Shan had a lot of experience with good fathering.

"Dee'eta didn't yell," Temar said in a defeated tone. "She gave me one glance, and then she started lecturing on how to recycle scraps."

Shan was confused. "So you didn't leave over that, did you?"

"I did." Temar practically leaped out of his seat and started pacing. Shan was more than confused now, but he held his tongue and waited for Temar to explain. Both Shan's brother Naite and Temar had suffered terrible abuse, but unlike Naite, Temar opened up if you gave him enough time and space to get the words together. But this time it took longer than normal. He stalked the room, his fingers running over the smooth, rolled metal edges of the tables and shelves. He was a tactile man, and sometimes touching a well-made piece of glass would soothe him enough to start talking. Shan gave him that space.

Temar stopped at one of the few pieces of furniture Shan had insisted on bringing out—a windwood chest with intertwining branches that Roget Ally had made for Shan's mother before she died. It was the only part of his father's farm he'd saved when the man's land and house were sold to pay his debts. Temar crouched down and let his long fingers dance over the intricate work and smooth joints. "How can she teach me if she's so afraid of me that she can't even tell me when I'm wrong?" he asked in a tired voice.

"She's feeling guilty," Shan said.

Temar turned and gave him an incredulous look. "Do you think I don't know that?"

"I know you know it," Shan said, "but maybe you—" Shan put his hand over his heart. "You and Naite know the pain of being hurt, but you need to know there's a pain and guilt to being not hurt." The moment he said that, he knew it sounded incredibly rude. It sounded like he was dismissing Temar's trauma, which wasn't his intent.

Standing up, Temar crossed his arms over his chest. "I know that, but do you really think I'm so weak that I'm going to collapse in tears if you rip me a new asshole for ruining a beautiful piece of work?"

"Me? No. I know you're stronger than that," Shan said in all truthfulness. He'd seen Temar's strength, and he knew it would take a lot more than a few words to bring the man down. Temar was worth waiting for, in part because of his strength.

Temar shook his head. "Naite is the only one who treats me normally."

"Not surprising. After the council assigned him to three years of slavery with you, he's going to go out of his way to make sure that he doesn't change, because he won't want to let himself act servile, even if he's serving. He knows the danger of letting a slave-sentence get to you too much."

"Not that he's actually a slave," Temar said in a disgusted voice. He leaned against the wall and closed his eyes.

Clearly something was wrong there, and that shocked Shan down to his core. Naite was a cantankerous, difficult man. Growing up, Shan had wanted to kill him more than once, but Naite had already been suffering their father's abuse. Well, they'd both been abused, but Naite had been the one raped while Shan had suffered only the cold disinterest of a man who had neglected and ignored him while seeming to shower all his love on the older Naite. However, it was Naite who understood Temar better than anyone else on the planet. Shan would have expected Naite to support Temar, not make him feel worse.

"What's going on?"

Temar pressed the heels of his hands to his eyes as though trying to block out some memory. "He ripped me open, left me about as raw as a sand-rat-chewed wound and stalked off."

Shan's breath left him. "He… what?"

Temar made a little huffing noise that was either frustration or amusement—Shan couldn't tell. "He told me I had a right to sell the balance of his contract, but I didn't have a right to ignore him after asking him to manage Ben's farm."

"Your farm," Shan corrected him.

"Well, apparently, I'm letting Cyla treat it like her farm, and Naite informed me that if I didn't get my head out of my ass and make my idiot sister stop acting like a sandcat, I wasn't going to have anyone to work the crops but him."

That did sound like Naite. When people weren't living up to his expectations, he could be a sandstorm, blowing in and destroying entire villages without slowing.

Temar sighed. "And the worst part is, he's right."

Shan leaned back in the chair and studied Temar. His shoulders were pulled in, and his whole body looked as tight as a person could get without having a heart attack. It bothered Shan that he'd driven out in this mood, because the sand dunes were unforgiving if you made a mistake, and Temar wasn't all that experienced on a bike.

"So," he said carefully, not wanting to make things worse, "you're upset that Dee'eta can't treat you normally, and you're upset that Naite is treating you normally?"

Temar had a self-deprecating half grin on his face as he shrugged. "I didn't say I was feeling logical. I can be annoyed with both of them and you all at the same time."

"With me?" Shan sat up straight, not sure when his faults had come into the conversation.

"With you," Temar echoed. "Are you attracted to me or not?"

Shan's mouth fell open, and he had to consciously close it and gather his thoughts before he could answer. Even before he'd blurted out his whole stupid infatuation while drunk, he'd been less than subtle. Apparently. Shan always thought he'd hidden his interest well—he'd certainly lived in denial. However, since leaving the priesthood, more than one person had clapped him on the back and congratulated him for finally having the strength to openly court Temar. Shan had to assume he'd been a little more obvious than he'd thought. "You know I am," he said as calmly as he could.

"So, you haven't changed your mind now that you're not a priest and you can sleep with anyone you want?"

"No." Shan studied Temar more carefully, sure the man had some hidden agenda for this question. "Have I ever shown any interest in anyone else?"

Temar crossed the room slowly. Since leaving the priesthood, Shan hadn't taken anyone to his bed. He hadn't wanted anyone in his bed, no one except Temar, and he'd been very open about both his interest and his willingness to wait, so he met Temar's uncertain gaze. Temar had such beautiful eyes—blue eyes that reflected more emotions than Shan could ever hope to understand.

Temar settled on the end of the couch. "Why don't you ever touch me?"

"I hugged you! When you came, I hugged you, so I know I touch you," Shan snapped. He had enough flaws of his own without Temar inventing reasons to be upset with him.

Moving slowly, Temar rested his hand on Shan's knee. "Why don't you ever really touch me?" he asked again. The warmth of Temar's hand soaked through the fabric.

"I do," Shan said, only this time his voice wavered. This was the sort of touch he generally did avoid.

"No, you don't. Shan, I know that you liked me before, but you were a priest, so it was safe for you to like me without thinking anything would happen. If you aren't interested—"

"I am." Shan cut him off, bringing his own hand up to rest on Temar's. He had long fingers and small hands, and Shan's big, scarred paw just about covered it. They were the hands of a mechanic, not a priest.

"Then why don't you touch me?"

For a second, Shan chewed on his lower lip and tried to control the growing hardness in his pants. He did want Temar. Too much. "I don't want to push things too far too fast."

"Shan, I need a little more pushing. Actually, I can do the pushing myself, but I need a sign that you're okay with me pushing."

Shan looked at Temar, but he didn't see any doubt or fear in his expression. He'd expected Temar to want to move slowly, to heal from his time in Ben's custody. Hell, Naite had been clear that it had taken years for him to get his own balance back after being abused, and Shan couldn't expect more of Temar.

After that uncomfortable conversation, Shan had firmly counseled himself about patience and the dangers of lust. That had been more than ironic. Naite wasn't exactly celibate, and he'd lectured Shan about not having sex. God could have a sharp sense of humor. Shan had even considered asking Temar to marry him before taking him to bed, wondering if the commitment would ease the fears. It would ease Div's mind to know that Shan was still taking the church's teachings so seriously. But now that he was looking into Temar's eyes, fear didn't live there; frustration did. "I take it I've been moving too slow?" he guessed.

Temar nodded. "I was starting to think you were trying to find nice ways to let me down easy. I thought maybe, like Dee'eta, you were too afraid to hurt me."

Shan tightened his hold on Temar's hand. "I don't want to hurt you, ever. But I want you. I want you more than I should."

"Then why aren't you showing any interest in having a relationship?" Temar asked. Shan's gaze drifted down to his own pants, where his hard cock pressed up against the seam. Temar chuckled. "Okay, so you're showing some interest," he added with some amusement, "but in my defense, that's the first time I've seen that."

Suddenly Temar pulled his hand away from Shan. "Wait, is this about you not wanting to show me a hard cock? Do you think that I'll confuse what Ben did with sex?"

Shan's sexual frustration was interfering with his ability to form coherent thought at this point. "You don't have a lot of experience...."

Temar gave a rough bark of laughter that didn't really match his normal shy manner. "Unless you have a few lovers Naite doesn't know about, I have more than you. He insists you're a big coward who doesn't want to admit that you're clueless."

"You talked to my brother about my sex life?" Shan demanded, hot anger rising up to vie with the sexual heat that was already making his skin warm.His anger couldn't maintain itself, though. In three months, he hadn't done more than offer a quick hug, so Temar had some cause to get a little insecure. "Of course you did. That sounds exactly like Naite, only without the profanity that he would have thrown in."

"He did have a couple of choice words. But without Naite, I wouldn't have had the nerve to do this. I would have sat home and given you time to move on because you clearly didn't want me." Temar set his jaw and glared at Shan, clearly not willing to apologize for going to Naite. "I love you, but I'm starting to doubt whether this is right for us. For you."

"It is," Shan insisted. Leaning forward, he captured Temar's hands and held them between his palms, their warmth mingling. "I admit that I haven't had many lovers. I took my vows seriously, and before the priesthood...." Shan thought back to himself as a young man, gawky and awkward and fumbling in the dark with a boy named Nuesis, and with two different women. Both of them kept warning him not to put his cock in them because pregnancy was serious and a man who got a woman pregnant had his life tied to her until the child was grown—neither of them liked him enough for that. "I don't have a lot of experience. But the main problem is that I would rather wait until you're ready than risk ruining the friendship we share."

"I'm ready," Temar said gently. "I'm more than ready."

Shan grimaced. "I should also mention that I'm not exactly good with relationships."

With a smile, Temar ducked his head. "Naite mentioned that."

"If we're going to do this, could we not mention my brother anymore?" Shan begged. There were certain topics guaranteed to send his cock into full retreat. Ben was one, and Naite was another.

The smile remained as Temar brought his hand up to rest against Shan's cheek. "Deal. But no more waiting. It's giving me a neurosis."

The heat was gathering in Shan's body, making his throat dry and tight, so he simply nodded. Temar slowly smiled, shifting forward on the couch so that he perched on the edge. It had been a long time since doing this, but Shan's body remembered. He remembered the slide of skin against skin, the aching need to touch, the hunger. Reaching out, he slid his hand under Temar's shirt so he could feel the hot skin hidden underneath.

Temar's hand came up to stroke Shan's arms, fingers reaching up under the loose sleeve. "I'm not sure what you want," Temar murmured before he ran his fingernails down Shan's arm hard enough to make three tiny trails of white on Shan's olive skin.

"I'm open to anything," Shan said, and he meant it. He was nervous about it because his experience with men was limited to some touching and sucking, but this was Temar.

"Funny enough, me too," Temar said with a smile that Shan couldn't resist. He leaned forward and caught Temar behind the neck and pulled him close. Temar came off the couch and put his knee on the edge of the chair, leaning close so Shan could press his lips to Temar's. He smelled of sand and salt and soap, and Shan groaned..

Temar pulled back a few inches. "Problem?" he teased.

"Yeah," Shan said. "And I'm too old to do anything about it in a chair."

Temar laughed. "You're not that old."

"I'm old enough not to give up a good bed for a small chair," Shan countered. Temar must have agreed, because with a smile he stood. Shan didn't realize Temar had caught hold of his shirt until the fabric pulled tight.

"Then the bed it is," Temar said, tugging on the shirt to urge Shan up. Shan's cock was painfully hard as he pushed himself up and followed.

Coming Soon to
DSP Publications

Desert World: Book Three

Desert World Immigrant

By Lyn Gala

Lieutenant Commander Verly Black is ready to leave the atrocities of war behind and immigrate to the planet of Livre, where he can build a future away from the ghosts of his past. He doesn't expect to find a kindred spirit in councilman Naite Poli—a man with secrets as dark as Verly's own and bearing the scars to prove it. Both men have done what was necessary to survive—Verly in battle and Naite in defense of his family—and they're haunted by memories that leave them wary of trusting others. As they circle each other, the political maneuvering around them grows more dangerous, with the outer worlds trying to force Livre into one alliance or another. Some still view Verly as a killer and a spy, and they're determined not to let him forget what he's done. Others fear the implications of a military officer sharing the bed of a councilmember. When the rebel alliance moves beyond threats, Verly and Naite must push through the pain of their pasts and stand together to fight for the future of their world.

http://www.dsppublications.com

LYN GALA started writing in the back of her science notebook in third grade and hasn't stopped since. Westerns starring men with shady pasts gave way to science fiction with questionable protagonists, which eventually became any story with a morally ambiguous character. Even the purest heroes have pain and loss and darkness in their hearts, and that's where she likes to find her stories. Her characters seek to better themselves and find the happy (or happier) ending.

When she isn't writing, Lyn Gala teaches history in a small town in New Mexico. Her favorite spot to write is a flat rock under a wide tree on the edge of the open desert where her dog can terrorize local wildlife. Writing in a wide range of genres, she often gravitates back to adventure and BDSM, stories about men in search of true love and a way to bring some criminal to justice… unless they happen to be the criminal.

Don't miss

Eagle's Blood

Mountain Spirit Mysteries: Book 1

By A.J. Marcus

Brock Summers is a Colorado Parks and Wildlife Officer who loves his job and takes it very seriously. When he discovers a video of golden eagles being shot and learns of a nest in trouble, not even a blizzard can stop him from trekking up the mountain in an attempt to rescue them.

When Brock returns with the one eaglet he manages to save, Landon Weir, the local wildlife rehabilitator, patches up the bird and the injury Brock suffered during the rescue. Though they have been friends and colleagues for years, they discover a shared passion for protecting wildlife and vow to work together to protect the majestic birds from the criminals preying on them. It isn't long before another video of eagles being killed comes to their attention. They must face inclement weather, a dangerous mountain, and armed poachers if they want to ensure the eagles'—and their own— survival.

http://www.dsppublications.com

Also from DSP Publications

Greenwode

The Wode: Book 1

By J Tullos Hennig

The Hooded One. The one to breathe the dark and light and dusk between....

When an old druid foresees this harbinger of chaos, he also glimpses its future. A peasant from Loxley will wear the Hood and, with his sister, command a last, desperate bastion of Old Religion against New. Yet a devout nobleman's son could well be their destruction—Gamelyn Boundys, whom Rob and Marion have befriended. Such acquaintance challenges both duty and destiny. The old druid warns that Rob and Gamelyn will be cast as sworn enemies, locked in timeless and symbolic struggle for the greenwode's Maiden.

Instead, a defiant Rob dares his Horned God to reinterpret the ancient rites, allow Rob to take Gamelyn as lover instead of rival. But in the eyes of Gamelyn's Church, sodomy is unthinkable… and the old pagan magics are an evil that must be vanquished.

http://www.dsppublications.com

Also from DSP Publications

The Relics of Gods

Between Heaven and Earth: Book 1

By Yeyu

What is worse: Being so broke you can barely afford food, getting hired for dangerous missions way out of your league, suffocating under mountains of unanswered questions—or wanting to sexually dominate someone who can kill you without lifting a finger?

Lu Delong is a mercenary who evaluates antiques most of the time and deals with the paranormal on rare occasions—even though it's supposed to be the other way around. When he joins a dangerous quest for an ancient artifact, he meets and becomes strongly attracted to a mysterious and powerful immortal named Cangji. Despite his friends' warnings and Cangji's icy, unsociable demeanor, Delong is unable to resist befriending him. However, Cangji is deeply involved in a matter beyond mortals, and Delong is drawn into a chaotic struggle by both visible and invisible forces.

Always the pacifist who wanted to live a simple human life, Delong never imagined he'd end up involved in a conflict that will affect everything from the lowest insects on earth to the highest gods in heaven.

http://www.dsppublications.com

Also from DSP Publications

Wolf's-own: Ghost

Wolf's-own: Book 1

By Carole Cummings

Untouchable. Ghost. Assassin. Mad. Fen Jacin-rei is all these and none. His mind is host to the spirits of long-dead magicians, and Fen's fate should be one of madness and ignoble death. So how is it Fen lives, carrying out shadowy vengeance for his subjugated people and protecting the family he loves?

Kamen Malick means to find out. When Malick and his own small band of assassins ambush Fen in an alley, Malick offers Fen a choice: Join us or die.

Determined to decode the intrigue that surrounds Fen, Malick sets to unraveling the mysteries of Fen's past. As Fen's secrets slowly unfold, Malick finds irony a bitter thing when he discovers the one he wants is already hopelessly entangled with the one he hunts.

http://www.dsppublications.com

Also from DSP Publications

Infected: Prey

By Andrea Speed

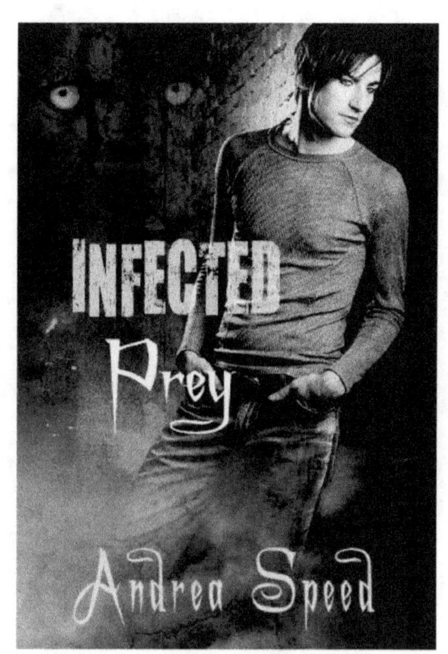

In a world where a werecat virus has changed society, Roan McKichan, a born infected and ex-cop, works as a private detective trying to solve crimes involving other infecteds.

The murder of a former cop draws Roan into an odd case where an unidentifiable species of cat appears to be showing an unusual level of intelligence. He juggles that with trying to find a missing teenage boy, who, unbeknownst to his parents, was "cat" obsessed. And when someone is brutally murdering infecteds, Eli Winters, leader of the Church of the Divine Transformation, hires Roan to find the killer before he closes in on Eli.

Working the crimes will lead Roan through a maze of hate, personal grudges, and mortal danger. With help from his tiger-strain infected partner, Paris Lehane, he does his best to survive in a world that hates and fears their kind… and occasionally worships them.

http://www.dsppublications.com

Also from DSP Publications

Third Eye

By Rick R. Reed

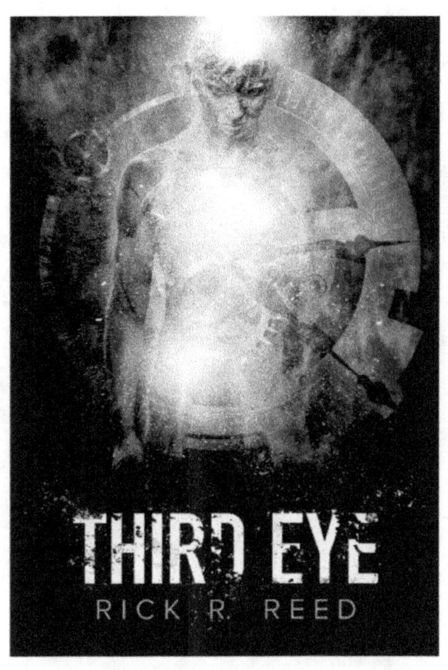

Who knew that a summer thunderstorm and his lost little boy would conspire to change single dad Cayce D'Amico's life in an instant? With Luke missing, Cayce ventures into the woods near their house to find his son, only to have lightning strike a tree near him, sending a branch down on his head. When he awakens the next day in the hospital, he discovers he has been blessed or cursed—he isn't sure which—with psychic ability. Along with unfathomable glimpses into the lives of those around him, he's getting visions of a missing teenage girl.

When a second girl disappears soon after the first, Cayce realizes his visions are leading him to their grisly fates. Cayce wants to help, but no one believes him. The police are suspicious. The press wants to exploit him. And the girls' parents have mixed feelings about the young man with the "third eye."

Cayce turns to local reporter Dave Newton and, while searching for clues to the string of disappearances and possible murders, a spark ignites between the two. Little do they know that nearby, another couple—dark and murderous—are plotting more crimes and wondering how to silence the man who knows too much about them.

http://www.dsppublications.com

*Also from DSP
Publications*

*Erasing
Shame*

By Yeyu

The son of a Han traitor who had let the Xianbei Mongols invade the borders, Jiang Shicai swears to restore his family's honor, hoping to better the Hans' lives through peaceful means. He believes violence is never the answer, but to gain respect, he finds himself fighting for the Xianbei.

Ten years later, an annoying but handsome playboy, Dugu Xuechi, arrives as the incompetent new military inspector of Shicai's region. Shameless, irresponsible, and obnoxious, Xuechi tests Shicai's patience almost every second. Despite their mutual dislike, Shicai finds himself drawn to the capricious man, especially when he sees the resemblance between Xuechi and his deceased best friend. Yet Xuechi's self-destructive behavior and refusal to accept help require attention that distracts Shicai from his goal for peace--and it doesn't help that Xuechi is Shicai's strongest political opposition. Haunted by a childhood promise he never had the chance to fulfill, Shicai must choose between his feelings and his values.

http://www.dsppublications.com

Also from DSP
PUBLICATIONS

Willow Man

By John Inman

Woody Stiles has sung his country songs in every city on the map. His life is one long road trip in a never-ending quest for fame and fortune. But when his agent books him into a club in his hometown, a place he swore he would never set foot again, Woody comes face to face with a few old demons. One in particular.

With memories of his childhood bombarding him from every angle, Woody must accept the fact that his old enemy, Willow Man, was not just a figment of childish imagination.

With his friends at his side, now all grown up just like he is, Woody goes to battle with the killer that stole his childhood lover. Woody also learns Willow Man has been busy while he was away, destroying even more of Woody's past. And in the midst of all this drama, Woody is stunned to find himself falling in love—something he never thought he would do again.

As kids, Woody and his friends could not stop the killer who lived in the canyon where they played. As adults, they might just have a chance.

Or will they?

http://www.dsppublications.com

Coming Soon

'Til Darkness Falls

By Pearl Love

A malicious deception…. An ancient curse…. A timeless love….

Brian Macon is a worn-out homicide detective whose job and life hold no meaning until he meets a gorgeous German man who turns his world upside down. Alrick Ritter has a poet's soul, a master cellist's skill, and a sniper's deadly accuracy, and though constrained by sinister forces to be a killer-for-hire, Alrick wants nothing more than to be with Brian. Helpless to resist the call of their hearts, Brian and Alrick begin a cautious affair, keeping secret the reality that places them on opposite sides of the law. But an ancient danger threatens to destroy their love.

Three thousand years ago in the burning sands of ancient Egypt, Prince Rahotep and his devoted slave, Tiye, were robbed of their lives, betrayed by a powerful woman's mad hatred and the cruel humor of an evil god. Now, destiny has reunited the lovers, joining them in an unquenchable passion even as a twist of fate casts them as potential enemies. Will Brian and Alrick be able to overcome the centuries-old curse to secure the love that should have always been theirs?

http://www.dsppublications.com

For more
great fiction
from

DSP PUBLICATIONS

visit us online.

WWW.DSPPUBLICATIONS.COM

www.ingramcontent.com/pod-product-compliance
Lightning Source LLC
Chambersburg PA
CBHW070432120726
47910CB00003B/752